EULOGY FOR AN IMMORTAL

BOOK 1

DAN ALLEN

ISBN: 978-1-7354765-0-6

Credit

Cover Artist: Ligia Gonzalez

Editor: Dr. Michael at FirstEditing.com

❀ Created with Vellum

To Miss Beccah, who made the whole thing possible.

1

Her sudden appearance caused the boy's heart to skip a beat. He reeled back, like a boxer avoiding a punch, dropping his armload of corn. Crouching down, the boy grabbed hold of a fallen cob, gripping it like a club. His eyes settled upon his opponent. Her eight long legs gripped delicate strands that kept her anatomy level with the boy's button nose. Horror swelled inside him as he watched her frame sway in the breeze.

"I oughta!" the young boy yelled.

Relaxing on her midair home, the arachnid displayed no sign of remorse. Her body was rigid as wisps of wind rocked her like an anchored boat on a choppy sea.

The child tensed; his eyebrows furrowed.

"Y'ugly monster!" he yelled.

Stepping forward, he readied himself to strike. But, in mid motion, he stopped. He'd never seen a spider quite like this one before. Across her body vibrant colors of gold and ivory wove in between lines of pitch black. The pattern resembled a dark ladder stretching across a beach soaked in golden sunset. Her eight long legs were colored in with alternating patches of dusty brown and sagebrush gray. Eight beady little eyes stared seemingly at the ground, but the boy knew that she saw him. In the sky, a cloud shifted, allowing the daylight to strike her home. The boy's jaw dropped.

Individual strands of silk glistened, revealing a stunning polygonal construction. The boy's eyes traced a linear segment of light from the center of the web to the stump of a skinny tree. The spider had anchored her home across the entire pathway. As the boy lowered his weapon, a large grasshopper flew over the top of the web. He watched the bug nearly collide into the silky trap as it twisted its way through the air.

Suddenly, he remembered dinner.

Looking down, he saw a gap between the bottom of the web and the ground. Tossing each ear of corn over the web, he crawled underneath the bottommost strand of silk. When he cleared the sticky gate, he scrambled to gather up the fallen load. After ensuring that the spider had not jumped off her web, the lad took off down the pathway.

Waning light pierced the sparse group of pines, showering the forest floor with shattered sunbeams. The boy's bare feet brought him out of the forest and into a field filled as far as the eye could see with rows and rows of ripening crops. Carefully hopping over a protruding root, he passed by a single oak tree that towered over all. Following the dingy dirt road slicing through the field, he finally made it to the narrow outhouse that stood just behind his home. Holding his breath, the lad sped past the rickety, wooden latrine, ignoring the shack's back door as he aimed his strides around the side of the quaint structure. The boy skidded to slow his pace before he officially rounded the front corner.

Looking to his left, he saw a lanky man stretched out in a rocking chair. With one mud caked boot propped up on an uprooted stump and the other stabilizing his position on a wooden column that held up the porch's roof, he appeared frozen in rigid relaxation. He occupied the space in front of the entrance, but the boy spotted just enough space.

As the boy marched up the two steps, the man's baggy eyes shifted from the horizon to the lad. His teeth chewed on the bit end of a smelly pipe. Withdrawing a foot from the wooden beam, Pa's weight shifted forward into a lean.

In a low tone, he said, "They wait'n on ya."

"Yes, Pa," the boy answered as he shuffled by.

The moment he entered the shack, a pair of disappointed faces looked up from their chores. One face belonged to a skinny girl not much older than the small boy, and the other belonged to a thin, wrinkly-faced woman.

"Nathaniel!" the thin woman demanded as she wiped her hands on her apron. "Where ya been?" She stepped away from the stove, "Water's nearly boiled out!"

"Sorry," Nathaniel mumbled as he unloaded the corn onto the round dinner table, knocking over a cup in the process.

With quick strides Ma reached the table and picked up the fallen vessel. "What took ya so long?"

Nathaniel's face brightened as he proudly explained, "I met a spider!"

Ma stepped back and exclaimed, "A spider?" Then she rushed to her son's side and began an immediate inspection. "Did it getch'ya?"

"Naw, Ma," Nathaniel grimaced as Ma's fingers checked his hair. "It didn't bite me. It was pretty!"

The girl laughed.

"Hush, Jane!" Ma snapped.

Nathaniel looked at the floor. "I only watched it."

Ma halted her frantic quest. "An' how ya know it didn't bite ya when ya turned yer back?"

"Spider's favorite food is eyeballs," Jane commented.

"*This* is why dinner's gonna be late?" Ma placed her hands on her hips. "It's not polite to keep hungry bellies wait'n on accounta yer own curiosities."

With eyes still on the floor, Nathaniel slumped down in the smallest dining chair. The rim of the circular table was nearly level with his chin.

"If ya stare at a spider long enough," Jane said, "ya become a one.".

"Hush, Jane! Boy, get yer idle hands shuck'n this corn!"

2

Nathaniel searched his eyelids for sleep. Tossing and turning, he looked high and low for where he had last put away his dreams. Jane grunted a few times before slowly escalating each corresponding breath into a louder snore. With each breath she shredded the air. He tried counting sheep. Then he tried counting how many breaths Jane was taking. An itchy sting struck the back of his neck. Slapping the area, he felt a mushy pile of gummy grossness stick to the palm of his hand. He wiped the bits of bug off on his sheets.

His eyelids snapped open. Looking straight ahead, he stared at the wooden barrier separating him from his parent's room. Nathaniel rolled over and looked through the scantily clad window drapes that barely obscured anything. Bright moonlight illuminated Pa's field.

Rubbing his eyes, Nathaniel sat up and glared at Jane. Somehow, she was sounding even louder now. Kicking off his covers, Nathaniel quickly escaped his bedroom. As he crept into the biggest room in the house, lingering, stale scents of grease and corn filled his nostrils. Reaching the front door, he carefully and quietly pulled it open.

Warm, fresh wind soaked through Nathaniel's thin shirt, sending shivers down his spine. Stepping out onto the porch, he hugged his chest and listened for any sign of pursuit. Satisfied, he skipped both porch steps as he dashed from the shack. Taking a right, he ran around the house. Following the path, he passed the outhouse and then the oak tree before halting his step just before the threshold of the dark forest. He waited for his eyes to find the dull moonlight that managed to fall onto the tiny shadowy path that cut through the trees. Leaning forward, Nathaniel carefully searched each inch of the air. Slowly, he made his way down the path until he caught a sudden glint of light. Using the moon as a backdrop, he eventually spotted a dark dot floating in midair. Dropping to his knees, the boy adjusted his vantage until she appeared as a shadow cast upon the fully reflective moon. She stood as rigid as ice in the top corner of her web.

The boy's ear perked as the sound of a large locust's flapping legs floated through the air. It landed with a dull thud, just behind Nathaniel. Keeping low to the ground, he turned around and formed his hands and fingers into a dome. Calculating the distance, he lunged forward and cupped his hands over his target. Desperate wings beat against and tickled the boy's flesh. The defiance inevitably succumbed. Nathaniel carefully clamped his fingers and a thumb around the tiny prisoner. Something dark and viscous pooled up under the hopper's mouth. Standing up, Nathaniel extended a hand and dangled his captive over the top of the web. Keeping two wide eyes on the critter, Nathaniel released his grip and the hopper plummeted. The two newly freed wings fought violently against gravity. The bug twisted through an erratic flight pattern before striking the silk trap. It broke several strands before its wings and legs became thoroughly entangled.

The arachnid reached the prey and halted its step as the hopper's legs burst forth with new found energy, entangling itself even further. The spider and the boy watched the locust's erratic spasms.

"Nathaniel?"

Panic erupted in Nathaniel's chest as he spun around. Jane stood in the middle of the path with her arms crossed.

"What're ya doin'?" Nathaniel demanded.

"What are *you* doin'?" Jane replied.

"I'm..."

A grin swept across Jane's face. "Looking for poison spiders?"

"I found the spider from before," Nathaniel yelled, "and he's *not* poison!"

Jane raised both index fingers to her lips. "Pa will hear!"

Nathaniel desperately clasped his loud mouth with both hands.

Lowering her hands, Jane stepped closer, "Where is she?"

"*Shhhheee?*"

Jane stiffened her raised a finger, "Spiders are girls."

Nathaniel angrily whispered back, "No they're not!"

"Yes they are," Jane answered. "The school teacher said so!"

"What teacher?"

"Miss Mathers." Jane patted her brother on the head, "You'll meet her someday."

Jane leaned in and searched. "Where's the spider?"

Stepping aside, Nathaniel presented the web. Jane squinted her eyes and leaned her face forward. His eyes alternated between Jane and the web. The boy jumped when Jane covered her mouth and let out a muted scream.

"Woah!" Jane declared. "She got a bug!"

"I know!" Nathaniel scrambled up next to his big sister. "I got her it!"

With inconsistent outbursts of rage, the locust struggled against silk. Its powerful wings broke through a sticky strand and gravity dragged it deeper into the webbing. The spider chelicerae twitched with patient anticipation. Moving with quick staccato, the spider reached her dinner and sank both fangs in. The victim barely fought as the spider utilized her front appendages to lift its meal and begin to rotate it. Lifting her larger abdomen, she aimed her spinneret as a pair of her rear legs wrapped layers of silk around her prey. Soon the only sign of the grasshopper was an ivory cocoon.

Jane leaned over and whispered, "She gonna put her eggs in there."

Nathaniel wrinkled his nose. "Gross!"

The spider dragged the silky package back to the middle. Anchoring the marinating meal to the center of the web the arachnid continued sinking its tiny fangs into her victim. The grasshopper twitched while the predator continued. With invisible speed she retreated to the top right corner. Sitting still, the spider's vibrant colors blended with the dim night light.

Nathaniel cast his eyes to the ground.

"Nathaniel?" Jane asked.

"Ya?" he answered still looking at the ground.

"Wanna see my fort?"

Looking up, his eyes brightened, "You have a *fort?*"

Jane pointed down the path, "Over the river."

"Are ya pulling my leg?" the little boy scrutinized.

Jane grabbed her little brother's hand, "I'll take ya."

Nathaniel grabbed Jane's other hand, he pulled her back and shouted, "Don't smash her web!"

Jane stepped back.

Letting go of his big sister's hand as he dropped down into a crawl, "Ya gotta go under."

When he finished crawling underneath the spider's web, Jane stepped off the path, walked around the tree the web was anchored to, and then reentered the path. She stopped in front of her brother. He blinked.

Turning her head, Jane waved. "Goodnight, Miss Spider."

Waving both hands, Nathaniel yelled twice as loud, "Bye, bye, Missus Spider!"

Jane placed both index fingers in front of a very serious face, "Shhhhhh!"

The boy shrank back as Jane took the lead. With each footstep, the width of the path shrank. The air grew humid as the sound of rushing water crept up behind their ears. The path sloped gradually downward, and the ground grew moist as they came upon a narrow clay beach. Nathaniel tugged back his arm and his fingers, slipping through Jane's grip. He stood at the threshold of the river, analyzing its waters. The broad body of water looked wider in the darkness.

Jane pointed to the forest on the other side of the slow-moving current. "Go for that big rock."

A large round portion of a boulder stuck up above the water. Nathaniel crouched down and stuck a hand into the river.

"Brrrr."

"It's fine," Jane assured, "Jus' roll your pants up."

Nathaniel backed up onto drier land before taking a seat and rolling up both pant legs.

"Ready?" Jane asked.

Nathaniel nodded as he stood up and stepped to the water's edge. A yelp escaped his throat, as he splashed down into the cold water. Jane took a few steps and hauled herself up onto the large stone. Turning around she offered a hand. He accepted her assistance and ascended the boulder.

As soon as her little brother gained his footing, Jane turned and pointed at the pine forest on the other side of the river, "It's deeper on this side."

Nathaniel took Jane's free hand.

"The barn's not that far after that," Jane insisted.

Letting go of her little brother's hand, she sat down and slid off the rock. Turning back she offered up both hands. The lad cautiously accepted the offering as he sat down. He dangled his feet into the water, and slowly slid forward into the river. With a solid stance, the boy stood listening to the rushing and swirling water.

Nathaniel smiled, "It's not as cold now."

"Yer getting used to it."

Stepping forward, Nathaniel planted a foot on a pointy, rough rock. The sharpness sliced through his balance. A yelp escaped his throat as he fell forward with a splash. His chin struck jagged solid stone and searing pain cut through his soft flesh. Water rushed into his screaming mouth, cutting off his cry. Jane screeched as she dove forward and grabbed her little brother. Pulling him closer to shore, Nathaniel felt the warmth dripping off his face.

"You okay?" Jane shouted.

Blood covered his hand. Stepping onto land, Jane ripped off the lower portion of her dress.

"Hold this!" Jane yelled, as she wrapped it around his chin and head.

Nathaniel held onto the wet cloth as Jane finished securing it with a shoddy knot.

Jane turned her back to her brother and squatted down, "Get on my back!"

Nathaniel clung to his big sister as she charged up the steep, clay bank. As the terrain leveled the path widened and Jane's speed increased. Trees rushed by in a nauseating blur.

Sudden panic filled Nathaniel as he cried out, "Missus Spider!"

Nearing the end of the forest, Jane quickly broke from the path, dashed around the spider's web, and exited the woods. With each step Nathaniel felt Jane's strength weaken.

Jane's left hand grabbed Nathaniel's arm and tugged at it, "Breathe," she gasped.

Nathaniel loosened his grip and slipped. His hands gripped her shoulders and he pressed his chin into her back. The bandage slipped as Nathaniel's face was dragged down to the ground.

She stopped at the tree and Nathaniel finished his slide. The moment he regained his footing, his hands held onto his wound. Grabbing him by the shoulders, she pulled him towards the shack. When they made it to the porch, Jane stopped and examined the damage in the moonlight. Peeling back the cloth, her little brother whimpered. Blood flowed from a two inch gash in his chin. She put the cloth back.

"I'm gonna get Ma," she whispered.

Nathaniel whimpered.

Jane took Nathaniel by the hand and led him inside. She pulled out his chair and gently pushed him into it.

"Mus' try an' be quiet," Jane begged. "Don' wake Pa."

Nathaniel tried to stifle himself but his skin leak hurt really bad. He squeezed his eyelids trying to hold back the tears. A soft whimper escaped. Jane's footsteps faded into the adult's room and Nathaniel waited in the darkness, trying his best not to cry or bleed.

The floorboards creaked as Ma took one look at her boy and coarsely whispered, "Boil some water!"

Moving to the front of her son, she slid him in his chair until he was directly facing her. Carefully, slowly, gently, she removed the torn, soaked cloth. The night air licked his wound while thick blood oozed down her son's face.

"Goddammit."

Keeping his face steady, Nathaniel glanced through his tear streaked peripheral vision as Jane struck a match.

"Hold still." Stepping back, Ma disappeared into her bedroom.

Upon her quick return, Ma quickly but quietly closed the door before returning to her child's side.

Placing a glass bottle and a wooden box on the table, Ma asked with a loud enough whisper, "That water boiled yet?"

"No."

Nathaniel felt his heart beating through the lacerated skin.

Opening up the wooden box, Ma retrieved a bent needle and stared at the tiny, metal instrument for a good while.

"This gonna hurt," Ma muttered.

Nathaniel looked confused, "It already does."

Putting down the needle, she picked up the glass bottle and uncorked it.

"Open."

Nathaniel's eyes grew big.

"It'll help the pain," Ma ordered.

Nathaniel opened his mouth.

A splash of nasty, spine twisting, tongue numbing liquid poured into the boy's mouth. Shock squirmed up his spine as he gagged and choked. The liquid spilled down his chin, lighting his bleeding cut on fire. The searing heat of a thousand suns swam over his open wound. Ma clasped a fresh cloth over her boy's mouth. With eyes blurred by tears, Nathaniel stared up at the ceiling.

"Hold the cloth in place."

Nathaniel's hands grasped the rag as the rest of him bled into it.

"Keep it there. Don't move it. Jane, how that water coming?"

"Ready enough."

"Can't wait any longer. Come stand by me, Jane, and bring the better light."

A nauseating rumbling swirled inside Nathaniel's tummy. Aside from the throbbing, his head felt light as a feather. Jane set the candle on the dinner table while Ma took a knee in front of her son. She removed the bloodied bandage from Nathaniel.

"Ya tired?" Ma inquired.

"Huh?"

"Jane, take hold yer brother's shoulders."

"Wha?" Nathaniel uttered as Jane's hands clamped down on him.

"Be strong, my baby boy," Ma said.

"Stuff something in his mouth," Jane suggested.

Ma folded the cloth to a cleaner section. "Bite down."

Nathaniel's tongue tasted dry, rough cotton.

Ma pierced the skin next to the cut with a strong, fine point. He felt the air drying his tears to his cheeks as the needle turned and Ma pulled it through. Nathaniel felt his loose flap of skin being yanked away from his face. But with each new piercing, the divide was drawn closer and closer together.

Jane shook her brother, "Don't fall asleep."

"Let him. You gonna stand there an' hold 'im in place if he does."

Nathaniel shut his eyes and searched for any part of his body that wasn't in pain.

3

D reamland shattered into a million pieces as Pa burst into the children's room, causing the whole shack to shudder as he shouted, "Let's go, let's move! Up and at 'em; we got work to do an' we losing daylight. C'mon! Chop chop!"

Nathaniel's eyes snapped open as he recalled the previous night's ordeal.

Pa stomped into the middle of the room, "Let's see some life!"

Quickly sitting up in bed, Nathaniel stole a glance at his still resting sister. Pa marched over and ripped off the blankets covering Jane. A disgruntled noise escaped from her throat.

"We're wastin' daylight!" Pa shouted.

"Let's waste some more," she grumbled into her pillow.

Pa grabbed his daughter by the ankles and dragged her halfway, off the bed.

"I'm up!" she stated.

"Nathaniel!" Pa bellowed.

Nathaniel sat up and aching, warm pain erupted just below his lower lip. Pa's determined face melted into confusion. His fingers caressed the scab caked and cracked cut that throbbed with his pulse. It was hot to the touch.

Pa pointed, "What's that 'round yer head?"

Jane's eyes snapped open.

"Kids went out on a walk las' nigh'," Ma stammered as she appeared at the door, "An' Nathaniel got cut up somethin' terrible."

Baffled, Pa shot his wife a look. "Last night?"

Ma laid a hand on his shoulder. "Yes."

Pa marched up to Jane. "You lead this young 'un 'round last night?"

"He wen' firs'," Jane rubbed her eyes, "I only want'd to...Yes."

"You get him all sliced up?"

"He fell, nearly drowned," Jane testified, "'cept I saved him."

"He'd need no save'n if you'd just kept yer asses in bed." Jane's eyes wandered over to the floor.

Pa looked over at his son, analyzing his bandage, "How bad?"

"Like this," Ma stated, placing an index finger over her chin at a diagonal angle.

"Dare I take a gander?"

"Best not."

"Fine." Pa raised his tone to a shout, "Jane, yer work'n right by my side all day."

Jane rolled her weary eyes.

"You hear me, girl?"

"Yeah!"

"Be ready in no more than one." Pa exited the children's bedroom.

With every passing heartbeat, pain throbbed through Nathaniel's chin.

From the other room, Pa shouted, "Jane, let's go!"

Grumbling as she stood up from her bed, Jane took clumsy, slow steps, over to the large wooden chest set in her corner of the room. She opened the lids and began flinging clothes onto her mattress.

Ma leaned forward and kissed her son's forehead. "Rest up, my baby boy." Nathaniel felt the air drying his mother's wet smooch as he closed his eyelids and fell back into his bed.

He was in church trying to listen to the preacher's sermon. Sounds of fire and brimstone exploded from the podium. All of the tall, standing bodies blocked his view. He couldn't see what the preacher was saying. Growing bored, Nathaniel got up and made his way towards the central aisle. Turning left, he made his way to the rear of the sanctuary. He stared up at the large portrait of Jesus residing above the house of worship's main doorway.

Pushing the doors open, he emerged into a small, wooden town. Sounds of laughter and conversation drifted out from the wooden walkways that lined the town's buildings.

A large horse drawing an even larger carriage pulled out in front of him. Reeling out of its way, Nathaniel turned his head and stared at the road that led back home. He followed the path. It led to a mansion.

The two-storied edifice had a row of four columns holding up the second story's veranda. Both of the building's dark, sapphire blue doors burst open, revealing two figures. Turning one hundred and eighty degrees, Nathaniel took off running.

A heavy, vague wetness wrapped itself around the boy's lower half. Looking down Nathaniel realized he was waist deep in a river. The moonlight shined brightly against the inky, black sky. His balance slipped and he plunged into the icy cold waters. He fought for air. Like a vice, suffocation gripped and squeezed his lungs. He felt the water melt away until he was laying on solid ground. Getting up, he spied a familiar path.

A smile formed as he recognized a silky structure. Rushing up to the symmetrical construction, the lad searched for its little architect. There she was, waiting patiently in the center of her web. Warmth blossomed in Nathaniel's chest as he reached out and gently caressed the eight legged critter. The spider looked up at him with bright eyes and reached her front legs up. Cupping his hands together the arachnid stuck to his skin and stepped off of her web. She scurried to the center of his palms. As the spider walked, Nathaniel shifted his hands around, turning his fingers into a treadmill.

Nathaniel's eyes snapped open. He was back in his room and his chin throbbed. The brisk wind gently swirled through the bedroom but a pile of blankets kept him bundled and protected. He closed his eyes.

4

Everything was white. It faded slightly to gray off in the distance, which seemed to stretch for infinity. The only thing Nathaniel could see was his own dark skin. Upon realizing he was standing, he looked upwards. He searched for a source of light, but found none. The horizon, the sky, the ground all blended into one bleak environment. Squatting down, Nathaniel reached to touch the floor but his fingers passed below the soles of his feet. Backing away from the floor, he stood and spun around.

"Hello?" he shouted.

A calm, clear, female voice responded, "Hello, Nathaniel."

Nathaniel whipped around. A spider, the size of a mule, stood ten yards in front of him. Eight lidless eyes, each the size of a dinner plate, stared at him. Nathaniel made out his own reflection in the large, shiny, black circles.

The boy took several steps back. The spider's head tilted. Nathaniel took a few more steps back. With an eerie grace, the spider drew near.

Just beneath her giant eyes, two chelicera parted as a calm, female voice enunciated, "You may refer to me as Key."

Nathaniel halted his retreat and the spider ceased her movement.

The spider named Key asked, "Am I frightening?"

"Yes."

The arachnid's palp twitched as she began shrinking in size. When she became the size of a puppy, Nathaniel recognized a familiar pattern of gold, ivory, and ebony decorating her bigger abdomen.

"You?!" Nathaniel exclaimed.

"My name is Key," Key said.

"Hi, Key," Nathaniel answered as he leaned forward.

"You are incorrectly associating my name with a device used to open locks." Key explained, "My title is a pronunciation of the acronym 'Q' and 'I'."

Nathaniel waited for Q and I to continue.

"One pronounces my name the same as the word 'key,' but it is spelled, Q, I."

"Okay," Nathaniel replied. "Qi."

"Exactly," Qi replied.

"You looking for bugs?" Nathaniel looked about, then he stopped and gulped. "Or you looking for somethin' bigger?"

"I do not hunger."

Nathaniel blinked. Her eight legs scrambled to move her body to the left of the boy. He couldn't take his eyes off her.

From the blank ground the top of a large, ocean-blue circle began to rise. The sphere rose until its bottommost point was the only part touching the translucent ground. Green and brown colors began bleeding into the blue, filling in queer borders of every size and shape. Suddenly, the features shifted and it became apparent that the sphere was spinning.

Nathaniel walked up and touched the globe and his fingers went through the surface. Withdrawing his hand, he asked, "What's this?"

"This is Earth," she answered. "It is the only orbital in this solar system capable of sustaining life forms. It is currently sustaining the two of us."

Nathaniel traced the shoreline of a large, green continent. "It looks so weird."

Utilizing a pedipalp, Qi tapped the earth and a bright cyan dot appeared. "The marked location is where we are."

The sphere disappeared as the cyan dot changed into a dark green color as it grew into a square. Squiggly blue lines and jagged, bumpy, brown inflammations appeared inside the green square. Another cyan dot appeared in the center of the shape, just below a thin watery zigzag.

Qi pointed. "This is where we currently are."

Nathaniel frowned. "What's this?"

Eight black eyes contemplated the earthling. "A view of your house from very far away."

"Up in the sky?" Nathaniel asked. "Like a bird?"

"Yes, like a bird."

Instantly, Nathaniel and Qi were surrounded by humans of all shapes and sizes. As far as the eye could see, there were men, women, girls, and boys standing exactly three yards apart from one another, in a grid-like formation. Their races, heights, and weights all varied. Some of them were naked but most of them wore clothing ranging from wedding dresses to full suits of armor. The only obvious similarity among them was their frozen poses and blank facial expressions. Qi meandered among them; Nathaniel cautiously followed.

"Variation in species is crucial for avoiding genetic erosion," Qi explained. "With earthling biology possessing great diversity, the reproductive system will sustain a potentially infinite variety of future generations."

Nathaniel stared at the angry metal face molded into a samurai's helmet. Then his eyes were drawn to the sword hanging down from the belt of a dark skinned pirate.

Qi continued, "Alterations can occur during conception, adding or removing crucial codes that make up a developing fetus. Usually, such abnormalities cause detrimental attributes that negatively affect survival."

A man with a sword appeared in front of Nathaniel. His enraged eyes focused on something that was neither the spider nor the boy. Then the blank features of the white room transformed. Soon, the angry swordsman was surrounded by half a dozen armored men wielding an assortment of weapons. They were on a wide steppe with stone huts sporting hay rooves. Nathaniel noticed columns of rigid smoke reaching up from the various tops of various huts.

"The angry human with the sword has been cataloged as Subject One," Qi said.

An armored warrior appeared in the same physical location as Qi. Her arachnid face stuck out from the warrior's body like a protruding belt buckle.

"He is the first earthling to ever project frequencies worth listening to," the spider added.

Nathaniel jumped back as the scene sprang to life. Subject One stabbed his sword into Qi's face. The armored man fell over while an unscathed spider continued to watch the killer remove his sword and slaughter two more foes with a single motion. Turning his focus to an archer pulling back on his drawstring, the swordsman threw his weapon. The blade easily punctured his target, forcing them to release their bowstring. Ducking his head, the unarmed warrior swatting the arrow and the projectile continued on until it struck into a stonewall.

Their surroundings returned to the featureless emptiness. The grid of statue-like humans returned. This time, all of them were nude with arms and legs spread apart, and floating above each of their heads appeared a number in bold font. The group did not stretch beyond the horizon but it was still a bigger crowd than Nathaniel would possibly wish to count. Without moving a muscle the humans started physically sliding past the boy and spider. The numbers above each statue's head grew into the thousands.

"In the past five centuries on earth, there have been thousands of human anomalies born with a variety of abilities."

Nathaniel tried to touch a nearby woman's belly button. The moment his finger made contact, sparks erupted from her fingertips. He jumped back, knocking into a man whose eyes began to glow bright red.

Qi watched the boy, "We are designed to find these subjects and sample their genetic material."

The boy's eyes widened, "What abilities do I have?"

"None."

"None?" Nathaniel's demeanor fell, "But you said I was designed."

"Modified," Qi corrected, "for a specific purpose."

He asked glumly, "What purpose?"

"Acting as the physical host, providing transportation and sample gathering."

"Sounds like more stupid work," he whined.

"The complete opposite," Qi snapped. "A lot of time and effort was put into our modifications. We are far beyond any scientific endeavor anyone on *this* planet has ever even attempted."

"This planet?"

One chelicerae scratched the other. "I will assist you with our journey."

"Our journey? What journey?" Nathaniel said.

Qi retreated from Nathaniel as a three-dimensional image of Jane grew out of the floor. Dressed in ratty clothes, she floated a few yards above the ground.

"This is the first earthling that you shall sample from," the spider explained.

"Her?"

"This is your sister,"

"I know who she is!"

"Excellent, then you should have no trouble collecting a sample of her."

Gazing hard at the image of Jane, Nathaniel asked, "What's so special about *Jane*?"

"We believe that she possesses an attribute that could be crucial to our creator's longevity."

The boy pondered, "What's her sample?"

As Qi scurried closer to Jane, every part of her anatomy disappeared, except for the head, which instead grew. A multitude of bright blue dots appeared all over her face.

"Hair, saliva, skin, tears, even teeth, are all suitable for sampling. Take hair for example, which is by far the easiest to procure." The rest of her face evaporated away as the image focused solely on one of Jane's hairs. Suddenly, a giant, disembodied version of Nathaniel's face appeared next to Jane. "Gathering it," Qi continued, "you will consume it like you would any other form of food."

The hair flew into the gaping maw of Nathaniel's floating head where it disappeared behind a set of chomping teeth.

"Send it down to the stomach, and I'll do the rest."

The images disappeared. Nathaniel stared at the spider's shiny, black eyes.

"Is this a dream?" he wondered.

"Yes."

"Oh." the boy laughed.

"You misunderstand. The information I am conveying is quite real regardless of your current state of consciousness."

"Sure, I'll go eat Jane's hair," Nathaniel looked around the sheer white exterior. "Where's she at?"

Qi's palps twitched. "You must wake up first."

"Right."

Nathaniel's eyes snapped open. The bedroom was brightly lit by the sun. It must be close to noon, he judged. Drifting in from the dining room came the sounds of Ma humming, accompanied by the percussion of a sweeping broom. As Nathaniel listened to the rhythm of each stroke, he remembered being asleep.

"What a strange dream," the boy mumbled.

He closed his eyes and tried to escape the pain on his chin. In the darkness, he could feel his hot heartbeat pounding through his laceration.

A gigantic arachnid towered over Nathaniel. In the midst of the white room, the spider seemed to be the size of a small mountain.

Qi's voice boomed, "I am real, Nathaniel. This dream is real!"

Nathaniel turned to flee but discovered he was surrounded by an army of similarly sized spiders. He spun in circles, his eyes darting from one towering monster to another.

In unison, the arachnids spoke, "Get a sample of Jane."

"I'm hurt!" Nathaniel pointed to his chin.

"You are physically capable of completing the task."

Before Nathaniel could reply, the angry spider faces dissolved into his bedroom's wooden ceiling. He blinked his eyes as he listened to Ma sweeping the dining room. Turning his head, he saw that his sister's bed had been made. Pushing away his quilt, Nathaniel placed his feet upon the floor. Creeping over to his sibling's bed, he leaned over and studied her pillow. A stray piece of hair stuck out among the array of shed hairs. Plucking the sample, Nathaniel placed it on his dry tongue. He exited the room and headed for the wooden barrel propped up in the corner near the stove. Taking a wooden ladle in hand, Nathaniel scooped a portion of water and drank.

"How you feeling?" Ma questioned.

Spinning himself around, Nathaniel grimaced through saying, "Hur'st'alk."

"Hmmmph," Ma grunted, "gonna put on some fresh bandages."

"Sleep."

Ma nodded, "Get to it."

Nathaniel hurried back to his room and jumped into bed, pulling the covers up to his hot, aching chin. Closing his eyes he quickly slipped back into sleep. The white room seemed grayer.

Qi greeted him with a friendly voice. "Congratulations on completing your first task."

"So?"

"Now I'll analyze the information, and you will grow into an ample enough body to start transporting us to our next target."

"Grow?" Nathaniel pondered. "How long is that gonna take?"

"Minimum amount of time is nine years."

"Nine? Nine *years*?"

"Yes."

Nathaniel threw up his hands, "That's forever!"

"No, it is nine years."

"But...I hav'ta wait? What'll I do?"

"Grow."

"I already do that!"

"Then there is no problem."

"No," Nathaniel mumbled. "But. Can't you get me to grow faster?"

"No."

"Nine years?" Nathaniel looked at his fingers and asked, "You know where we're gonna be in nine years?"

"Much can change between now and then, but I anticipate that we will be traveling north."

"North?"

"It is the opposite direction of south."

"What's there?" Nathaniel pouted. "What if I don' wanna go north?"

Qi's pedipalps twitched as they picked at her chelicera, "I'll worry about that. In the meantime rest and heal up from your wound."

Nathaniel faded away from the white room and dreamed about things he later forgot.

5

"**H**e fixed?" Pa asked as he took his seat at the dining room table.

"I clean 'n dress it everyday," Ma answered.

Pa poured himself a portion of rabbit stew.

"He may be fully healed by morning," Ma continued.

Pa hesitated taking his first bite. "Good, he can help us out tomorrow."

"Sick or not, he's too small."

"Hogwash, I was smaller than he when I first started." Pa addressed his son, "Ya like eat'n, boy?"

With his cheeks full of soup, Nathaniel nodded.

"Then yer gonna earn yer food like the res' of us. No more of this help'n with domestic chore bullshit."

"He's been very helpful," Ma retorted.

"Reckon he has. If you wanna work his spot and he can do yer house chores instead."

"Don't be ridiculous, he don't know how to operate the stove."

"I do," Jane pipped up.

"No," Pa pointed a finger at Jane, "don't even think 'bout try'n to skip out." His finger shifted to his son. "Yer gonna learn how to pick."

"May I please be excused?" Jane spoke up. "I'm finished."

Pa kept his eyes on his wife. "No!"

Jane slumped back in her seat. Nathaniel stared at his bowl of rabbit stew.

"Fine," Ma said, "but lemme freshen his bandages midway through the day."

"You said it's healed."

Ma hesitated.

"He's had plenty of rest," Pa said as he reached for another portion of food. "He should take the damn fool thing off his head."

Nathaniel touched the cloth bandage tied around his skull.

"He's gett'n soup stains all up in it," Pa commented.

Ma turned to her boy and reached out. "Let me do it honey."

Pa hit the table. "He needs to take it off hisself!"

Nathaniel's eyes shifted between his mother and father.

"Lose it!" the towering man ordered.

Nathaniel removed the soup catcher from his head and let it fall to the floor.

Pa returned to his half-full bowl of stew. "Tired a look'n at it."

6

Pa shook the whole shack as he burst into the children's room, his voice booming, "Up an' at 'em. Daylight's draining! Let's move!"

"Breakfast's hot!" Ma shouted from the dining room. Nathaniel's nostrils caught the steamy scent of food wafting into the bedroom while Jane grumbled. Opening his heavy lids, Nathaniel saw that Jane's eyes were still closed.

"C'mon!" Pa shouted.

Without looking, Jane crawled out of bed and stumbled over to the wooden box in the corner. Pa moved closer to his boy's bed. Nathaniel sat up like a released spring.

"Get dressed!"

Nathaniel walked around his father to the foot of the bed where he opened a wooden chest and pulled out a shirt. Fully clothed, Jane exited the room.

"Don' take too long," Pa instructed before departing.

When Nathaniel emerged, Jane was slumped in her chair while Pa eagerly watched the stovetop. As Nathaniel took his seat, Ma carried two bowls of steaming oatmeal to the table. Stomachs growled as she placed portions in front of family members. When his bowl arrived, Nathaniel stared into it, letting the hot steam pour over his face.

"Where's the honey?" Jane asked.

"None," Ma answered.

The children exchanged glances, and Jane sighed. As soon as Pa wolfed down his portion, he shoved his dirty dishes to the center of the table and stood up.

"Y'all bes' be out there in no mo' than five," he said as he grabbed a cotton sack from a wall hook and dashed out the door.

"Five what?" Nathaniel asked.

"Hours," Jane answered.

"Nooooo," Ma corrected, "minutes."

"How long is a minute?" he wondered.

"Sixty seconds," Jane snapped.

"How long is—"

"Three hundred seconds," Qi answered.

Leaning back, Jane squinted at the ceiling as she quietly mumbled some numbers aloud. "Eleven, zero seconds."

Both children slowed their feeding frenzies. After finishing her food, Ma scooped up her own dishes along with Pa's. She walked over to the stove and placed them in an already boiling pot of water. Jane shoved her empty dishes towards the center of the table before walking over and grabbing a cotton sack. She tied it around herself like an extra large satchel before exiting the shack.

Nathaniel's tummy hurt. Each mouthful became more and more of a chore. He stared at his remaining oatmeal.

"Finished?" Ma placed a hand on her boy's bowl.

Nathaniel nodded, and Ma whisked the dish away. She returned with an empty cotton sack.

"Stand up."

Nathaniel obeyed.

Scurrying over to her son's side, Ma adjusted the sack to Nathaniel's small frame. When it was finally secure, Ma placed the bunched up part of the sack inside Nathaniel's hands, "Keep a grip on it till yer out there. It'll snag on somethin' an trip ya up if yer not careful. Go on now! Stay close to Jane."

With the bundled up tail of his cotton sack in hand, Nathaniel walked out into the world. He almost tripped as he stepped down from the porch. The sun was up, but the day was still young. Pa and Jane were standing in two separate rows, collecting little white balls and feeding them into the ivory slugs that trailed behind them. Pa's sack already had a good bit of bulge to it.

Careful not to trip, Nathaniel walked over to his sister's side. Jane picked two white balls and handed one to her brother. As Jane removed the dark, dried up stem on the bottom of the fluffy white stuff, the little boy continued staring blankly at his own. Jane plucked another boll and handed it to him.

"Don't just look!" Jane hiss-pered at him.

Nathaniel grabbed the bur and pulled it off. He felt the bag slipping off his shoulder.

"Good, put it in the sack," she said.

She watched her little brother struggle, "Take it off. Help me fill up mine, then we'll fill up yours."

Nathaniel felt a weight lifted when the bag slumped to the ground. Grabbing an ivory ball, he removed the bur from it. He cast the locks into the opening of Jane's sack. Then he did so again and again, one at a time, over and over. The dried burs scratched his hands. His eyes wandered over to Jane's quick fingers, noticing the callouses in her palms.

"Hell," Jane muttered.

Nathaniel's attention snapped to the small bit of blood on Jane's right hand. Jane tore a section of cloth from the top of the sack and wrapped it around her hand.

As she continued to harvest, Jane said, "If you start bleeding much, go see Ma. Pa gets mad if ya stain the cotton."

After a while she started humming to herself.

"Girl, quiet!" Pa snapped.

Jane mumbled something under her breath before falling silent.

"Damned tall bastards," Pa muttered, "too damn tall."

Pa moved down his row, faster than the children moved. Jane waited for him to move some distance ahead and then started to whisper a song to herself. The further Pa moved, the louder she got. Nathaniel listened while his hands searched and plucked more and more locks.

"Let's hurry up," Jane whispered loudly. "Pa gets mad if we fall too far behind."

"How far is that?" Nathaniel asked.

"Depends on the time."

"Time?"

"Dunno," Jane grabbed another ball, "he's nicest right after lunch."

The children quickened their pace. Nathaniel tried not to think about the tedious motions, but just do them, over and over again. The sun was beating down. It was a great day for a swim.

After enough accumulation, Jane broke her song. "Fetch the other sack," she instructed him.

As he took off running, Jane tied up and left the bulging bag on the ground. Nathaniel returned and handed the empty sack to Jane. He watched her tie the sack over her shoulder. Then she continued harvesting.

"Keep going!" Jane hissed.

Nathaniel faced the plants and continued.

Keeping his tone low, Nathaniel asked, "How long do we go for?"

"Till the sun sets."

Nathaniel glanced up at the sun which was still making its ascent to the zenith.

"Every day," she said. "Until every last one of these damn things picked,"

Nathaniel slowed his pace.

"When the harvest quits, we go to school," Jane yelled, "hurry the hell up! I ain't missing no schooldays on accounta you bein' a slow poke."

Nathaniel ignored Jane until she grabbed him painfully by the wrist. Jane's eyes burned with serious anger. Nathaniel felt his own fury rushing through his face.

"I don't wanna still be in this field come late autumn," Jane declared as she threw Nathaniel's hand at the plants.

Nathaniel's heart pounded in his ears. He stared at the ripe plants. Nathaniel felt the blood flowing back into his wrist. His other hand grabbed some more white lint. His heart pounded in his ears as her words and tight grip cycled through his memory. Plucking the bur, Nathaniel removed and released it from the lint before tossing the white fluff into the sack. He did this over and over, and over and over, again. Behind Jane, Nathaniel could see Pa keeping an eye on them.

From the porch, Ma called, "Lunch!"

Pa glanced at the shack where a small wisp of smoke was emanating from the chimney. Jane tied up and dropped her sack on the ground. She took off towards the shack, and Nathaniel did his best to follow suit. As he stepped onto the porch, he saw steam escaping through the top of the doorway. The table had been set with three bowls of leftover rabbit stew. Every pot, pan and kettle the family owned was cooking water atop the stove. A steady cloud of steam rose up.

Ma emerged from her bedroom carrying two full buckets, "Where's Pa?"

She moved to the stove and poured water from a bucket into the various containers, topping them off.

"Prolly still picking," Jane said.

"Get him 'fore his soup get cold!" Ma snapped.

Jane quickly departed from the shack.

Nathaniel took a bite of soup.

"Wait," Ma said, "we ain't thanked the Lord yet."

Nathaniel placed his spoon on the table and gulped. The food felt warm as it trickled down into his gullet.

"What's all this?" Pa demanded as he stood in the doorway.

Steam mixed with sweat and condensed down into droplets before dripping off the brim of his hat.

"Mr. Gibb is coming by," Ma looked up. "We gonna smell like rosebuds when he get here."

Pa grunted as he strode over to the water barrel and grabbed the wooden ladle.

Jane emerged from the parents' bedroom and sat down at her seat.

"Deary," Ma said as she poured water into a pan, "would ya fetch me the trough?"

"After I eat," Pa grunted as he took his seat. "Thank ya, deary."

"You kids need to hurry up," Pa announced as he took hold of his spoon. "I've done nearly three times the amount y'all done."

"Ya reckon two small children oughta be outwork'n a full-grown man?" Jane inquired.

"Outwork'n more than a third my pace," Pa said. "Damn the sundown, y'all ain't coming in till ya pick as many pounds as I do."

"Don't make them work late today," Ma pleaded, "not when Gibb's visitin'."

Pa grunted then shoveled down a load of rabbit stew. He finished his bowl quicker than Nathaniel could empty his water glass. With his second portion, Pa took a slower pace.

When he finished, Pa stood up and said, "Y'all finished?" then he turned and exited the shack.

Ma removed the dirty dishes. Jane shoved her empty bowl to the center of the table before exiting the shack. When Nathaniel finished, he jumped down from his seat.

"Nathaniel," Ma called, "fetch me them dishes."

Nathaniel glared at the center of the table. He ascended his chair again, and reached out for Jane's bowl. With a quick glance at Ma, Nathaniel crawled onto the table and gathered up the leftovers. He slid the pile over to the edge before sliding off. Ma walked up and grabbed the pile. She let them go into one of the larger boiling pots.

Without turning around, Ma said, "Get back out there."

As he moved to leave, Pa moved through the threshold carrying a pig trough over his back. Nathaniel stood back as Pa maneuvered the heavy load.

When Pa cleared the doorway, he glanced over at his boy and said, "Go help Jane."

Nathaniel dashed out the door.

As Nathaniel approached, Jane quickly explained, "This is where Pa said to start."

Nathaniel took the spot next to her and started harvesting. The porch steps creaked as Pa descended them rapidly. He walked slowly, giving himself ample time to assess the children. He joined in next to Nathaniel, and within minutes, they started on a new plant. Pa studied his boy's hands out of the corner of his eye. The boy quickened his pace but his fingers fumbled with the rough, raw texture.

Pa placed a hand on the boy's shoulder. "Here."

Nathaniel's upper body went limp as Pa's ginormous hands closed over his own. They guided his fingers to the plant.

"Like this."

Closing his son's digits around the boll, he pulled and Nathaniel added some strength too. One hand held the bulb steady while the other pulled the dried burs off. Soon the lint was loose.

"Lower yer bag," Pa commanded.

Jane lowered her shoulder.

Together, Nathaniel and Pa placed the cotton inside the her sack.

"Keep it within reach," Pa said.

"Yessir," Jane answered.

Stepping away from the boy, Pa continued his rapid pace. The repetition increased Nathaniel's speed, but out of the corner of his own eye, he witnessed his family members picking at much faster rates.

Boll by boll, plant by plant, second by second, the sun slowly dipped. Bit by bit, the day cooled. Covered in sweat and dirt, Nathaniel felt a burden in his heart evaporate when Ma shouted, "Come on n' get washed!"

The children watched their father.

Pa grunted as he tied up his bag. "We're done for today."

"Come on!" Ma shouted even louder.

"We're coming!" Pa yelled back.

Nathaniel almost took off sprinting for the shack, but Jane interrupted his jump start. "Get the other sack we filled up first."

Nathaniel immediately switched to frantically searching his surroundings.

Jane gestured, "We left it a few rows back."

Sprinting past the rows, Nathaniel searched each one for the sack. He spotted it halfway down a completed row. Grabbing the sack by the strap, he pulled it towards the shack.

"Don't drag *it!*" Pa shouted. "You'll put holes in it!"

As Nathaniel struggled to lift the load, he watched Pa deposit his sack into the cart's bed. Then Jane tossed her sack atop of Pa's before following him up the front steps. The weight caused the cart's handles to fly up into the air. When the two disappeared into the shack, Nathaniel dropped his bag down and dragged it. Abandoning the sack beside the cart, Nathaniel dashed into his home.

Hot, moist air radiated from within the shack. Inside the atmosphere was dense with steam. The trough was now filled with steaming, hot water and exhaustion.

"Nathaniel," Pa commanded, "pass me the bar a soap."

Taking a chair by the top rail, Nathaniel dragged it over to the only pair of shelves built into the shack's back wall. When he found the right position, he stood up on the chair, reached up, and pushed a dingy ABC's book out of the way to grab hold of a bar of ivory colored lye. Jumping down, Nathaniel walked over to Pa and offered up the item.

"Thanks."

Leaning forward, Pa revealed a horizontal and diagonal collection of cascading scars that covered nearly every inch of his back. Bending back his limbs, Pa reached back and placed suds on his shoulder blades. Ma moved closer and spread the soap to regions he could not reach.

Cupping her hands together, Ma splashed and rinsed his skin. Nathaniel stared at the elevated creases of excess scar tissue. Pa's eyes rolled back as Ma rubbed his neck. His eyes grew heavy as he leaned forward and Ma planted a kiss on his spine. When she stepped back, Pa's head sank into the water. Nathaniel counted many Mississippis, and then some more, before Pa finally surfaced. Ma placed a clean towel in his hand, and he buried his face in it.

Turning around, Ma pointed at her son. "Yer next."

Nathaniel looked away as his fingers grabbed hold of his shirt. Waiting for Pa to enter the bedroom, Nathaniel finally finished taking off his shirt. Removing his undergarments and positioning himself beside the trough, Ma came up behind and lifted her boy up. When he plunged into the warm, soapy water, Ma immediately started splashing her son. Squeezing his eyes shut, Nathaniel waited for the soapy water to fall off his face. Her fingernails dug the dirt from out of his hair. Nathaniel cringed. Finally, a damp towel covered his face. Ma lifted him from the bath. Without opening his eyes, Nathaniel was held steady in midair until he regained his footing.

Jane entered through the back door carrying a bucket of water and shouting, "Is this enough? Am I done yet?"

When he wiped his face dry, Nathaniel opened his eyes.

Ma sighed, "Jus' 'bout. Pa, help me empty this."

Emerging from the bedroom fully dressed, Pa took the trough onto the porch. After lifting up one side and emptying it, Pa dragged the trough back into the shack. As soon as he set it down, Ma was pouring freshly boiled water into it.

Pa placed a hand on his son's shoulder. "Give the women some peace."

The boy followed his father onto the porch. The rocking chair creaked as Pa sat down while the lad plopped himself on the top porch step. Pa took a dried up cob and a long, hollow twig from the front pocket of his overalls. Sticking an end into a hole in the side of the cob, he placed the connected lip of his homemade pipe in between his lips. Reaching into a side pocket, he produced a small, dark brown bag. As he untied the leather strip, the strong scent of dried tobacco filled the air. Pa poured dried leaves into his right palm. Biting down on the stem, Pa began filling the pungent plant into the bowl. After putting away the bag, Pa padded down the tobacco in the chamber with his left thumb.

"Shoul' coun' yerself lucky," Pa stuck the stem in his mouth. "When I's yer age, I'd earned mos' my collection." From his other pocket, Pa pulled out a short book of matches. "Young skin scars easy." He lit the match and let the flame lick the bowl. With every inhalation, the fire stretched for Pa and the blue smoke built up with each puff. Shaking his hand, Pa extinguished the tiny, growing flame. Then he sat back in his chair, adding, "Too easy."

Dueling columns of blue smoke seeped through the tiny slit between his barely separated lips. Placing a foot on a beam, Pa slowly rocked himself. "Suppose the war won that much, ya don' got no scars like I." He eyed the boy. "Ya never got beat on the regular."

At the sound of footsteps, they both glanced back just in time to see Ma emerge from the shack. She offered each of them a plate of boiled corn and beans before disappearing back into the house.

Pa carefully set down his still smoking pipe on the floor next to him before commenting, "Gotta shoot 'nother rabbit." He chomped down on his corn. "Maybe even get a rattler."

The growling in Nathaniel's stomach subsided as he devoured the nutrients.

Taking a break from his food, he said, "I like rabbit."

"You'll like whatever I catch."

The men folk ate until there was nothing left on their plates save a dirty spoon and a barren cob. Pa bit off a chunk of husk and chewed.

Sudden movement drew Nathaniel's eyes to the horizon. Some ways out above the path, two riders approached, kicking up a cloud of dust. Putting down his empty plate, Nathaniel stood up, tapped Pa on the shoulder and pointed in the direction of the path. Pa followed the boy's finger to the incoming guests.

Galloping hooves became louder. As they neared the shack, the larger of the two riders took a slight lead. A vicious scar streaked diagonally over the leader's right eye, leaving a bald spot in the middle of his brow. He pulled up before the shack, and his undamaged eye studied the beams holding up the slanted roof. With reins still in hand, he jumped down from the horse and hitched it to the nearest beam. The second rider, a thin white man, pulled off one glove and scratched his left mutton chop. The larger man took hold of his stallion and secured it to the post before its rider dismounted.

Grinning at Pa and Nathaniel, the white man declared, "Evening!"

"Why's Goober here?" Pa inquired.

Nathaniel's eyes shifted to the large visitor. His attention focused on the man's missing eyeball.

"To assist me," Mr. Gibb responded as he approached the porch. "And who is this little roly poly?" He took off his other glove and placed them both in a jacket pocket.

"This's my boy," Pa answered, "Nathaniel."

Crouching down to Nathaniel's eye level, Mr. Gibb smiled.

"Salutations, Nathaniel. I'm Mr. Gibb. What happened to your chin? It looks like you fought off a troll!"

Nathaniel mumbled, "Sir," before shifting his gaze back to Goober. The boy touched his own scar.

"Goober look meaner than he is," Mr. Gibb glanced at his comrade. "Been my best friend since 'fore I was even born."

"Hello, Goober!" Nathaniel waved.

"'fraid he can't say much," Mr. Gibb said.

Nathaniel dropped his hand. "Why not?"

"Got his tongue cut out," Mr. Gibb said. "Wasn't much older than you when it happened."

Nathaniel's clenched his jaw, but then blurted out, "Why?"

"For ask'n too many questions," Pa replied. "Why don' ya go inside."

Nathaniel scurried through the doorway. Inside the shack, both Ma and Jane had pulled chairs up to the wall. Their ears were pressed against the barrier. Breaking from her vigil, Jane grabbed her brother by the wrist and pulled him away from the doorway.

Jane put an index finger to her lips as they heard Mr. Gibb say, "Help's lack'n these past few harvests."

Jane loosened her grip. Turning away from the window, Nathaniel almost collided into the trough. He entered the children's room and flopped belly first onto his cool, breeze-kissed sheets. Nathaniel placed his chin atop his soft, refreshing pillow. Staring at the roundness of the logs in the wall, his ears strained to distinguish the outside conversation.

After a futile moment, Nathaniel tried, "Qi?"

A frown formed as he listened to the indiscernible sounds of adult conversation.

The bantering went on and on.

Nathaniel hopped out of bed and opened up his chest. Ignoring the stacks of clothes, Nathaniel took out a wooden box and placed it upon his bed. Opening it up, he pulled out a gun shaped stick. It had a long barrel and even a bit of a bulge where a cylinder should be. He aimed down its sights and quietly shot the bad guys hiding in the walls and ceiling. Tossing the gun on his pillow, he grabbed a ball made out of tightly wound string. He hurled it against the wall.

With a thud, it bounced weirdly off a log. Stretching out, Nathaniel caught the bouncing sphere with one hand. He threw it and caught it again. Ma's wild eyes came bursting into the room.

"Stop that!" She hiss-pered.

Nathaniel froze as the ball hit the floor and rolled under Jane's bed. Ma disappeared from view. Nathaniel laid down on the bed and stared upward. He picked up his stick and quietly shot at the bored ceiling.

The adult's conversation subsided and soon after that, the horses started galloping. They moved out of earshot.

A little while after that, Pa's voice boomed, "Where's the boy?"

Nathaniel jumped up from bed and hurried to the front of the house. As he skirted onto the porch, Ma held out an arm to catch her son before he stumbled into his sister.

"We're assistin' Mr. Gibb with haul'n the harvest." Placing a foot on the beam, Pa rocked himself. "Labor's short this year, jus' like last," He sucked on his pipe. "He wants a child to come along."

"He say what for?" Jane said.

Smoke wafted from Pa's speaking lips. "Reckon it's to fit some-place we can't."

"We'll get pay?" Nathaniel wondered aloud.

Pa halted his rocking rhythm. "Y'all *should* get paid a day's wage."

"'specially if he asked for 'em *specific'ly* ," Ma said.

"Matter of fact," Pa said, "I'll mention it next time I see him."

"How much is a day's wage," Nathaniel asked.

"For you?" Pa assessed. "You'll be happy with a quarter."

"Y'all gonna hav'ta go ta Freemont," Ma said, "if ya ever intend on spen'n it,"

Nathaniel's thumb rubbed his chin's scar. "Why can't I spend my money in town?"

A hush fell over the family. Nathaniel's wide eyes wandered from Pa staring at the dirt to Ma staring at nothing, to Jane biting her lower lip.

"Can't buy noth'n but trouble in Oaksville," Jane stated. "No one will sell to us."

"Why not?"

Jane stood up. "'cause we black."

Pa nodded his head, "Best to avoid that town. But it's the nearest rail for Gibb. 'less he wanna go all the way up to Montgom'ry."

Ma studied her children. "Gibb must be desperate."

Chewing on the bit of his pipe, Pa answered, "Reck'n so," He stood up from his chair. "I'mma go hunt for some meat."

Nathaniel brightened. "Can I go?"

"No." Pa entered the shack.

"Don't blow that smoke in the house," Ma pleaded.

Jane quickly occupied the vacated, rocking chair.

Nathaniel descended the porch steps. "I'm gonna go play."

"Jane, go play with yer brother." Ma said.

"I don't wanna."

"I didn't ask ya what ya wanted." Ma called after Nathaniel, "Don't go 'yond earshot!"

Nathaniel followed the pair of horseshoe tracks that led away from the shack.

"Get up, Jane!"

With a huff, Jane went after her little brother. Ma sat down in the rocking chair.

Following the prints all the way out to where the path ended at a T-intersection. Nathaniel's feet stopped, but his eyes followed the prints as they turned left and merged onto the cross road.

"What are ya doin'?" Jane cried as she hurried to catch up.

Only the brightest constellations sparkled in the pink, purple twilight sky. The longer he studied, the more he saw space's twinkling freckles. Jane stopped and looked upwards.

"You can look at stars back on the porch," Jane said.

"Go back," Nathaniel said.

"Ma said I havta."

"I came out here to be *alone*."

"Let's go back."

"Ma's not giving up her chair."

Jane sighed and sat down crossed legged on the path.

"What's the farthest you been from here?" Nathaniel asked. "'side from town."

"Not count'n town," Jane pondered. "The schoolhouse."

"How far 'way is the schoolhouse?"

"'Over a mile."

"Oaksville?"

"Few more, takes nearly half a day to get there an' another half coming back."

Nathaniel studied Orion's belt, wondering how far away it was. The sound of a shotgun erupted into the air. Another blast followed not too long after.

7

Nathaniel stared at the rows of cotton that ran parallel to the road that led to town. Without looking down, he tugged on the lip of Jane's sack with one hand while his other hand chucked in some seedy lint. Stealing a gander upward, at the great timepiece in the sky, he asked, "What happens when we finish the last row?"

"Then we pick the other side," Jane said.

Nathaniel picked another boll. He stared at it, then stuffed it into the sack.

Jane halted her harvesting to point at the road, "Someone's coming!"

Shading his eyes with a hand, Pa squinted at the horizon. The shadowy silhouette of a horse and rider was approaching.

Standing fully erect, Pa declared, "It's **preacher** Malachi!"

"Pastor Malachi?" Jane said, "What he doing here?"

Pa knotted up his sack and let it fall to the ground, "The one an' only," he mumbled as he stepped over a row.

He moved up to the brink of his territory and casually placed a hand in his overall's front pocket. Removing his cap, he fanned himself with it. The clopping of the horse's hooves grew louder.

"Af'ernoon preacher," he called, "Long way from home?"

Pastor Malachi waved and slowed his steed before speaking in a deep, melodic tone, "God bless me; it's Ezekiel. Good to see a friendly face. I pray you are enjoying this wonderful day."

"As well as any working tenant farmer can." Pa wiped his brow.

Dismounting from the horse, Malachi took the reins and held them loosely as he meandered over.

"Mmmm, same ole', same ole', huh?" he said glumly before brightening, "My, my, yer children have grown! Is that, now don't tell me, I remember. I could never forget a face so pretty; it's Jane, right?"

Despite blushing and looking away, her reply was crystal clear, "Yes, sir."

"My, how you've sprouted," his gaze shifted to the little brother. "And who is this fine, young gentleman? I don't recall."

"Nathaniel," Pa prompted.

"Right, already old enough to be work'n 'longside his pop."

"We here, Mary an' I. Ain't noth'n more exciting than watch'n young'ns grow old and yerself grow even older." Pa brushed aside the air, "What is happening with you? Last I heard you was a sitt'n senator."

"Was. They gonna force me and other colored politicians to stand up from our elected seats." He smacked the stone wall with his horse crop. "It's damned! I can either stay an' fight *and* die." Turning his head he looked to the horizon. "Or I can go on ahead before it gets bad."

"Meet up with yer wife," Pa said.

Malachi shook his head. "Sarah died back in seventy–childbirth. The baby survived and been liv'n with me up until recent. I sent her on ahead to New Orleans about four months back. Now, I'm gonna catch up with her and my sister, her aunt."

Pa nodded as he stared vacantly at the dirt.

"Hoping to make a fresh start as a schoolteacher in one of them mixed schools. If white children bein' taught there along'side my own, ain't no one but a deranged person gonna burn *that* building down."

"That's security." Pa gestured toward the children. "Me and some other folks just rebuilt ours two years back."

"Thank God. Send yer children every day ya can," Pastor

Malachi looked down at the ground. "Take my word for it, they pulling out the federal troops, all of them, soon."

"I've never seen a single federal troop out here," Pa admitted.

Placing a gentle hand on Ezekiel's left shoulder, Pastor Malachi said, "If you keep work'n for a white man, ya ain't never gonna ever be no better than a slave without its market price. Ya need to move yer family close to Tuskegee, be with a good community that looks after its own."

Pa shook his head, "If no one notices me, I can't be targeted."

Malachi's brows furrowed, "That's what they inten!" Sadness washed his features. "Though I cannot deny the truth you speak, brother. I cannot swear that where I go, I will be without risk. But thankfully, I know God is with me."

"God ain't black."

Malachi was hushed for a good moment before he forced himself to say, "When we get to heaven, we'll claim a piece of it without any white folks on it."

"Or children."

Both men cracked a laugh.

Pa shifted his weight. "You should stay the night, dine with us, give yerself and yer steed a chance to rest."

"Thanks brother, but I cannot. I have a baby daughter I must attend to. I must go. God bless thee for thy offer," Pastor Malachi raised his hat then mounted his horse. "Although if I pass through these parts again, I will be certain to accept yer invitation. Hyah!"

The preacher took off down the road. With a vacant stare, Pa watched the rider go. He marched back to his row of cotton, crouched down, and restarted plucking.

Snatching up a boll, Nathaniel waited for Jane to open up her sack. He glanced at the preacher as he disappeared over the horizon.

"It's open," Jane stated.

His eyes snapped back to the bag. He chucked the boll in before grabbing for another.

They continued for a good many more hours. When they finished the row, they moved across the path and started on the other half of the fields.

A loud, female voice blasted inside Nathaniel's head, "TESTING!"

Clasping his hands over his ears, he screamed out, "Gaaaaahhh!"

Everyone froze in mid motion.

More quielty Qi's voice spoke inside his head, "Tell them an insect flew into your ear."

"Wha's gotten inta ya, boy?" Pa demanded.

"A bee flew in my ear."

"A what?"

"A bee!"

Pa blinked, "Stung?"

Nathaniel nodded.

"Ya good to work?"

Nathaniel shrugged, "Guess."

Pa grunted and went back to working. Nathaniel grabbed another boll and twisted off the bur. With each laborious harvesting, the rough trichomes rubbed against Nathaniel's skin; relentlessly grinding upon his soft flesh.

"I apologize for startling you," Qi said.

Nathaniel whispered under his breath, "Don't *do* that."

"Think your response. No need to voice your reply. No one else can hear me save you."

"What do you want?" Nathaniel thought.

"I finally got the conscious communications working," Qi said.

"What does that mean?"

"It means I can communicate with you at any time."

The boy paused, "I don't have to be asleep?"

"Exactly."

"Great," Nathaniel mumbled as he added another boll to the bag.

Pa removed his hat, wiped his brow, and looked up at the sun, "Let's hurry it up," he announced, "I want out of this hellish sun."

They didn't even make it halfway through their row before they officially quit for the day.

8

A fit of loud, hacking coughs snapped Nathaniel from his deep slumber. Turning his head, his heavy eyelids parted, revealing Jane curled up upon her bed. She remained motionless until another round of violent coughs escaped from her lungs. Kicking the blankets off, Jane lets out a low moan as she rolled over and hugged her pillow.

After a few seconds of quiet, Nathaniel closed his eyes and tried to release his tense, tired body. Jane moaned, then groaned. Her steady stream of sounds echoed inside Nathaniel's sleepy skull. Rolling over, Nathaniel covered his head with a pillow. Energy surged through his blood, invigorating him to sit up and discard his blankets. Rubbing his eyes, Nathaniel wondered what on earth he was doing awake. Jane coughed.

Ma appeared at the threshold. After a concerned pause, she hurried over to her daughter's side. Halting her step, she leaned over and felt Jane's forehead. Pulling her hand back, she slowly reached down and picked up Jane's fallen blanket. She placed it over her child before taking a step back. Jane let out a feeble groan, followed by an even feebler cough.

The ground shook as heavy footfalls filled the air. Pa appeared at the threshold of the room.

Nathaniel tried not to breathe as he watched Pa march over to the women to demand, "What's all the ruckus?"

The boy laid back down in his bed and covered himself in blankets.

"She's sick," Ma replied.

Pa cussed under his breath.

"She can't work," Ma stated.

"Goddamnit,"

"You'll live,"

"Mr. Gibb say he need a young'n."

Jane wheezed.

"The boy," Pa uttered.

Nathaniel's eyes grew huge.

"You said you wouldn't!" Ma retorted. "He's too young!"

"Bosh! I worked the fields when I was younger an' littler."

"As did I!" Ma retorted.

"An' now, it's our dime on the line!" Pa turned around to address the boy, "Wana work like a man today? Earn a man's wage?"

"Uh..."

"Sure ya do." Turning back, Pa addressed Ma. "Gibb can pay him Jane's share."

Nathaniel's mouth stayed shut. "Take me where?" he wondered.

"Town," Qi answered.

"What's in town?" Nathaniel inquired.

"Railroad," Qi replied.

"Why we going there?"

"To transport all the cotton your family has harvested."

Pa pointed a finger at his boy, "Be ready in five."

The whole shack shuddered as Pa exited the room. Ma scurried over to the foot of her son's bed. She opened a wooden trunk and began gathering up a suit of clothes. The boy rolled over and closed his eyes. A strong, bony hand grasped his ankle.

Pa called from the dining room, "Godamnit; where's the coffee grinder?"

"Get up and get dressed!" Ma hissed as she departed.

Placing his feet on the dirt floor, Nathaniel shot an angry glare at his sleeping sister. Her coughing fit seemed to have miraculously eased up.

"Get dressed," Qi commanded.

Begrudgingly, Nathaniel got up and moved closer to his clothes.

"Mr. Gibb hauls his own damn cotton," Nathaniel thought.

"Not this year," Qi replied.

"Why not?"

"Can't afford the extra help."

Nathaniel crawled into his clothing with the speed of a depressed turtle.

Pa boomed, "Is he ready yet?"

Despite Pa lowering his tone, Nathaniel still heard him say, "Go check on him."

By the time Ma entered the bedroom, he was in his cotton shirt and faded brown overalls.

Ma dropped a pair of worn black shoes on the floor.

She pointed at the bed, "Sit!"

Nathaniel obeyed. Ma's left hand grabbed her son's right shoe while her right hand shoved the corresponding foot into it. Grasping the shoestrings, she pulled the long laces tightly together before tying both strings around the boy's ankle. Nathaniel looked down at his right foot; his big toe stared back at him.

"Is he ready?" Pa shouted.

"Yes, sir!" she shouted back.

Jane rolled over.

Ma grabbed her son by the hand and pulled him from the room. With each awkward step, the shoes slipped and slid while the laces dug into his ankles.

Pa was sitting at one of the dining room chairs, lacing up his boots.

"Coffee ready?" Pa grunted.

"In a minute," Ma released her son.

Rubbing his heavy, itchy eyelids, Nathaniel sat down in his chair.

"Getcher hands ou'cher eyes," Pa snapped.

Lowering his hands, Nathaniel wondered, "What's his problem?"

"Sleepy and grumpy," Qi answered.

After placing a simmering bowl of oatmeal in front of each male, Ma addressed Pa, "Yer coffee's almost ready."

Nathaniel pushed his bowl away, "I'm not hungry."

"You need to eat," Qi said.

Pa strangled his spoon with his right hand he watched as his son quickly grab his bowl and begin gulping down spoonfuls of hot porridge. Pa's mouth fell open but no words fell out. After watching Nathaniel eat for a few straight seconds, Pa returned his attention to his own breakfast.

Nathaniel had never felt so hungry. The oatmeal never tasted so good. It filled his starving belly with solid warmth. By the time Pa finished his meal, Ma had placed a tin of steaming, hot coffee on the table.

"Let's be ready," Pa announced before taking a careful sip of the piping hot beverage.

Soon, Nathaniel had finished too. Pushing his dishes to the center of the table, Nathaniel stood up from his seat.

"We'll leave in a minute," Pa murmured as he struggled with his steaming beverage.

"I'm gonna wait on the porch," Nathaniel announced.

"*Sit* there!" Pa pointed a finger at the vacated chair, "And *don't* move!"

Nathaniel's mouth fell open an instant before his feet took him back to his seat. Pa grunted, and Ma came over and cleared away the empty dishes. Pa managed to get a gulp of coffee down. He waited before risking a second sip. The third attempt came sooner and the forth sooner still. Not long after that, the cup was empty.

"Ready?" Pa asked.

As Nathaniel stumbled towards the door, Pa watched the boy's oversize shoes.

"Ain't we got nothing better for his feet?" Pa asked.

"Noth'n 'sides they Sunday shoes, but I'd hate to ruin 'em with work."

"Right," Pa replied.

Outside, it was dark, with a blue gray and shattered streaks of linear sunlight on the horizon. The distant tree lines were painted in shadow save for the group directly blocking the rising sun.

Pa made his way to the cart and took hold of its handles. Lifting it up, Pa started off. Nathaniel caught up to the rear of the cart and sat down on the bed's wooden edge.

"No mule today," Nathaniel commented.

"I would advise against riding like this," Qi said.

"Like what?"

The cart came to a sudden stop; jolting Nathaniel in his seat. Heavy footsteps rapidly fell as Pa stormed his way to the rear of the bed. His nostrils flared as he grabbed his son by the collar. Ripping his child from his seat he held the boy above the ground like a rag doll. Pa's lips quivered and his irises burned. Nathaniel's small hands desperately grabbed at Pa's iron like strength. A blast of angry spit and sound erupted from Pa's crooked maw. "It's too early in the Gaw-damn morn'n for such Tom fool'ry!"

Lowering the boy, Pa tucked his son's head between his legs. Staring at the ground, the boy could not move his head. Pain erupted from his ass cheeks as Pa's hand slammed into them again and again and again. Nathaniel cried out like a bursting dam. Each shockwave sent more tears and snot streaking down his face. Finally, after countless strikes, Pa stepped back, allowing his son to fall onto the dusty ground. Half wailing and half panting, Nathaniel lay there whimpering. Rolling on his side, Nathaniel frantically and viciously rubbed his stinging rear. Time pulsed on, intertwined with agony.

Pa walked to the front of the cart. "Get up!"

He tried to stand. The pain thawed into numbness as he listened to the wooden wheels creak. He struggled onto one knee and then onto one foot. Limping after the cart, he positioned himself just behind Pa's peripheral vision. A gust of wind chilled his neck where his ripped shirt collar dangled.

"Quit sob'n."

Squeezing his eyes closed, Nathaniel clenched his fists and rubbed his wet, itchy eyeballs. A whimper drifted from his drooling lips.

They came to the T intersection and turned left. Glancing back, Nathaniel saw that the shack was now dark. Looking to his right, Nathaniel kept his attention glued to the raggedy stonewall lining the road.

Raging hatred for Jane filled his soul.

Slowing his step, Nathaniel noticed that the wall was failing to contain the various weeds and grasses from making a generational jailbreak to the road. Out in the middle of the field, Nathaniel saw the remains of structure. Two of the building's sides were gone, allowing Nathaniel to see a pair of charred stairwells protruding out from the rubble and up into the sky.

Passing by a gap in the stone wall, he spotted an overgrown pathway leading to the blackened shell of the building. Wind stirred up a scent of ash and jostled stained, infested cotton bolls. Beyond the wounded mansion was a group of smaller houses, similar in size to the shack.

Their feet took them until Nathaniel could no longer see the remnants. The stonewall ended at a wooded area that eventually led to another enclosed field. They passed the remains of a few more large homes. Most of them had been abandoned or destroyed.

Qi announced, "In a tenth of a mile, your destination will be on the right."

A long, gray rooftop was sticking up just above the shortest sections of a far off tree-line. As they traveled closer, specks of the white painted building peaked through the gaps of the trees.

"Go on an' check on the gate," Pa said, "make sure it open."

Nathaniel took off down the path. A tall, red brick wall kept the trees from ever touching the road. There was a giant, wrought-iron gate in the wall. Giant letters carved into the gate spelled, "GIBB MANOR." Nathaniel pushed the left side open, splitting the words.

Moments later, Pa pulled the cart through the gate and onto a private path. Nathaniel secured the barrier behind him before following after his father.

Directly ahead, obscuring the view of the manor, was a large, smooth stone fountain. Pa maneuvered the cart around its circular rim while Nathaniel stopped in front of it. Atop of the tallest tier stood a statue of a well attired man. Most of the man's left shoulder and arm were gone, broken off by some force, yet the man's isolated hand remained stuck to his thigh. The man's fully intact right appendage pointed back towards gate. Just above the second tier, bolted onto the outside of a cylindrical water pump, was a plaque that read, "Alabama cannot ask of me what God cannot empower me to do. -Doctor Mason Charles Gibb, 1822-1864." Every letter shared the same bold, gold engraved font, save for the last two digits, which had been roughly chiseled into place.

"Catch up to Pa," Qi said.

Panic swelled inside Nathaniel's chest. High tailing around the fountain, Nathaniel quickly caught up to Pa but made sure to remain in hindsight.

Pa halted as a flood of torchlight came pouring from the manor. Two figures emerged from the building. With bright light at their backs, their features remained silhouetted. Moving forward, they emerged from between, central white-washed columns that supported the roof of the second story's veranda. The men's foot-falls ceased to sound quite so loud as they transitioned down to the hardened earth. They entered the fetal morning light, revealing Mr. Gibb wearing blue jean overalls and a striped engineer's cap, while Goober donned his usual bleak attire. In unison, both stopped two yards from Pa.

"I brought my cart, dolly, an' boy," Pa greeted.

"Won't need the cart. The boy I'll utilize," Mr. Gibb stated as he turned his back. "Come."

Abandoning the cart, Pa followed after the two men. Nathaniel lagged behind as the trio moved around to the right side of the white washed manor. Once the boy rounded the corner, he caught sight of a large stable, the height of a three story building. A pyramid roof crowned its head, while its sides were constructed of polished, unpainted lumber.

Goober took hold of the left portion of the stable's giant front double doors and slid it open. The stable's interior was completely dark save for the reflection of a rogue sunbeam. Mr. Gibb entered the building first, followed closely behind by Pa and Goober. Beyond the adults, he spotted a big, long looming silhouette of cold metal machinery.

Slowly, Nathaniel was able to make out what the object was, "Train."

"With a caterpillar track." Qi added.

Goober jumped up into the cab while Mr. Gibb explained instructions to Pa.

Nathaniel stepped closer to the all-inclusive tread that ran the entire length of the locomotive. Moving to the closest sprocket, Nathaniel reached out to touch it.

"Do not stick your hands in heavy machinery," Qi said as Nathaniel froze in place. "That's a good way to make a mistake you'll have to permanently live with."

Nathaniel looked to the front of the metallic beast and wondered, "Why is its face open?"

"It gives access to a section of the engine."

Nathaniel spotted Mr. Gibb standing just outside the threshold of the circular opening. The white man gestured for the boy to come hither.

"Let's get a wiggle on, chum," Mr. Gibb called. "We gonna make this baby ace high."

As he drew near, Nathaniel eyed the long, thin metal instrument in Mr. Gibb's hands. One end had a series of rigid bristles, and the handle was long, smooth and flexible.

Mr. Gibb's eyes widened. "I need a li'l bugger like you to hop on up and clean'er out," he said as he offered the tool to the boy.

"You gonna pay me a dollar?" the boy asked.

Cracking a smirk, Mr. Gibb replied, "I'll pay ya a dime."

Mr. Gibb released his grip and Nathaniel took the rod. The adult moved around, behind the boy, and stuck both his hands underneath the lad's armpits and lifted him up.

"Mind your head," Mr. Gibb said as he let go.

Nathaniel ducked his head as he landed inside the interior of the locomotive. Nathaniel found himself kneeling in layers of soot and ash. Struggling to put his weight onto his feet, Nathaniel eventually managed a squatting position that allowed him to maneuver forward. A pair of metal pipes blocked his path.

"Stick the bristly end inta those openin's back there," Mr Gibb pointed. "Twist an' clean 'em out."

Nathaniel stared through the pipes at the vaguely hexagon shaped wall filled with circular holes behind it.

"Know what they called?" Mr. Gibb asked, "They called flues."

"How do I get back there?" Nathaniel asked.

Mr. Gibb pointed at the gap, just below the elbows in the pipes, and ran into the opposite sides of the machine. "Go under them pipes."

There were layers of dust and rubbish covering the floor.

"Can I clean it first?" Nathaniel asked.

Mr. Gibb licked his lips, "Hang on."

He disappeared from view but soon returned with a shovel in one hand and a broom in the other.

As Mr. Gibb placed the shovel on the ground, he commanded, "Jump down."

Nathaniel did.

"Stand back." Mr. Gibb began sweeping.

Plumes of dark dust erupted into the air. Covering his nose with the collar of his shirt, Nathaniel took two quick steps back.

After a brief moment of elbow grease, Mr. Gibb wiped his brow, "It's better now. Get ya back up in there."

Climbing up into the smoke box, Nathaniel crawled face first through the less dirty crawlspace. Pulling his legs through, he took a squatting position and readied the cleaning utensil.

"Start in the top left corner," Qi said.

With both hands, Nathaniel aimed the bristly end at the metallic hole. With a thrust he jammed the cleaning instrument into its target.

"Twist," Qi said.

Nathaniel did.

"Twist more; a little more," Qi instructed, "Pull."

Pain blasted up his arm like exploding frostbite as Nathaniel's elbow collided into a heavy metal pipes.

"Gah!" Nathaniel screamed as he crumpled to the floor clutching his throbbing appendage.

"Wha's the matter?" Mr. Gibb demanded.

"Funny bone!"

Mr. Gibb grimaced as he clutched his own elbow, "I hate that," he mumbled, "You gonna be alright?"

Breathing heavily and with tears welling up, Nathaniel waited for the agony to dwindle.

"Y'alright?" Mr. Gibb questioned.

Nathaniel grunted as the pain receded to a dull throb.

"Ya gonna be able to keep goin'?" Mr. Gibb asked.

"I'll get 'em clean!" the boy snapped.

Mr. Gibb stiffened. He watched the child massage his wound until he was ready to pick up the fallen rod. Facing the flues, Nathaniel went back to work.

"Yer Pa ever talk to ya 'bout bein' 'round white folks?" Mr. Gibb inquired.

Nathaniel twisted the rod. A puff of ash drifted from the cold metal.

Mr. Gibb raised his tone. "Ya hear me, boy?"

With his hands still grasping the rod, Nathaniel snapped his eyes back at Mr. Gibb, "I'm get'n it done, ain't I?"

"I oughta smack ya for talk'n smart to me!" Mr. Gibb barked. "Folks won't give a damn how cute a'n* yar, if ya start giv'n 'em any smart lip. Reckon ya don't know a continental about the real world. Reckon your pa forbids such talk."

Nathaniel yanked the brush from the flue and a giant cloud of dust erupted. He quickly squeezed his eyes shut and looked away. When he dared to open them, Mr. Gibb was gone.

After removing rubbish from thirteen more flues, Pa's voice boomed louder than the train's thick metal could muffle, "Boy!"

Nathaniel froze save for a gulp in his throat.

"Answer me!" Pa demanded.

Nathaniel mustered up all his desperate loudness. "Yes?"

The volume lowered but the authoritative tone remained, "Speak with me after yer finished! Understood?"

Nathaniel listened to his pounding heart shaking his entire body.

"Understood?" Pa yelled even louder.

"Yes!" Nathaniel mustered back.

He slowed his pace, and had done only thirty something flues clean when Pa appeared at the threshold of the smoke box.

Mr. Gibb loudly addressed Pa. "Is he done?"

Pa shout echoed around the engine, "Are ya done?"

"There are twenty seven flues remaining," Qi said.

"I got twenty-seven left," Nathaniel yelled back.

Pa repeated the number.

Mr. Gibb replied, "Why don't ya go assist Goober wi—"

"You told me I *need* to talk with my son, did ya not?"

Nathaniel could not discern Mr. Gibb's response.

Pa clapped his hands together. "Hurry up! It shouldn't take ya all damn day."

Pa waited. He shifted his weight. Eventually, he managed to awkwardly sit down on the relatively small cowcatcher.

As Pa fanned himself with his hat, he muttered, "How the hell he gonna get this engine hot before sundown, I dunno."

It took ages for Nathaniel to get down to fifteen flues, and even longer to finish. When he finally did, he slid the cleaning rod through a gap first. Cautiously, Nathaniel slid underneath the pipes. With firm strength, Pa lifted his son from the smoke box and planted him gently on the ground. Dropping to one knee, Pa removed his hat, revealing heavy eyes. His skin hung loose upon his face.

In a low, serious tone, Pa said, "Son."

Nathaniel held his breath.

"Ya gonna havta be careful in town today," Pa said. "On the farm we got the privilege of avoid'n," Pa took a glance around the side of the locomotive before continuing, "—crackers," he looked back at his son. "But we got no choice today."

"Crackers?" Nathaniel pondered.

"White folks. See, it's a white folk's town we going to. An' you gotta be on yer best behavior. It's a white law. It don't protect black folks. Matter of fact, if we weren't accompan'n Mr. Gibb, the town's folk wouldn't want us around at all. I ain't say'n this is right but it is how this world, this life, is." Pa looked directly into his son's eyes, "Ya remember Senator Malachi?"

"Yeah," Nathaniel said.

"He was making law up in D.C. And I mean making 'em, writing 'em, vote'n on 'em, til the big white majority start fight'n an' sendin' all coloreds outta town. Hard as ya may try, ya can't pass no law that can change a man's bias. He still gonna have his feelings no matter how fancy the letters ya scribble down to proclaim otherwise."

Nathaniel blinked.

Pa continued, "If ya ever do find yerself stroll'n through a town, stay off the sidewalks. Almost a sure way to get trouble is using the sidewalks. Just avoid them. Never stare at a white lady for too long, matter of fact, don't stare at a white lady. Listen for 'em and know every directions yer not supposed to look in. Don't ask why, just know, punishment for such a sin is much worse than you can ever imagine." Pa leaned in close and whispered. "That's how Goober lost his tongue. And he is lucky," Pa relaxed a little. "Remember what I said, stay in the cab; under no circumstances are ya to go exploring by yer lonesome. There ain't no tell'n what some white folks might think."

"Qi?" Nathaniel wondered. "Is this true?"

"Pa is not lying." Qi replied. "This is a serious threat supported by local law enforcers."

Mr. Gibb popped his head around the side of the locomotive. "Everythin' fine? I sure could use some help."

"Finish'n up," Pa answered.

"Nathaniel," Mr. Gibb said, "there's no need to worry. Stay in the cab the whole time and nothin' will happen. Understood?"

Nathaniel nodded.

"It's a cinch. Zeke, help Goober load water."

Pa stood up from the cowcatcher. Turning around, Mr. Gibb led the way back to the cab. But Nathaniel tugged on his father's trousers and halted their progress. The adult looked down and saw his son gesturing for him to come closer.

Leaning down, Nathaniel whispered into his father's ear, "Wha's a n*?"

Pa stiffened, fury flushing his cheeks.

"Y'all coming?" Mr. Gibb called.

"Still learn'n!" Pa shouted, then turned to continue his conversation with his son, "It's a horrible word. People that use that word are bad people who think colored folk are beneath them. But we ain't n* no more," Pa looked deep into his child's eyes, "understood?"

Nathaniel nodded.

"Lotta men died to make it so." Pa took his boy by the hand and guided him alongside the train, towards Mr. Gibb.

"Learned him?" the white man asked.

"Well enough," Pa said.

"Got another errand for the boy," Mr. Gibb said, "go help Goober fill the water." Letting go of Nathaniel's hand, Pa took hold of the metal ladder and climbed. Wrapping a long arm around the boy's shoulders Mr. Gibb drew his face very close to Nathaniel's.

Mr. Gibb gestured to the locomotive. "Betcha never seen nothin' like this."

Nathaniel nodded.

The adult grinned. "It's three cars in one. The cab in front, the coal bin in the middle and the flatcar acts as caboose."

Nathaniel nodded.

"She's built with Confederate pride, built to knock back every damn Yankee that dared come lower than Virginia." He pointed to the flatcar with a tower of cotton bales tied into a neat rectangle atop of it. "Three Gatling guns, each bigger than a full-grown cow, would be mounted there," Mr. Gibb wiped his brow, "We go'n to oil her."

"What?"

Mr. Gibb led the way away from the train to a side of the stable where piles and piles of equipment lay, "We're going to lube 'er sprockets up. Keep 'er treads turn'n."

There was a vague sort of order to what had been tossed into the corner. Nathaniel stopped at the edge of the piles of farming tools. Mr. Gibb stepped through the metal foliage and made his way to three long shelves bolted into the back wall. Every inch of shelf was taken up by an oil can. Picking up the closest one, Mr. Gibb shook it, listening to its contents like a doctor inspecting a patient's heart. He placed it back on the shelf before checking another.

"Step back," Qi said.

Nathaniel did so, just as a full can came flying over the piles before landing on the dirty ground. Walking over to the fallen can, Nathaniel stooped down and tried to pick it up. Mr. Gibb emerged from the disorganized tool storage with his hands full.

"Use both hands," Mr. Gibb said as he led the way back to the locomotive.

Nathaniel gripped the handle with both hands as he followed him back to the machine. Mr. Gibb stopped at the rear end of the tread. The boy stared up at the tower of cotton bales while the adult aimed the can's spout and then squeezed the trigger. With a clunk, a dark viscous liquid spurted out.

Looking over at Nathaniel, Mr. Gibb commanded, "Pay attention!"

Nathaniel's eyes snapped to the can's spout. Mr. Gibb oiled up every nook and cranny, where the metal would twist and grind with motion.

"You give it a try," Mr. Gibb presented the oil can. "Don't miss an inch."

Taking the can in hand, Nathaniel aimed and squeezed the trigger. He looked up at Mr. Gibb.

"Keep yer eye on yer target. Yer doin' fine." Mr. Gibb leaned back and yelled, "Y'all finished up with the tinder?"

"Jus' about!" Pa yelled back.

"Let's get a wiggle on!" Mr. Gibb disappeared around to the other side of the locomotive.

Cyan dots appeared in Nathaniel's vision, covering the train's tread in color.

Nathaniel muttered, "Even the damned spider's ordering me around today."

"If you do not properly lubricate," Qi explained, "the machine will generate too much friction during travel and potentially break. I doubt you would enjoy having to wait for this trio to repair such a machine."

Nathaniel squirted oil, and one by one removed each dot.

Jumping down from the cab, Pa and Goober moved to the back of the stable where they exited the building through a back door. Looking beyond the doorway, Nathaniel spotted a field outside.

When the door closed, Nathaniel returned to work. His mind wandered further and further away from the lubing. Mr. Gibb reappeared and walked alongside the tread, inspecting the lad's work. When he reached the youth, he had a big smile on his face.

"Looks great," Mr. Gibb admitted. "Ya didn't miss a spot. Maybe one day, you'll be a Pullman Porter. How many ya got left?"

"Just these."

"Come up to the cab when yer done," Mr. Gibb said before heading there himself.

When Nathaniel oiled the final dot, he quickly chucked the empty cans in the midst of the unruly heap of discarded inventory and headed for the ladder.

Scurrying up the ladder, Nathaniel had reached the final rung when Pa appeared above him. Reaching down, Pa grabbed hold of his son and lifted him up into the cab. Placing the boy on the wooden floor of the cab, Nathaniel stared at a podium made of polished mahogany. It was rectangular in shape, though its top was crowned with the top half of a metal semi- circle. The numbers, '-15, -10, -5, 0, 5, 10, and 15' were painted in black ink on the metal semi circle and protected by a convex shield of thick glass. Sprouting out of the crux of the half moon and aiming straight for the sky was a dark polished throttle with a thin, gray metallic clutch. On the opposite side of the cab stood an identical twin podium.

At the front of the cab was a vertical jungle of pipes and valves. Most of it was blocked by Goober squatting in the center of the metallic symphony, and Mr. Gibb standing behind him. Mr. Gibb held down a lever while Goober grabbed from a box of kindling and fed it into the mechanical beast. Orange light flickered.

"Don't touch noth'n," Pa instructed.

Stepping back, Nathaniel leaned up against the rear wall of the cab.

Mr. Gibb released the lever and the fiery light stopped bouncing off the walls. He turned around and spotted Nathaniel.

"Boy, git over here," Mr. Gibb commanded.

Nathaniel cautiously stepped forward.

"Quick!" he gestured frantically before placing a hand on the lever he had just been holding, "Yer in charge of this lever. It controls access to the firebox."

Nathaniel reached up and grabbed hold of the handle with both hands. He stood outstretched, with barely any control of his appendages.

"Got it?"

His small, sweaty fingers squeezed tightly around the lever and then slipped slightly but not enough. Nathaniel nodded.

Mr. Gibb looked back at Pa, "Where's yer other kid?"

"Jane?"

"Yeah. Why ain't she here?"

"Sick."

"Too bad," Mr. Gibb pointed at the boy. "Yer responsible fer open'n that lever."

"Uh…"

Mr. Gibb crossed his arms. "Understood?"

"Nod your head," Qi instructed.

Nathaniel nodded his head.

"Good, now see this other lever?"

Nathaniel noticed the knobby control being indicated and nodded.

"That's the regulator. Don't touch it, don't bump into it. Goober an' I will worry about mucking with the regulator. Just stand back but when yer Pa needs to put another shovel of coal into the firebox, you gotta fulfill yer responsibility." Mr. Gibb tapped on the boy's responsibility. "Ya got that? Need I say any of it again?"

Nathaniel grabbed the lever and let his weight pull down, sliding the two thick, metallic semi circles apart and spilling orange light into the cab.

"Great, let go. Only do it when yer pa has a load; too much air is bad for an engine. It'll explode."

"Too much air burns the fuel faster," Qi said. "Overloading the firebox and running her at full tilt for too long will make her explode. Faulty machinery will make her explode."

"How long we gotta wait for her to be hot 'nough to travel?" Pa inquired.

59

A smile cracked Mr. Gibb's face. "I know a few tricks. She heats up quicker than a nickel girl."

"Maybe I'll use yer technique on my stove."

"Ya'd blow that shack up."

Pa snorted. "But it won't blow up yer train?"

Mr. Gibb glanced back and winked before facing the engine.

"I'll believe it when I see it," Pa snickered. "Ya should've let us sleep in til noon; it take a good long while for an ice cold engine to get fully hot."

Mr. Gibb pulled out a timepiece, "She quicker than ya think," he said, and placed the pocket watch back in his jacket, "Goober, I'm go'n up front."

When Mr. Gibb departed from the cab, Goober moved to the back and picked up a wooden crate with the word, 'DANGER' hand painted onto it. He moved to the front of the train and opened it. Pulling out a smaller, wooden box that resembled a large six sided die. Sliding away a removable segment from the top of the cube, Goober retrieved a glass cylinder, uncorked it, and began pouring its powdery contents into the bigger box's base. When he was satisfied, he placed the glass tube inside the wooden box and closed it up again.

Climbing into the cab, Mr. Gibb called out, "Now."

In one quick motion, Goober picked up the wooden box and tossed it into the burning maw. Nathaniel released the lever and the fire-door slammed shut. Goober returned to his throttle while Mr. Gibb positioned himself near his own control. With a vacant look in his eye, Mr. Gibb stared down at the cab's floor.

"Are they waiting for something?" Nathaniel wondered.

"Yes."

Mr. Gibb put a finger to his lips. They all stood in silence, feeling the heat of the fire grow. The crackles grew louder. The entire loco-motive rocked as a muffled explosion occurred within the firebox.

"Let her have air!" Mr. Gibb shouted, "Boy! Open'er up!"

Nathaniel jumped up and grabbed his lever. A blast of sticky heat cascaded over him as long flames poured out of the maw.

"That's hot," Mr. Gibb smiled, "Fo' five!"

With a uniform metallic snap, the men shifted their levers

forward. Steam hissed out the side of the train as dark smoke shot out of the stack. The momentous initiation was punctuated by the treads digging into the earth, lurching the train forward. Smoke filled the stable as the vessel crawled towards the exit.

"Fo' ten!" He clicked his throttle another notch forward. "'nother load, Zeke!"

Biting his lip, Nathaniel continued holding the lever.

"Get ready with that lever," Mr. Gibb shouted.

Pa fed the beast a shovel full of coal.

"Close the firebox!" Mr. Gibb shouted.

Nathaniel's heart leaped into his throat as he let go. The lever snapped back and the fire-door closed.

"Goober, halt!" Mr. Gibb shouted.

Goober's tread stopped and Mr. Gibb's tread continued turning the locomotive.

"Fo' ten!" Mr. Gibb shifted his throttle forward.

The locomotive's speed picked up as the left tread regained momentum.

Suddenly the sound of cracking stone filled the air and everyone stumbled forward as the locomotive struck something solid. Metal scrapping stone screeched through the air as the train pushed and wrestled against a heavy barrier. Mr. Gibb fumbled to regain his footing while Goober lunged for his comrade's throttle. Pointing the control to the ceiling, the tread stopped spinning.

When Mr. Gibb regained his footing, he stuck his head out the window and announced, "We hit the fountain. Back five!"

Goober hurried back over to his throttle and adjusted it one notch back.

The treads lurched into reverse. Mr. Gibb braked and Goober's tread turned the train.

"Fo' five."

The train switched to forward motion. The statue had a slight lean to it, which may or may not previously have been there.

"Zeke," Mr. Gibb said, "open the front gate."

"You gonna stop?" Pa inquired.

"It's slow."

"I ain't risk'n breaking a leg."

Rolling his eyes, Mr. Gibb called out, "Halt!"

The momentum faded and died. Gripping his shovel tighter, Pa moved to the top of the ladder.

"You won't need that," Mr. Gibb pointed at the shovel.

Nathaniel stiffened as the metal spade clattered against the coal bin as Pa exited the cab.

With all attention gone from him, Nathaniel focused his own on the plethora of hissing pipes, joints and valves that made up the front portion of the train.

Mr. Gibb tapped the lad on the shoulder, "Ya wana go n' grab another load for the fire?"

Nathaniel's face brightened. He scurried to the back of the cab and picked up the fallen spade. Twisting the door handle open, Nathaniel dug the shovel into the pile. With all his might, put as much the chalky black rock upon shovel blade as he could.

"Dump half," Qi commented.

Nathaniel obeyed and carried the lighter load back to the firebox.

Mr. Gibb snapped his fingers. "Help the lad."

Goober took a step, reached out, and yanked the lever. The air instantly turned hot as it poured over Nathaniel. Squeezing his eyes shut, the boy took a step back from the heat.

"Hurry up!"

With a quick aim and prayer, Nathaniel tossed the coal and Goober released the lever.

Standing up, Mr. Gibb moved over to the right side window and popped his head out, "Ya done yet, Zeke?" he shouted.

By the time Nathaniel returned the spade to its originally fallen spot, Pa appeared on the left side of the cab. Moving back to the lever, he popped a squat by his shovel.

"Fo' five!" Mr. Gibb shouted.

The treads bit into the earth and Nathaniel steadied himself with the lever.

Pa walked over to an edge and peered over it. "Cuttin' up mo' ground than a plow."

Mr. Gibb looked back at his tread's turning wake.

"Seed it on the way back," Pa suggested.

A snort escaped Mr. Gibb's nose.

Nathaniel moved to the back of the cab.

"Stay by the lever," Qi said.

Nathaniel stopped walking and thought, "I wana *see!*"

"Halt!" Mr. Gibb screamed.

The men adjusted the train to idle.

"Goddamn carriage," Mr. Gibb remarked.

Moving to the back corner of the cab where Pa was not, Nathaniel stuck his head out the door. An older man, dressed in a dusty, brown suit, bow tie and hat, sat in a one mule buggy. His white hair contrasted with his angry; red face.

"Goddamn sonofabitch!" the driver shouted. "Get this damned devil bastard out of my way!"

"Go around!" Mr. Gibb shouted back.

Shaking a fist, the driver managed to yell even louder, "Damn'd machine's take'n up the whole road!"

"Pull off!"

"I got'smuch right to the road as any!"

Mr. Gibb pulled his head back in. He looked up at a yellow wire running along the underside of the cab's narrow ceiling.

Smiling, he said, "Cover yall's ears."

The full blast of the train's shrill whistle forced Nathaniel to slap both his ears as he tucked his chin into his throat and crumpled to the floor. The sound vibrated his entire body. When Mr. Gibb released the wire, Nathaniel could still hear the echo ringing through his hands.

"Fo' five!"

The train started up again. After a few forward feet, Nathaniel caught sight of the mule and buggy stuck on a crumpled stonewall. Anchored by its reigns to the trapped carriage, the mules could do nothing while the massive load of metal shook the earth. Nathaniel's attention remained fixed on the animal's wide, black eyes as the train passed.

"Get back to your lever," Qi said.

He made his way back to the lever. Everyone had their head outside the cab except for Nathaniel.

"Zeke, mo' coal," Mr. Gibb declared.

Retrieving the shovel and digging in, Pa soon arrived at the fire-box. With all his might, Nathaniel pulled down on the lever and his father tossed in the coal.

The residents of Gibb Manor returned to their controls and Mr. Gibb yelled, "Fo' ten!"

The smoke grew darker as their pace quickened.

"Fo' fifteen!"

At their current speed, Mr. Gibb began ordering a new load so often Pa remained in constant cycle.

"Fo' ten!" Mr. Gibb shouted.

Pa leaned his head out the side.

"Fo' five!"

The locomotive crawled. Nathaniel tried to see out the window but only managed a boring angle of the sky.

"Keep her steady," Mr. Gibb instructed, "straight shot down main street. There she goes! Watch that wagon, Goober! Don't want no lawsuit."

With his eyes remaining on the prize, Mr. Gibb grabbed the yellow wire. Squeezing his palms over his ears, Nathaniel tucked his chin into his neck. The shrill whistle blasted through the air. Mr. Gibb seemed overjoyed by the intense sound. The boy did not release his grip on his ears until the adult released his on the wire.

"Halt!"

Goober braked. The right tread gradually shifted their facing. Nathaniel moved to the cab's left side and stuck his head out the window. They were passing by a red brick schoolhouse. A heavy hand gently grabbed Nathaniel's head and pulled it back. When Goober withdrew his fingers, they both had a view of the building's front door opening up. A mother and child emerged. Their step stopped as their matching green irises locked onto the steel stallion. The little boy smiled and lifted a hand. Goober and Nathaniel waved back. The mother's mouth fell open.

"Fo' five!"

The metal beast shifted its forward speed into a gradual turn. Angling its way around the schoolhouse, Nathaniel glanced up at the metal rooster residing atop of the bell tower.

"Halt!"

Mr. Gibb's tread continued to turn the vessel.

"Fo' five!" Mr Gibb shouted. "Halt!" A brief moment passed. "Fo' five! Zeke!"

Jumping down from the window, Nathaniel hurried back to the lever, just in time, to pull it open for Pa. Mr. Gibb continued to call out positions as the train awkwardly angled itself around the red brick schoolhouse. Finally, he called for a complete stop.

Then he addressed Pa. "We gonna go meet 'bout the gin. And yer gonna make sure *no one* gits up here and messes with *noth'n*."

"What if some strange white folk push their way up?" Pa inquired.

"Fine," he turned to Goober, "Make sure no one pushes their way up here." He turned back to Pa, "Zeke yer with me!" Mr. Gibb turned to leave but then; looked back, "An' make sure yer boy stays put."

Mr. Gibb's departure was promptly followed by Goober's. Pa jumped down to the ground, spun around, pointed a finger and commanded, "***Don'*** *touch noth'n!*" before turning around.

Nathaniel's eyes remained on his father until the man disappeared inside the nearest building. A sign above the door read, "Oaksville Gin."

Standing up, Nathaniel moved closer to the wall of long, bending pipes. He reached out towards a particularly brilliant valve.

"Don't touch that," Qi said. "You'll burn yourself!"

Nathaniel lowered his hand. He felt a blue dot appear behind him. Turning around, he spotted the colorful circle residing on the left opening of the cab.

"Exit the cab there," Qi instructed.

"Leave?" Nathaniel whispered, "Pa'll bust my ass off!"

"We will be back before anyone notices."

"How do you know?"

"I can see everyone."

"How?"

"My orbital friend."

Nathaniel walked silently, towards the blue indicator, wondering, "You're sure I'll get back in time?"

"Everything will be fine."

Nathaniel peeked his head outside the cab. A vague wooden two story building sat directly behind the red brick schoolhouse. A dot appeared in the alleyway that ran between the two structures.

"Move quickly."

With swift, silent steps, Nathaniel jumped down before rushing towards his destination. Beyond the alleyway, he made out a row of fences that divided the rear ends of the main street properties. The dot sat on a fence a few acres down.

As Nathaniel jogged, he kept a wary eye on the pine trees to his right. They were interwoven with bramble and thistles. Multiple footpaths made the feeble forest patchy. Splashes and giggles could be heard coming from a group of children playing in a river not too far away.

"Stay on target."

Whipping his head back, Nathaniel caught sight of the light blue dot residing on a back fence. Moving up to the gate, he unlatched it and the cyan dot teleported to a darkly colored back door. Nathaniel moved up to it and peaked through a crack. While his nose smelled of rotten wood, his eyes adjusted to the dark corridor that lay beyond the rickety barrier. The ceiling bulged as the underbelly of a stairwell leading to the second story stole most of the hallway's head space. Pulling back on the door, his small stature easily slipped through the crack. Taking a few steps inside, he froze. Somewhere in the main area, someone mumbled something to someone. Standing in the dark hallway, Nathaniel listened and smelled until he realized that he was in the back of a grocery store.

To the boy's left a light blue dot appeared on set of shelves. It was shorter than the boy, and looked more like an extra-long cubby hole. Old, smelly knitted socks and gloves were cast about, while a single row of books was bookended by two different glass mason jars filled with dirt. Only a few bundles of pages had thick enough spines to proclaim their titles.

"Take a book," Qi said.

Nathaniel hesitated, "Which one?"

Dots appeared on every literary spine the bookshelf had to offer.

Nathaniel picked up a book and read the cover, "Tom Smith,

Indian Hunter." He flipped through the first few pages until he reached,

TOM SMITH

THE

INDIAN HUNTER

BY MS. ANN EPHENS.

BEATLE AND COMPANY
NEW YORK: 111 WILLIAM STREET.
LONDON: 42 PATERFOSTER ROW.

Entered according to Act of Congress, in the year 1860, by

IRWIN P. BEATLE & CO.,

In the Clerk's Office of the District Court of the United States
for the
Southern District of New York.

The red man's stealthy tread-

"Just look," Qi interrupted, "I'll remember."

The boy blinked, then looked at the next page.

"Faster."

Nathaniel turned the page and blinked.

"Faster."

Nathaniel flipped and reached the end of the chapter.

"Learn anything?" he wondered.

"Yes. Keep going."

Eventually, Nathaniel had looked at every single page in the book. As soon as he reached the back cover, he closed it and placed it back on the shelf.

A blue dot appeared on the biggest book in the group. Nathaniel stared at the nine gold letters printed on its black spine. "HOLY BIBLE."

Taking the book in hand, Nathaniel opened it up and saw,

OLD AND NEW TESTAMENTS

THE ORIGINAL TONGUES:

AND WITH THE

FORMER TRANSLATIONS DILIGENTLY COMPARED AND REVISED

Turning the page, Nathaniel dragged his eyes across the inky blobs, not reading their words but seeing their shapes.

"Turn."

Laying the open book atop of the short shelf, Nathaniel turned the page.

"Turn."

Nathaniel obeyed.

"Turn."

Over the next few minutes, as he flipped each page, he gradually felt the heavier weight shift from the right side of the book to the left. When it neared the end, he noticed some of the phrases were inked in a bold red color. When Nathaniel flipped to the final page, he let loose a loud sigh.

"Hello?" an unidentified male voice questioned.

The room held the silence. The front door burst open.

"Howdy Chuck," a strange male voice greeted.

"Morn'n, Rusty," Chuck returned. "Ya hear that damn ruckus this morn'n. Broke my damn'd nap up."

"It Gibb day 'gain. Almost wished I missed it like I did last year."

"Reck'n the boys down at the gin are the only ones celebratin'. Well, I ain't goin' nowhere near the damn depot today, might not even leave the store; main street will be crawling with gawkers."

Rusty laughed, "Ya need to get out mo'."

"That damn contraption don't do noth'n more than clog up main street and scare the horses n' women and excite the children."

A blue dot appeared on the backdoor.

"She lost that shine she had back in sixty six," Chuck said.

Qi said, "Lift the bottom of the door while you open it, limit the noise."

"Why don't I wait for him to leave?"

"Do it now. They're distracted by conversation."

Nathaniel grabbed the rotted bottom of the old door. Hugging the vertical rain damaged plank close to his chest, Nathaniel scooted one foot in front of the other, slowly inching his way across the threshold. A blue dot appeared at the gate.

"Forget closing it," Qi said, "we need to hurry."

Taking off sprinting, Nathaniel took awkward strides in his big shoes. Heading for a wooden crate that had been left next to the fence, he planted one foot atop of the crate while he lifted the other foot over the barrier. Its big toe caught on the toothy peak of a fence and Nathaniel went crashing into the dusty ground. Rolling to a stop, he slowly lifted his head from the ground.

"You're fine, get up."

Standing to his feet, Nathaniel felt a bit of aching in his lower back and knee. His eye refocused on the blue dot that was still indicating the far side of the abandoned building. With a quick pace, Nathaniel walked off the remaining pain as he headed for the circle.

Rounding its back corner, Nathaniel came to a sliding halt when he spotted two older boys gawking at the trackless train. Both of them glanced at Nathaniel but they quickly returned their attentions to Gibb's machine.

"I saw it last year," the shorter boy bragged, "an' the year 'fore that."

The taller one replied, "If I owned it, I'd make a name for myself."

Nathaniel saw the blue dot shining brightly through the short boy. Stepping to the side, he peered around the boy and spotted the train.

"M'pop's says Gibb's a n* lover," the shorter boy said.

Qi asked, "What're you waiting for?"

"Maybe these boys want a new friend," Nathaniel thought.

"You don't want to be friends with these boys," Qi said. "Get to the train."

"Betcha too chicken to slap its boiler," said the yellow haired one.

"Bet *yer* too chick'n to slap it," the smaller boy retorted.

"Move!" Qi said.

Nathaniel placed one foot in front of the other.

The taller boy raised a clenched fist, "Betcha I lick ya silly, you call me chick'n again,"

The other lad lifted up his arms, "You're too chicken to touch it."

"Touch it yourself, betcha a penny ya won't."

"Run for the back," Qi declared.

Nathaniel took off.

"That li'l n*'s gonna touch it," the smaller boy announced, "you more chicken than a li'l n*?"

Anger halted Nathaniel.

"Keep going," Qi insisted.

He shot a furious glare back at the boys as he wondered, "What's their problem?"

"Ignore them; keep moving."

The shorter boy yelled, "What ya look'n at, n*?" Nathaniel

turned and ran for the ladder. Stopping at the top rung, he looked back at the boys, "Let's beat 'em up!"

"*Get* in the *cab*!" Qi shouted.

Nathaniel shuffled into the cab and covered his ears but could still discern that the boys were yelling at him. Scurrying to the center of the cab, Nathaniel hid behind Goober's control. His lungs chased his breath all over his chest.

A blue dot appeared on the nearby spade.

"You might need that," Qi advised.

Like a bullet, Nathaniel jumped up and grabbed the shovel before returning to his hiding spot.

"The hell ya damned kids doin'?" Mr. Gibb yelled. "Get 'way from there!"

"A l'il n* climbed aboard yer train!" a boy answered.

"We goin' a catch 'im by the toe!" the other boy added even louder.

"The hell you are! That n*'s mine!" Mr. Gibb yelled, "Now scat before I brain the both of you!"

"You can put the shovel down," Qi said.

Nathaniel didn't. Mr. Gibb scrambled up into the cab.

Remaining on the top rung of the ladder, he scanned the cab and found the boy.

Pointing an index finger, Mr. Gibb yelled, "Don't move from there! We'll be leaving soon 'nough. Don't stick your darky nose outside this chamber." He went to leave but then, hesitated and climbed up into the cab instead.

Reaching into his overall pocket the adult pulled out a small black book. He placed the book on top of his control. Nathaniel stared at the little black book.

Pointing the same finger, Mr. Gibb commanded, "Keep an eye on this book. Make sure ya get it back to me in one piece. That's your responsibility. Understood?"

Nathaniel nodded as he looked over at the little black book. As Mr. Gibb departed from the cab, the boy noticed a small, thin pencil resting inside a leather holster attached to the spine. Once the white man was gone from sight, Nathaniel crept over to the book and picked it up. Opening it, his eyes poured over the cursive letters and numbers penned in between the perfectly printed blue lines and brackets. In the top right corner of the page, Mr. Gibb had scribbled 'August of 1868.' Nathaniel flipped through over half of the book until he ran into blank pages.

He turned back a few pages, until he reached "October 24th 1873, cotton sold at .10 cents per lb. Fourteen bales at 550 pounds sold for 770 dollars. 6/14 - Gibbson." The line above it read "October 15th 1872, cotton sold at .11 cents per lb." The line above it read "(Twelve bales at 500 lbs per bale nets 660 dollars. 4/12 Gibbson)." Flipping back a few pages, Nathaniel found "cotton at .08 cents per lb. 32 bales at 525 lbs nets 1344 dollars. Eight hundred extra bushels of corn at .25 cents nets 200 dollars. Ten cows at $25 and two bulls at $95 nets 440 dollars." The numbers made him sleepy.

"Look at every page," Qi commanded.

Nathaniel groaned.

"Be gentle."

Nathaniel propelled the pages from one side of the book to the other.

"Be gentle."

When he finally, carefully finished, he closed the book and placed it in the front pocket of his own overalls. Leaning his head back on the throttle podium, he closed his eyes. He felt the rumble of the idling engine. Opening his eyelids, Nathaniel stared up at the ceiling.

"Qi?"

"Yes?"

"Can you read me a story?"

"Which one?"

"The one about the Indian Hunter."

Qi's voice smoothed out and grew gently louder, "The red man's stealthy tread remained undetected by the fair, young maiden. She was returning from a brief personal journey into the foliage, just beyond the view of the rest of her party. Upon completion of her necessary, she returned to the trio of wagons that were stalled and awaiting her return. The girl's father strode forth to greet her but unbeknownst to anyone in the party, the most savage of all Apache chief's lay hidden amid the wild thistles and thorns. A veteran warrior with skin as red as his savage blood, he had been watching the pretty, fair maiden's feminine gait for quite some time. With salivating lips, he patiently considered the perfect time to strike. The chief's skill at hurling a tomahawk was unmatched by any fighter in the known world.

When the fair maiden clasped her hands together, the savage sprang into action, throwing the deadly tomahawk. Her father cried out in such agony as he clutched his mortally injured bosom. Wasting no time, the savage grabbed the fair maiden by her delicate hair and dragged her back into the forest. Her cries and screams, pleading for help, echoed throughout the valley."

Nathaniel sat up.

Qi continued, "Tom Smith heard the shrill cries of agony and hastened his trusty steed into a gallop. He unholstered both of his trusty Colt revolvers and followed the savage's footsteps. The maiden's screams never ceased until they suddenly stopped.

The night was filled with silence save for the sounds of Raven's gallop, Tom's loyal steed. Tom expertly navigated the desert, hot in pursuit of the savage's trail. He took a short cut through the mountains but when he found the trail, he was still hours behind. For days he traveled in pursuit of the murderous chief," Qi's tone shifted, "Mr. Gibb is coming back. We will be departing soon."

Nathaniel opened his eyes just in time to see Mr. Gibb come, bounding up into the cab.

"Let's get a wiggle on!" he shouted as he headed for the firebox.

Nathaniel jumped up.

"Let's go!" he yelled. "Take the lever, son!"

Scrabbling over to his responsibility Nathaniel thrust his entire self into pulling the lever down while his employer dumped an armload of kindling into the circular opening. Pa climbed up into the cab.

"Zeke, grab a load!"

"Give me a second."

"The quicker we get her hot," Mr. Gibb barked, "the quicker we get home!"

Pa picked up the shovel while Goober entered on the left side of the cab. Goober walked up behind Mr. Gibb and inspectated his fire-starting skills.With a shovel full of coal, Pa halted just behind Goober.

"'scuse me, sir, but the boss needs this right away."

"I'm not ready for it yet," Mr. Gibb curtly explained, "but keep it ready."

Goober moved back to his control.

Turning his head back, Mr. Gibb addressed Goober, "Should we go in reverse? Or go out 'roun' the town? Try an' skirt by the river?"

Goober stuck his head out his side of the cab. He looked behind them and sneered. After glancing forward, he shrugged.

"We'll haveta aim true, not take her for a swim. Reckon it'll be wider than main street. Zeke, load!"

"My arms are get'n tired," Nathaniel admitted.

Pa fed the flames.

"Let go," Mr. Gibb ordered.

Nathaniel gladly crumpled to the floor. Mr. Gibb marched back over to his throttle and pulled on the whistle.

"Fo' five!" he shouted.

As they shifted their levers in unison, a familiar lurch shifted the train. Nathaniel felt the vibration of the treads through his back. He listened to the rhythms of the engine. The sounds of snapping branches filled the air and Nathaniel sat up.

With an ear to ear grin, Mr. Gibb declared, "We oughta hire her out to clear land!"

Scurrying to the rear of the cab, Nathaniel stuck his head out the open left side of the cab while Pa looked out the right side. The tread's wake scarred the earth deeply, leaving crushed huckleberries and bramble behind them. They bushwhacked alongside the river until the reached the end of the block. Mr. Gibb called for a brake and the train turned left. They emerged onto the main road and Goober pushed his throttle forward swinging the vehicle to the right. After straightening themselves out, they took up most of the road. Only a pair of single horsemen managed to get by while the massive metal, behemoth bottlenecked main street. A giggle escaped Nathaniel's lips as he watched a young rider almost get thrown from a horrified horse. After they completed the maneuver the metal beast picked up speed.

Someone shouted, "That damn thing belongs on tracks!"

Glancing back, Nathaniel saw several people shaking their fists at the departing train. Swinging his head forward, he watched the world rush towards them. He closed his eyes and felt the wind rustle his hair and his cool face.

Looking up at the sky, Mr. Gibb declared, "Looks like rain." He glanced over at Goober. "Let's be quick getting her back in the stable." Then he looked at Pa. "Got it?"

Pa muttered something.

Facing front, Mr. Gibb stated, "Let's get another round of coal in."

Reeling himself back in from the window, Nathaniel dashed to the front of the cab and pulled the lever. Pa dumped some more black rocks into the firebox and Nathaniel let go. Both males returned to their previous positions. Nathaniel stuck his head out the window, and watched a familiar sight from an unfamiliar perspective. With fewer loads being called for, Nathaniel saw more of the passing views. It felt much quicker to return to Gibb Manor than it had been to reach Oaksville. Pa opened the gate and then the stable doors. He climbed back aboard just in time to hear Mr. Gibb declare, "Let the fire burn itself out," before stretching deeply, which ended with him cracking his neck.

Goober was the first to depart and Nathaniel was the last to reach solid, immobile ground. The men huddled around, Pa stood with anticipation. Mr. Gibb reached into his overall's pocket and produced a wad of greenbacks. He slipped some bills from the bigger bundle and handed them to Pa. Placing the money back into the pocket, he offered his other hand to the boy. A shiny coin lay in the center of his palm. Mr. Gibb smiled at the lad.

"Ya earned it, today." he said, "you were very responsible." He pinched the lad's cheek.

The adult released it into his fingers and Nathaniel felt the weight of the coin plop into his hand.

"Mr. Gibb did not pay the correct amount to your father," Qi said.

Straightening his posture, Mr. Gibb offered Pa a hand.

"Mr. Gibb owes Zeke for six bales. The market price is ten cents a pound; each of the six bales weighed at least 545 pounds with the largest being 552. The price should be 330 dollars, but Mr. Gibb paid Zeke 100. He still owes him 230 dollars."

"C'mon Nathaniel," Pa declared, "let's get home."

Walking together, the adult hurried the child out of the stable. When they exited the stable, their pace relaxed. As they walked around the cracked fountain, Nathaniel stopped in his tracks.

"Pa?" the boy said.

Halting his step, Pa's eyes snapped down to his son.

"Mr. Gibb still owes you two hundred and thirty dollars."

Pa halted his stride. "Come again?"

Nathaniel quickly explained, "Yer six bales fetched 330 dollars. He only paid ya a hundred."

Taking a knee, Pa met his child's eye level and explained, "I only get a third of my total crop. The rest of that money pays Gibb for the seed, feed we buy and the land we live on."

"Did he say a third of the total crop?" Qi inquired.

"Did you say a third of the total crop?"

Pa raised an eyebrow, "Yes."

"Then ten dollars is still owed," Qi stated.

"He still owes you ten."

"Ten?" Pa's eyebrows widened and then furrowed, "How ya figure?"

"Six bales weigh'n 550 lbs at ten cents per pound fetches 330; a third of that is 110 dollars."

Reaching into his front pocket, Pa took out his wad of bills and quickly counted. When he reached the end of his second count, his eyes widened. "*That* son of a *bitch!*" Jumping to his feet, he pocketed his money and kicked the dirt. "He shook m'damned hand!"

Pa marched himself around the fountain, up the blue porch stairs, in between the white columns. Stomping in front of the dark blue double doors, both his fists began assaulting the barrier. Nathaniel cautiously meandered over to the fountain and popped a squat on its edge.

"Gibb!" Pa shouted, "Open the damn'd door, Gibb!"

The briefest of moments passed before Goober cracked the door open.

Pa immediately halted his strikes, "That jackass owes me ten! He *shorted* me!" Pa panted, and then said in a slightly calmer tone, "Please go get that *cheat* for me."

The door closed. With his hands on his hips, Pa scuffed his feet, mumbling to himself. Nathaniel Jumped down from the fountain and inched his way closer to the porch. Pa scratched the back of his head as he leaned up against a column. The front door opened.

Standing just inside the threshold, Mr. Gibb asked in a calm tone, "Zeke, what seems to be yer problem tonight?"

"You shorted me ten dollars!"

Crossing his arms, Mr. Gibb continued, "I compensated you one hundred dollars, a third of your total production as is established *perfectly clear* in our contract."

Pa took a step closer to the door, "That's not a third, Mr. Gibb, ten mo' dollars is a third."

"My good, sir, 100 dollars is what I owed you and paid you! And furthermore, most sharecroppers end up *owe'n* their landlords."

Sliding down from the rim, Nathaniel cautiously approached the debaters.

Pa crossed his arms, "You think I don' kno that? I'd *never* ever *ever* consider werk'n these fields if it was not the best deal by far," Pa poked his index finger at Mr. Gibb's torso, "Ya think I'm *grateful* I don't end up like my cousin? Work'n the same crops, year after year, and now in *mo'* debt than when he started?"

Mr. Gibb waited for silence before holding up three fingers, "I made three hundred today, a third of that is one," Lowering two fingers, Gibb continued. "How's that so difficult ta understand? You illiterate!"

Reaching into the front pocket of his overalls, Nathaniel displayed a page from the little, black book, and said, "Yer log book says the market price is ten cents a pound."

With wide, furious eyes, Mr. Gibb glanced down at his log book.

"You wrote that you made three hundred and *thirty* dollars," the boy continued. "A third of that is a hundred and *ten* dollars."

Mr. Gibb grabbed for the book but Nathaniel shuffled back. Pa stepped in between Mr. Gibb and his son.

The white man's brow furrowed as he blurted, "Give that back you thief! I demand you to give it back!"

Retreating a step, Mr. Gibb pointed a finger. "Command him to give me back my book! He can't read it! It's *my* property!

"That ten dollars is *my* property!"

"Goober!"

The dark skinned giant emerged from the house. Walking around the group, Goober stopped in front of the child. Crouching down into a squat, he held out his hand.

"Give him the book," Qi instructed.

Nathaniel placed the book inside Goober's enormous palm. Goober's free hand picked out the pencil from the spine. Standing up, he walked over to Mr. Gibb. Flipping to a naked page, Goober scribbled something quickly in the book before displaying the message to the white man. Letting out a sigh, Mr. Gibb reached into his overalls and started counting his money.

"I don't have a ten," Mr. Gibb shook his head, "I will need to retrieve a ten from my office."

With the book still in hand, Goober brushed past Mr. Gibb and entered the manor.

"Didn't need to ruin a whole page writing that," Mr. Gibb muttered.

Pa moved closer to his son. Mr. Gibb gave the boy a wary glance.

Leaning down, Pa whispered into his son's ear, "We'll be goin' home soon."

Moments later, Goober reappeared, holding a small leather sack. Coins clinked as Goober offered the sack to Pa.

Pa opened the sack and analyzed its contents. After a brief moment, Pa said, "C'mon Nathaniel!"

Hurrying to his father's side, Nathaniel grabbed Pa's free hand. They walked back towards the cart.

"Ya better not have given them anymo' than ten," they heard Mr. Gibb whine. "We can't afford no extra charity."

Extending his hand out, Pa offered the sack of coins to his son, "I need my hands free for carrying the cart home."

Taking the coins, the boy felt the weightiness of their dense metallic mass. Pa positioned himself between the cart's handles and soon the two were heading towards the gate. Looking back, Nathaniel watched a light in one of the upper windows. Passing through the gate and bearing left, they continued on towards home.

Keeping a steady pace, Pa glanced over at his son and inquired, "Yer literate?"

"What that mean?"

"Don't play dumb with me. It means ya can read. Who **taught** you?"

"I found yer ABC book."

"My alphabet book."

"Ya."

"That's it?"

"Ya."

"Ya taught yerself to read with only an alphabet book?"

"Yes."

Pa's eyes zoned out, "The hell am I doin' wrong then?"

"I also tooked yer Bible."

"*My* Bible?"

Nathaniel nodded.

"Gran'pappy's Bible?"

Nathaniel nodded.

"I thought I told ya *an'* Jane *never* to touch my bible!"

Nathaniel winced.

"I'd never guess in a thousand years ya'd have learned to read with it. I always suspected ya would just rip it up, an' damage the pages. Never would have dreamed ya would have learned yerself to read with it." Pa pondered for a while, "Praise God." With one eye on the road, Pa placed his other on his son, "See that money there in yer hands?"

Nathaniel glanced down at his hands, "Yes sir."

A smile crept onto Pa's face, "That money's fer school. You'n Jane are attend'n. Goddamnit."

Nathaniel looked down at the sack.

"Matter of fact," Pa added, "I'll visit the schoolteacher next week an' place *that* money *directly* in their hand. Ya did great today."

A smile cracked Nathaniel's face.

"That was mighty dangerous lifting that book off of Gibb," Pa stated, *"don't* make a habit of doin' those sorts of things. Good way to wind up dead."

"I didn't lift it," Nathaniel objected. "He told me to look after it."

"He gave it to ya to look after?"

Nathaniel nodded.

"Oh," Pa grinned. "Good," he chuckled. Pa's laughter grew until he could no longer hold onto the cart. Stabilizing himself on the vehicle he let the laughter out. Nathaniel joined in. Wiping his eyes, Pa straightened himself up

He knelt down and hugged his son. "Ya did great today."

Pride swelled and swirled into the thundering of his chest.

Releasing from the hug, Pa picked up the handles. "C'mon, race ya home!"

With furious legs, Nathaniel charged forward and took the lead. Pa caught up and held a constant pace beside the boy. By the time they passed the burned-out shell of a mansion, the weight of the coins was much less pleasant. Nathaniel watched the property, as permanently damaged features showed slightly differently in the dusk. The coins felt heavy. Nathaniel wished to spend them but there was no store in sight. His arms and legs grew tired. Pa slowed and stopped beside his son.

"Hop on," Pa said.

Nathaniel gave the cart a wide-eyed stare.

"I'll take ya home."

Nathaniel moved to the rear of the bed and jumped in. He sat down beside the dolly and found his balance as Pa picked up the cart.

"Ya good?"

Nathaniel nodded, "Yes."

Pa kept a careful and consistent pace. Nathaniel watched the path disappear into the dusky horizon behind them. Turning his head, Nathaniel spotted their 'T' intersection. Taking a right, Pa carted his son back to their home.

"Ma!" Pa called out. "Com'on out here!"

"Wha? Ya early! I need ta finish up dinner!"

"Nevermin' tha'," Pa placed the handles on the ground, "jus' grab some of the good stuff an' bring yer ears out here."

"The *good* stuff?"

"From my trunk!"

"Ya...ya sure?"

"Am I slur'n my words?" Pa ascended the porch steps and plopped himself down in the rocking chair. "An' brin' out a chair for the boy."

"I'm fine here," Nathaniel answered softly as he sat himself down on the top step of the porch.

Ma emerged from the shack carrying a corked bottle and dragging Nathaniel's chair.

"I don't know why you keep this in with yer clean clothes," Ma handed over the container. "Gonna spill, one of these days, get all in yer cloth and never come out, smell up the whole house, mark my words."

One hand took the bottle while the other pointed at his son. "Boy, tell yer Ma 'bout yer day."

Shifting her weight from one foot the other, Ma crossed her arms.

"I helped Pa with the harvest," the boy explained.

Pa chuckled as he uncorked his beverage and took a swig.

"Very nice," Ma said.

Pa blurted, "He done helped me make sure Gibb paid me proper."

"He done what now?"

Pa lifted the sack of coins, "He made sure Gibb didn' bilk me ten dollars."

"He done *what* now?"

Pa gulped down a healthy sum before declaring, "Mr. Gibb shorted me ten dollars on the haul and Nathaniel spotted it."

"He spotted it?"

"Sure did. An' I confronted Gibb. Told him I won' stand for no bilk'n!"

"The boy helped ya figure? How'd he figure?" she turned to address Nathaniel. "How'd ya figure?"

"I…"

Pa answered, "He read Mr. Gibb's account book!"

Ma's eyes narrowed. "You stole an account book from a white man?"

Nathaniel shook his head. "He gave it to me to look after."

"Why he give you his book to look after?"

"He told me to watch after it while they finished up."

"Bet he didn't think ya coul' read," Pa beamed.

"You can read?" Ma questioned. "Since when?"

"I…I learned myself."

"Took my Bible an' took my alphabet book. Then he looked at them an' all the words clicked." Pa stared blankly at his son. "One day."

Nathaniel nodded.

Ma eyed her son. "Yer sharp."

"Earned his keep," Pa laughed

Ma gently placed a hand on Pa's bent arm, "Bes' save some of the good stuff for the future."

Pa pulled his arm back, "I ain't presently finished."

"C'mon honey," Ma said, "best take yerself inside."

Pa thrust the bottle at his son's face, offering the bottle, "Take a drink! Ya was a real man today!"

Ma pulled back on Pa, "Don't give him that filth!"

Lifting his jug Pa stood fully erect and Ma shrank back as he yelled, "He got us paid! He earned himself a drink, fair!"

Nathaniel's eyes lingered on the sloshing alcohol.

"Decline," Qi said.

"Damnit boy!" Pa shoved the liquor toward the boy. "Yer a man!"

Ma stepped in between the boy and his father and Pa shielded the container from spillage.

"He don't wan't *none*," Ma raised her voice.

Nathaniel shook his head, "I don't want none."

Stumbling back, Pa almost missed the first step as he retreated down the steps and stumbled onto the bare earth, "The hell wi' ya!" he shrieked.

Ma's grip tightened on her child. They watched Pa stagger into the field.

She let go of her boy and said, "Go inside."

Nathaniel watched his mother hurry after Pa. Standing up, Nathaniel moved over to the rocking chair and popped a squat.

"Where's Ma run'n off to?" Jane asked.

Stretching out his leg, Nathaniel rocked himself with the tip of his shoe, "I thought you was sick to death."

Jane held a fist to her lips and coughed.

"It's a good thing to that ya didn't go," Nathaniel admitted, "else we'd be short ten dollars."

Jane crossed her arms. "What're ya going on about?"

"Gibb tried bilk'n Pa."

"He always bilk'n us."

"Well, today, he didn't. We rich now, cause you didn't go."

"We ain't rich!" Jane hissed.

"We'd made no money if you'd gone 'stead of me," Nathaniel smirked.

Pain exploded in Nathaniel's face. His hands furiously rubbed his tender cheek where Jane had slapped him.

Jumping up from his seat, Nathaniel yelled, "Pa! Pa! Jane hit me!"

"He can't hear you," Jane taunted.

Spinning around, the boy shrieked, "You stupid, damn!" and kicked Jane hard in the shin with the floppy toe of his shoe.

As Jane grabbed her leg, Nathaniel pushed past his chair, sprinted into his bedroom and flopped down on his bed. Burying his stinging, hot face into the cool cushion of the fresh pillow, angry tears pressed through his closed eyelids. The cold softness of the pillow absorbed his rage like pouring a boiling pot of water into a snow bank. He cried until fatigue and exhaustion put him to sleep.

9

Pale blue eyes reflected upon the mirror. Long, thick fingers caressed a gray beard that garnished a dry wrinkly face. The other free hand lifts a silver razor to its cheek. With a swift stroke, the left sideburn was removed.

Through the only window of the dull, gray room, a youthful voice called, "Land! Land ho!"

The door burst open as a redheaded lad came dashing into the quarters, bringing a gust of cold air in with him.

"Mr. Beechcroft?!" the lad shouted.

"Busy," Beechcroft's slipped his answer through tightened lips.

The youth's smile threatened to rip his face apart, "We made it!" he declared before dashing from the room.

"*Close* the damn'd door," Beechcroft hissed.

The salt flavored the air, chilled his lungs and sobered his mind. Grabbing a fresh towel, Beechcroft pressed the absorbing softness to his face. Folding it up, he laid it over the rim of the dirty porcelain sink. Picking up a dark crimson cane by its rounded goldenhandle, Beechcroft tested himself upon it. After several successes, he felt sufficiently satisfied enough to exit the room, sealing the door shut behind him.

Dense gray clouds muted the daylight and cold moisture clung to the air. Tiny snowflakes either melted on the uncovered regions of the deck or upon the frigid ocean. A bitter, sooty stench clung to the back of his throat. He ensured every button of his tan overcoat was thoroughly fastened before popping up his jacket collar. Glancing up at the dueling smokestacks, his eyes fixated on the thick, dark clouds being pumped into the sky. Tiny red sparks burned out and transformed into featherweight ash that drifted down onto the deck, mixing in with the tiny flakes of snow. Unfastening a single button, he slipped his hand into an inner pocket, then pulled out a silk handkerchief, with which he covered his face. Proceeding up towards the bow, he stopped to catch his breath at the top of the stairs. He saw a crowd gathering at the westernmost point of the guardrail. Descending the steps again, he made his way towards a familiar flash of fiery, red hair.

To his right, a long banner caught his eye. A steamship was displaying an advertisement with two ridiculously happy children and their equally estatic grandparent drinking glasses of what presumably contained what the bright bold letters proclaimed to be "Dr. Hood's Sarsaparilla, a cure for your entire life."

The lad leaned over the railing. "Isn't she beautiful?"

Looking out at the distant skyline, Beechcroft tightened his grip on his cane.

"Not as filthy as London," the lad added.

"All cities are full of shit."

The lad quickly laughed and turned his head, "Oh wow, you shaved it."

"Do I look terrible?"

"That won't matter in this city. Y'ever been here before?"

"Only vicariously."

A twinkle entered the lad's eyes, "Ya can have a gay ole' time if ya know where to go. As soon as I debark, I'm heading straight to fifty fifth." The lad leaned closer in, whispering, "Ya know anything about parlor houses?"

"A building comprised of nothing but parlor rooms?"

The lad chuckled and slapped his companion's back, "Never had a run in with a feral badger?"

"Are you referring to a brothel?"

The lad winked as he pulled a small, black book from a back pocket, "If ya need to know how to properly avoid New York's filthiest corners, I can let ya 'ave this 'ere book at a special rate; I know the author of the publish'n 'house personally. I even filled in a few certain details myself."

Reaching out, Beechcroft took the book and flipped it open on the last page.

"Each page is an education." the lad held up two fingers. "I can't bear to part with it for anything less than two dollars."

"I can visit the publishing location on West Houston Avenue and pick up any additional copy for a single dollar," Beechcroft closed the book and offered it back to the lad, "rip the last few pages out before you try to make a fool out of someone else."

The lad took back the book and Beechcroft walked away.

"I'll lower the price," the lad cajoled, "save you the trip."

As Beechcroft made his way back to the stairwell, the lad pocketed the book and returned to staring at the approaching city. Beechcroft returned to his room and headed for the sink. Picking up a container of cream, he placed it inside a white leather shaving kit. After buckling up the kit, he placed it inside one of the suitcases before ensuring that both of his pieces of luggage were secure. Shoving the cases to one side of the bed, Beechcroft laid down on the space remaining. As his eyes wandered about the room, his lungs inhaled the sweet, crisp, salty air. Turning his head, he focused on an open razor blade balanced precariously on the folded up towel placed on the rounded rim of the porcelain sink bowl. With a groan, Beechcroft sat up and placed his brown cowboy boots on the floor. Returning to the sink, he picked up the knife, folded its shiny blade back into the handle, and placed it inside his overcoat.

As he returned to bed, someone knocked on the door.

"Come in," Beechcroft announced as he flopped down on the mattress.

More cold air blasted into the room as a bulky, young sailor entered, followed closely behind by a silver haired, wrinkly faced fellow donning a captain's hat.

The older gentleman spoke with a deep, gravely tone, "Mister Beechcroft?"

Reaching into another inner jacket pocket, Beechcroft produced a tied up wad of bills. The captain nodded to the sailor, and the young man stepped forward and took the cash before retreating. The captain took the money and counted each bill twice. After completing his third count, his sharp eyes snapped up to the Englishman.

"Gratuity," Beechcroft explained.

The captain smiled, "You will wait in here until the other passengers have debarked," his smile faded. "Do not leave until an associate of mine has come to retrieve you."

As both men turned to leave, Beechcroft spoke up, "I am traveling with a lad. He is quite useful to me."

The captain raised the bills. "Got another cluster for him?"

"Not unless you count my gratuity."

Shaking his head, the captain answered, "I don't."

Beechcroft picked at one of his thumbnails.

"He gets off at Castle Garden," the captain said, "Any taxi can get ya there. You can even hire one to pick him up from there and drop him off wherever ya please."

"Could you recommend any other captains able to provide the services you do, should I return here at a later date and find you unavailable?"

The captain turned around to meet the Englishman's eyes. "When ya coming back?"

"Whenever I finish my journey."

"How long is that? A month? A year?"

"I have no way of knowing that at the present moment."

The captain shrugged and glanced over at his companion, "Bes' jus' find someone when the time comes. I'm sure it won't take you too long to find someone. As a general rule the summer has more available ships than winter. I must go now, very busy."

Exiting the room, the young sailor closed the door shut behind. Dwindling frigid currents lingered in the room. As Beechcroft fell back into the bed and listened to the sound of the engines churning, the cold cot stole much of his heat. He waited for the sheets to slowly absorb his warmth. Feeling the subtle movements of water beneath him, his lids closed and he drifted.

At some later moment, a loud metal clunk came from the door. The redheaded lad rushed into the room.

Halting at the foot of the bed, he asked, "Ready?"

"I'm getting off at the next stop."

The lad smirked. "All foreign passengers get off at Castle Garden."

Beechcroft sat up. "*You* are debarking at Castle Garden."

The lad straightened up. "I beg ya pardon?"

"Yer pardoned."

From inside his overcoat, Beechcroft produced a revolver. The lad stiffened as his employer aimed the weapon at the area just beneath his hairline. With his free hand, Beechcroft reached into his waistcoat pocket and tossed a few coins onto the floor. The money clattered before rolling in opposite directions.

Beechcroft gestured with his gun barrel, "Take your fee."

The lad stared at the money for a moment, then he sprang into action, scrambling on his hands and knees, scooping up the sovereigns as he went. The instant he'd retrieved all the coins, he dashed for the deck.

"Close the damned door!" Beechcroft shouted as he holstered his gun.

Standing up, he lumbered over to the door and closed it. Returning to bed, Beechcroft learned that he had lost his perfect pillow position from before. With his neck at an awkward angle, he listened to the general buzz of the crowd wafting in from the main deck, punctuated at regular intervals by the shouts of the workingmen.

The engines started rumbling again. The movement jerked Beechcroft awake.

When the boat regained momentum, he closed his eyes.

A knock came from the door. "Mr. Beechcroft?" a young voice inquired.

"Come in."

The door opened and the captain's muscular companion entered the room.

"I'm here to carry yer cases," the young sailor announced.

"What's your name?"

"Kenny."

"Nice to meet you, Kenny," Beechcroft smiled. "Thank you."

The floor creaked with each of the large lad's heavy footfalls as he moved to the cases.

As Kenny picked up both suitcases he asked, "Shall we?"

The Englishman creaked his way off the bed and meandered over to the door. The sailor led the way and Beechcroft closed the door behind them. He turned back to face his escort but Kenny was already halfway down the stairwell. A gust of salty wind circulated soot and slaughter up into the chilly air. Pulling out his handkerchief, Beechcroft covered his mouth as he headed for the stairs.

When he reached the top step, Kenny stated rather loudly, "I got stones of work, sir!"

Beechcroft saw Kenny standing at the bottom of the steps. The young sailor stepped back onto the first step, allowing another sailor steering a wheelbarrow to maneuver past him.

"Ya goin' to the parlor house, Kenny?" the wheelbarrow-wielding coworker inquired.

"As fast as god allows it," Kenny responded.

The moment Beechcroft was about halfway down the steps, Kenny spun around and headed for the gangplank. By the time the Englishman had made it to the gangplank, the youthful sailor was traversing the dock.

"Careful!" Kenny shouted as a dog came sprinting down the dock.

Firmly gripping his cane, Beechcroft stood off to the side. As soon as the canine had passed the Englishman, Kenny turned and headed for the street. Only when he reached the cobblestone did the sailor stop and wait for the Englishman to catch up. After a while, Kenny set down the cases. When Beechcroft finally caught up, the strong lad offered a hand.

"There are plenty of cabs," the sailor explained.

Taking the lad's sturdy hand, Beechcroft placed a sovereign into his palm. "Thank you."

Kenny lifted up the brim of his hat before turning and dashing back to the boat. Looking down, Beechcroft saw that he was in between his two suitcases. He took a moment to listen to wooden wheels rolling over the cobblestone streets.

From out of the street cacophony a rough voice inquired, "How ya doin'."

Opening his eyes, Beechcroft spotted a bearded man piloting a handsome hansom cab.

"Head'n up to Fifth Avenue, high roller?" the bearded driver inquired.

Lifting a hand, Beechcroft reached out to inspect the horse's snout. The animal shifted its neck back before Beechcroft could finish his caress. Picking up his luggage, Beechcroft maneuvered around the vehicle, halting his step on the threshold of the street. Mounds of horse droppings, mixed with slushy snow, filled the street like a frozen river. The tall thin wheels of the various vehicles cut through the waves of shit, ever reshaping it with multitudes of parallel slices.

"I can get ya anywhere," the driver said.

"No, thank you," Beechcroft replied.

Snapping his fingers, the driver yelled, "Earl, give this gentleman a sweep! He wishes to cross the street!"

A skinny gent with wrinkly skin and a red, wool hat stood up from a wooden barrel and grabbed an industrial strength broom. Marching over to the street's edge he started brushing and plowing the crappy snow away. Cleaning a square shaped pathway, it quickly grew into a rectangle as the sweeper led the way across the street.

Without missing a stroke, the old gent asked out of the corner of his mouth, "Ya come'n?"

A carriage that had been moving up the street stopped and its irritated driver waited for the sweeper to finish. As the traffic built up, Beechcroft took the hint and picked up the pace. When they reached the other side, he handed over two gold coins.

"One of thems for your friend," Beechcroft declared.

The older man nodded as he pocketed the two coins. Recrossing the street, the old man took his seat back on top of the wooden barrel. Beechcroft watched as the vehicles immediately started undoing the sweeper's latest contract.

Carefully setting his cases down on the side walk, Beechcroft looked for the nearest hansom cab. Its driver sucked on a fat unignited cigar as he rested his foot on his cab's parking brake. Lifting up the brim of his bowler hat, the rider kept one hand on the reins as he kicked his boot and clicked his tongue. The horse trotted forward, stopping just in front of the foreigner. Removing an ivory white glove, Beechcroft scratched the equine's chin. The beast snorted as its lips checked the stranger's palm for any sign of food.

"Where ya headed?" the driver inquired.

"The best room around."

The driver nodded, "I know the place. Take your cases?"

Nodding his head, Beechcroft moved forward. The weight of the vessel shifted as the Englishman occupied the seat. When luggage was secure, the driver clicked his tongue and the horse merged into the traffic.

Taking out a handkerchief, Beechcroft placed it over his face. It muted the scent of sour, burning coal, rotting excrement, freshly spilt blood, and decaying flesh. Up ahead, a group of people sat around the large open entrance to a warehouse. Internal heat blasted out from the building, melting a large region in front of the large double doors. People mingled on the spot of naked sidewalk, just barely outside of the building. Some were eating lunches while others watched them eat.

"Ya picked a good time to visit," the driver complimented, "In the summer, the city smells even worse and there are flies."

The horse picked up its pace as the cabbie declared, "Hyah! Hyah!"

They turned onto a different street and the odor of gas was replaced by the smell of super-heated metal being shaped into machinery. As they passed an enormous warehouse, Beechcroft caught sight of a blinding light illuminating men standing an arm's length apart as they pulled on massive chains.

Further down the road, they came upon another carriage with a stalled engine. The driver quickly took advantage of a gap in traffic and maneuvered around the cart attached to a dead horse.

Beechcroft's eyes lingered on the perished creature. "I do hope the hotel is not too far."

"The hotel is the first of its kind to supply hot and cold water in every bathroom."

"Really? Splendid."

The horse slowed down as urine poured from its rear end. The yellow stream mixed into the manure and melted snow. When it was thoroughly done dripping, the horse resumed its previous pace.

As they moved away from the docks, Beechcroft looked down and could see some area of cobblestone. The masonry of the buildings improved in quality. Occasionally, a peddler would be parked upon the snow, still trying to make a sale. One monger announced their wares in German, and then went on to repeat the same message in English, and then in Italian.

The carriage slowed and pulled to a stop in front of a chic rectangular edifice. Beechcroft craned his neck as his eyes followed the central portion of the structure, all the way up to the enormous flags flying high above the roof, dancing in the breeze.

Glancing to his right and left, the Englishman realized that the edifice took up the whole block. He counted twenty-two windows across and seven windows tall. It looked quite sturdy.

Two bellhops approached the carriage.

"Welcome to the Windsor," they both announced.

The driver handed over the luggage to one of the bellhops while the other assisted the Englishman with dismounting. The weight of the carriage shifted as Beechcroft exited the vehicle. Offering a coin to the driver, the Englishman turned and followed after the hotel employee. Another bellhop opened the door for his comrade and new arrival.

A large chandelier dangled from the apex of the domed ceiling. The room was carpeted with a sophisticated blood red rug that led all the way from the front doors to the front desk while also branching off and moving up the middle of a large, marble staircase that divided in two as it reached for the second story. Several gentlemen sat upon the crimson velvet cushioned furniture, and many of whom turned their heads to observe the newcomer. A fire roared inside the large fireplace, imparting a pleasant warmth to the room.

When Beechcroft reached the front desk, a well-groomed,

bespectacled clerk eyed him from top to bottom, "Welcome to the Windsor Hotel, sir. What may I scribe as your title?"

"Benedict Beechcroft."

"How long do you expect to be staying, Mr. Beechcroft?"

"At least tonight. Maybe more. Probably tomorrow. Undecided."

The clerk gave a wide smile, "Well I do hope for our sake, that you decide to stay for quite a long spell. Are you peckish? Our chef has outdone himself today. Shall I have a portion of the daily special sent up?"

Beechcroft watched a gay couple exiting the hotel grocery store. "I would prefer to dine in my room this evening. I was told there are bathing arrangements in each room."

"You have been informed correctly, sir" the clerk congratulated him. "We do indeed have the finest bathing arrangements in the world. You can either control the dials yourself or we can have a representative show you exactly how the temperature is regulated. Shall I have room service and a representative sent up?"

"As long as room service includes roast duck, garlic potatoes, and poached green beans," Beechcroft smiled, "I will be more than willing to order a helping." His smile faded. "What's my room number?"

"I'm sure the chef will be able to accommodate your request," the clerk replied as he raised an arm.

A young bellhop dashed to attention.

"Two-fourteen," the clerk answered and he dropped the key into his coworker's hand, "*James*, will escort you. Enjoy your stay, Mr. Beechcroft. And please let us know what your future plans may be as soon as conveniently possible."

Moving over to the bottom of the staircase, the bellhop waited for Beechcroft to come within a professionally polite enough distance to continue. As Beechcroft ascended halfway up the stairs, he held onto the handrail as he rounded the corner. Looking up, Beechcroft spotted a bright, cheerful dining room at the top of the stairs. The buzz of conversation and the scents of the cuisine radiated from within. The Englishman followed the bellhop past the enormous room and into a spacious but narrow hallway.

Taking a right, they soon parked themselves in front of room two-fourteen. With a single practiced motion, the worker unlocked and opened the door. Entering the room, the worker stood aside, encouraging the guest to take it all in. Beechcroft stopped in front of the bellhop and held up his hand, and the bellhop placed the key into it.

"Would you like me to draw the curtain, sir? Perhaps I may light a few candles?"

"A few candles would be pleasant," Beechcroft answered as he removed his coat.

"Would you care for me to draw you a bath?" the lad inquired as he pulled out a box of matches.

"Show me how it operates."

"Absolutely."

The bellhop finished lighting some candles before leading the way towards the bathroom. Igniting a few more lights, he illuminating the environment's features. Engraved woodwork furnished various aspects of the sink and toilet. The porcelain tub, toilet, basin and sink were all stenciled with an artist's rendition of purple grape vines. The vines wrapped completely around each of the rims of the smooth, shiny furnishings. Sections of fluffy, pink squares of rug carpeted the tile floor.

The bellhop moved directly to the giant tub in the center of the room and gestured to the valves, "This is the hot water, the other is cold water."

"Interesting," Beechcroft answered slowly

"Would you care for a hot or cold bath?"

"I have no desire to freeze any further."

The bellhop chuckled politely, "Absolutely, sir" he twisted a valve and water rushed from the facet.

Beechcroft smirked. "I didn't expect to find this sort of advancement outside of my own property." Leaning forward, he placed a few fingers in the current and a large smile melted onto his face. "Very good."

"Will there be anything else? Are you hungry?"

"I believe your friend at the front desk has taken my order."

"Very good, sir. Are you perhaps in need of some reading material? I could have a Harper's magazine or a Frank Leslie newspaper sent up."

"No need, I have plenty. I would like my clothes cleaned, pressed, and to be ready by morning."

"Very good, sir. Would you like me to retrieve them from your suitcases?"

"No need, I shall pick them out myself, and leave them by the door."

"Excellent, sir. If you leave them on this corner of the bed, I will take them for cleaning once I have gone to inquire about the status of your meal."

"Here," Beechcroft flipped the lad a coin.

A big smile broadened the lad's face. "Thank ya, sir."

The moment the door latched shut, Beechcroft picked up a suitcase and plopped it on the mattress. Opening it up, he removed multiple articles of clothing and stacked them near the door. Returning to the side of the bed, he emptied out his pockets and placed the contents on top of the nearest dresser. Stripping naked, he folded and placed his clothes in the dirty pile by the door before retiring to the bathroom. A pleasant steam had filled the air. Beechcroft moved closer to the tub and plugged the drain. He listened to the water flow as he watched the tub fill.

His mind filled with thoughts like a tub and he muttered, "I fucking hope it's close."

Beechcroft slid into the tub. Hugging his knees, he listened to the pitch of the crashing liquid changed as its depths increased. A minute shock wave of icy cold shot up his spine as he relaxed his back against the cold porcelain.

At some point later on, a familair voice called from outside the bathroom, "Dinner, Mr. Beechcroft!"

"In here," Beechcroft shouted, "bring it in here."

Opening the door, the bellhop guided the cart into the bathroom, "Enjoying a dinner and a bath, eh?" He parked the food beside the bath, took out a corkscrew and stuck it into the bottle of wine. "What is the point of such luxury if one cannot enjoy it exactly the way one is inclined to?"

Beechcroft chuckled. "I don't suppose you have a decent brand of cigar with you?"

A knowing smile swept across the bellhop's face as he finished pouring his guest a full glass. After handing over the wine, the bellhop opened up a small side drawer in the middle of the mobile table and retrieved a box of Havana Optimates. He waited for Beechcroft to gulp down his wine before carefully placing a cigar inside the Englishman's mouth. Picking up a lighter with both hands, the employee pushed a button and a narrow but tall flame ignited the tobacco leaf. Beechcroft inhaled and puffed, filling the bathroom with thick, blue smoke.

The Englishman sat up in the tub, "What's on the menu? I hope the kitchen is not out of anything."

"No, sir, the chef executed your request without obstacle," the lad replied as he parked the cart within arm's reach.

Retreating, the employee asked, "Will there be anything else, sir? I see the clothes you desire to be cleaned are by the door."

Beechcroft took another drag on the cigar before dipping its tip into the bath water, "That will do for now."

Trading in the cigar for a fork and knife, Beechcroft dug in. The smoked duck skin was crispy while the meat was soft, moist and dripping the savory sweetness of the honey roasted figs. Pairing it with a French vintage of an ancient, dark, rustic, grape, the palate was thoroughly cleansed in between bites. The wine quenched his thirst, warmed the belly, and buzzed the skull. The green beans were crunchy yet tender. The dill and rosemary roasted potatoes were the perfect option for mopping up the plate's mixture of poultry, fig, and green bean juices. When he finished the last bite, he scraped the plate with his knife, making a rapid, scraping sound. Licking the blade clean with his tongue, Beechcroft wiped his face and hands with his fancy linen. Picking up the wine with his less greasy hand, Beechcroft carefully poured himself another glass. He let out a hearty belch before chasing away the bad breath with another gulp of alcohol. Without spilling a single drop, Beechcroft crawled over the side of the tub and stood up on the soft, pink cushion. Keeping the glass level, Beechcroft reached down and unplugged the drain. Picking up the cigar, he placed it in the corner of his mouth before grabbing the lighter. With the push of a button, he rekindled the tobacco. Plumes of smoke filled the room as he watched the water drain out of the tub. When he exited the bathroom, he found that a warm, crackling fire had been lit. Beechcroft sat his aching body in the chair closest to the warmth. Setting his beverage down on an empty table, he watched the fire. The flames licked one another in an eternal dance.

He glanced over at the closet. Setting down the glass, Beechcroft stood up and walked over to that portion of the room and picked up a suitcase. Placing the luggage down on the bed, the Englishman proceeded to unlatch it. Each packed item had molded to its particular confinement. Sticking out from among the perfectly folded clothing was a black jewelry box. Taking the box out of the suitcase, Beechcroft spun around and picked up a key from off the nightstand. Inserting the key into the box he turned and opened up the metal container. Sitting down on the bed, he removed stacks of American and British currency from within. With the money gone, Beechcroft stared at the stiff red cushion that covered the base. Removing a long pin from his hat, Beechcroft pressed the tip into a back corner of the container then worked it along the back edge. Suddenly, the long, thin piece of metal disappeared beneath the surface of the cushion. A metallic sound clicked as the bottom of the box popped out of place. Beechcroft picked up the dislodged square piece of board and placed it on the bed. Beneath the false bottom, a single crimson colored hand almost shined in contrast with the white polished face that stared up at the Englishman. Twelve jet black sets of roman numerals encircled the single hand.

Picking up the timepiece, he spun it around in his palm. When he stopped its spin, he watched its single red hand wander back to the direction it had previously been pointing to. Grabbing a silver compass, Beechcroft laid the two pieces down, side by side, and saw that the single hand was pointing in a south-westerly direction.

"How far?" he grumbled as he placed the time piece on his nightstand.

Picking up the false bottom, Beechcroft placed it back in the jewelry box. After returning the money, he shut the lid and locked it up tight. After placing the compass, pocket watch, and the hat pin on the dresser, Beechcroft packed up the black box and secured it inside a suitcase before returning them both to the closet. Closing the closet door, Beechcroft returned to the cushioned seat in front of the fire. He picked up his half smoked cigar and reignited it. The nicotine stretched his eyelids as blood rushed to his head. He sipped his wine, smoked his cigar, and watched the flames dance. When the fire's rhythm waned, Beechcroft found himself too tired to get up and put on another log. He closed his eyes and felt the tired warmth of the flickering heat wash over his exhausted lids.

10

T he clean-shaven waiter promptly removed the extra setting as the Englishman sat down at the dining room table. Tying a fancy white linen around his neck, Beechcroft grabbed the nearest silver fork.

"And what are we having this morning?" the waiter inquired.

Staring up at one of the many bedazzling chandeliers glistening in the morning sunlight, Beechcroft answered, "Five strips of bacon, two poached eggs, a warm croissant, coffee, orange juice, and hollandaise sauce. Got all that?"

"Indeed," the waiter assured, "There is fresh, hot coffee already in your cup, sir."

Beechcroft glanced down at his coffee cup. As he leaned over the mug, the steam to washed over his face. Picking up the mug, he inhaled deeply. An intense buzz of conversation came from the other side of the dining room. Opening his eyes, he spotted a group of smartly attired men gathered around a number of tables that they had pushed together. Armed with a cup of coffee, Beechcroft stood up from his table and ventured forth. Stopping just behind the crowd he peered in between the shoulder's of two gentlemen, and caught a glimpse of a checkered board with black and white pieces upon it.

"You should've accepted the offered handicap," one gentleman exclaimed.

"If you don't stop yap'n I will deliver thee a handicap," another retorted.

"If you are ever in doubt of my abilities I would be more than happy to display them officially in a ring."

"You are quick to trade a test of chess for a test of violence."

A chuckle erupted among several of the gentlemen. One of the men sitting down at the table moved a black rook to a light square.

Beechcroft's nose noticed the waiter emerging from the kitchen armed with several plates of food. Hurrying back, he promptly plopped his butt down onto the poor chair. Grabbing a spoon, he dipped its tip into the hollandaise sauce before tasting it with the tip of his tongue. It was perfectly seasoned with a pinch of paprika and or cayenne. He poured the sauce over his entire plate. Utilizing his fork, he punctured the egg, spilling the runny yoke. Beechcroft ripped a piece of steamy croissant and began soaking up the mixture of hollandaise sauce and egg yoke. Grabbing his glass, he washed the whole filling experience down with orange juice and then gulped down the rest of his hot coffee. The waiter refilled his juice just as Beechcroft picked up a piece of crispy bacon and bit into it. He devoured the three strands of pig before poking his fork into the final egg. Scooping the mess of protein with a spoon, he plopped the whole thing on top of the croissant. He ate the wounded breakfast sandwich in two bites, then washed it all down with a gulp of coffee before wiping his face. The waiter refreshed his water glass. Beechcroft finished his orange juice and then sipped on the glass of ice water. The last strip of bacon was dripping in hollandaise sauce and yolk. He crunched through the chewy meat. He finished off the coffee and then gulped down the water. The waiter approached and removed all of the dirty dishes. He stared at the empty linen spotted with grease stains.

Standing up from the table, Beechcroft shuffled his way to the door. He returned to his room and enjoyed the luxury of the indoor plumbing. Some time later, Beechcroft emerged from his room clean, fully dressed, and perfumed.

The moment he exited the lobby, he heard the shrill cry of a youth declaring, "Extra! Extra! Read all about it! Exclusive information on the Boss Tweed trial!"

Aiming for a parked taxi, Beechcroft did his best to maneuver around the young peddler.

"Read all about it!" The boy spotted the Englishman and extended his paper wielding hand closer. "Mista', ya heard the recent corruption of Tammany Hall? They stealing all of our taxes! Learn the latest from the trial of Boss Tweed!" The boy stared at the foreigner until he took a step back, then yelled even louder, "Extra! Extra! Corruption in Tammany Hall! See and read the latest cartoon from Thomas Nast!"

Beechcroft halted his journey in front of a driver feeding an apple to his steed.

"Sir," the cabbie acknowledged without losing focus on the feeding. "where ya headed'?"

"South."

"Not too far then, eh?"

"I need to get out of the city moving in a south-westerly direction."

A smile cracked over the caretaker's face as he watched the equine devour the remainder of the core. Retrieving a second piece of fruit from his pouch, the professional continued to feed his animal.

"Mister, if you want me to take you out of the city I gotta deliver you north to Hoboken and that's more than a days travel. Unless ya got an aversion to boats I would recommend getting yerself across the river via one."

"Take me to the closest ferry."

"Alright. I can do that easy 'nough. Hop on in." The driver waited for the horse to finish the snack and his customer to be seated, then with nimble steps, he jumped up into the driver's seat and declared, "Hyah!" Their wheels added to the cobblestone cacophony as they rolled out into moving traffic.

Shifting about in his seat, Beechcroft managed to take out his compass. Despite the shaky ride, the Englishman discerned that the instrument was still pointing in a south-westerly direction. He put the tool away just in time to read a street sign declaring, "Twelfth

Avenue." Beyond the edge of the road, steam and wind powered vessels clogged nearly every inch of the water.

"What's this river called again?" Beechcroft wondered.

"Hudson," the cabbie replied as he stopped his hansom in front a small gathering of individuals.

The cabbie pointed. "It's a big crowd. It's a good sign they've been wait'n and she'll show soon." He lowered his other hand. "That'll be thirty five cents."

Beechcroft handed up a sovereign.

"Thank you, sir," the driver smiled as he pocketed the pound, "Hyah!"

Turning around, Beechcroft stared across the river. His eyes scanned the various sails and decks that were floating upon the water. A pedestrian maneuvered around Beechcroft and took a position at the back of the queue. Stepping forward, Beechcroft brought up the back of the line until someone else took the spot behind him. At the front of the line, Beechcroft saw a clerk manning a ticket booth. The line shifted as another couple approached the barred window.

Keeping his place in line, Beechcroft turned and stared out at the Hudson River.

Across the river, various columns of smoke drifted above the rooftops and eventually dissipating in the sky. Rooves garnished the horizon and were occasionally blocked by the passing sails of a ship. The line of people shifted, as did Beechcroft but he kept his eyes on the view.

Looking down, he checked the pocket watch's hand and then double checked the direction with his compass. Pocketing the instruments, he returned to staring and waiting. The wind bit into him. The cold slowly seeped into his flesh.

"Next!"

Startled, Beechcroft quickly reached outward with his cane and scurried forward.

Reaching the window, the Englishman instinctively took out his wallet.

A wrinkly old man barely met the new costumer's eyes. "What ya need?"

"I would like to purchase a ticket to get to the other side of the grand river."

"Which port were ya looking to end up at?"

"Um...whichever one is the most southwest."

"Southwest?" the old man adjusted his glasses, "Uh...you wana go to Jersey City?"

"I do?"

"It is the southernmost port any of our ferries run to. If you wish to go any further, I would advise chartering from another company."

"Nope, Jersey City will do just fine."

"Excellent. I'll sell ya a ticket for the next available Pavonia ferry. Do you want one way or two?"

"What's the difference?"

The clerk rested his chin on his hand. "One is three cents and only gets you there. Two is five cents, but you will be able to return, but you must do so within a twenty-four-hour limit. If you purchase a first-class ticket, then you may return whenever you desire."

Placing a sovereign in the slot beneath the barred windows, Beechcroft said, "I'll take first-class two-way."

"This is British."

"Indeed."

"Do you have anything smaller?"

Beechcroft shook his head, "Keep the difference."

"Sir? It is quite the difference."

Beechcroft shrugged.

The clerk eyed the coin and then instantly pocketed it before signing and stamping a dense piece of paper.

Handing it through the open slot underneath the rows of wooden bars, the ticketmaster leaned back and cried out, "Next!"

Beechcroft took the official certificate before leaving the head of the queue. Retreating into the crowd, he found an empty spot on a bench and waited. Popping his collar and pulling down his hat, he watched the boats traveling towards the open water, wondering which ones were simply moving to another region of the city and which were going out onto the ocean.

. . .

"The ferry to Jersey City is on time!" a uniformed employee shouted, "All passengers must wait for all incoming passengers to debark! Then all first class passengers will enter followed by the rest of you lot."

Men and women grabbed their things, while the sensitive children whined and cried before being promptly silenced. Beechcroft headed for the front of the crowd as a double decker boat emerged from the crowd of vessels. Its speed slowed as it maneuvered closer and several constables took positions on the dock. When anchor was dropped large gentlemen began checking the validity of the tickets from the people at the front of the line. The moment the plank struck dock arriving shoes started pounding down it. The line moved as efficiently as the inspector's inspections. Holding out his ticket, Beechcroft was waved quickly aboard. Immediately, he tried to locate the quietest region of the boat. At the stern, he found a well dressed large family that were busy securing a corner. Staring out the back, Beechcroft watched the waters ripple. He remained in the brisk, misty area until the ferry reached Jersey City.

11

Off in the distance a bell tolled. Looking up from the ground, Nathaniel saw the road bend around a group of trees. Above the treeline, a thin wisp of dark smoke flew up into the air. As he made his way around the corner, he saw that the path led through an open field. The rest of the meadow rolled into various crescendos, creating wallowing depths with their flexing heights. Patches of trees grew in scattered groups all over the mostly open field filled with only the heartiest flowers and wild crab grasses managing to survive. To the left, some ways up ahead, an unpainted building stood close to the road. Nathaniel could see a gang of people gathered in front of the structure.

"Jane!" Ma called "Wait up!"

Stopping at the crux of a gradual hill, Jane jumped up and down as she waved to someone some distance off. When Ma arrived at the peak of the crest, Jane quickly regained her previous speed. Nathaniel hurried after her, but could not catch her speed. The tolling bell ceased.

Up ahead the people had formed into a line and were slowly trickling into the schoolhouse. Women and children nodded and greeted the tall, pale faced lady standing at the front door. Men removed their hats as they offered a more formal salutation.

Finally Jane reached the back of the queue. By the time Nathaniel did, she was chatting with the teacher.

"This is my little brother, Nathaniel," Jane explained giddily. "It's his first day."

Stopping in front of his big sister, Nathaniel lifted his eyes up to the towering white lady. Above her auburn hair, was a sign that proclaimed, "Centron County Schoolhouse."

Leaning her face closer to his, the teacher smiled sweetly and said, "I'm Miss Mathers, welcome to your first day at the Centron Schoolhouse. Is that your mother coming up behind you?"

"Yes, Ma'am."

Miss Mather's gestured to the doors, "Please find a seat at the front of the class with all the other little ones. Jane, will you show him where to put his stuff?"

As Nathaniel followed after his big sister, he passed by an older gentleman handling a shotgun with great care. As the older gentleman waiting for the little child to remove himself from the doorway, he smiled down at the child and said in an unnaturally high pitched tone, "Gonna do some learn'n today?"

Nathaniel's eyes widened and he forgot how to nod.

"C'mon, Nathaniel." Jane took his hand.

Nathaniel was hurried into a much warmer and bigger room filled with thick air. The classroom was brimming with many tall bodies and a large, dark metal wood stove. Long, wooden, backless pews, covered every inch of floor save for the sides, front, back, and the central aisle. The stove was built into the center of the room, forcing the most adjacent pews to be pushed flush with the wall. Tightening her hold on her little brother's hand, Jane ushered him to the front of the class.

Letting go of her sibling's hand, she pointed at the young children sitting in the front row and said, "Sit there." Then, turning her back to him, she merged into the crowd.

Nathaniel watched his big sister approach a similarly sized lady and immediately strike up a conversation. Looking to his left, he spotted a small girl in a dirty dress sitting with one foot up on the pew, sucking her thumb and staring straight back at him. Looking to his right, he saw a boy, about an inch or two shorter than him, dressed in a pair of ratty, single strap overalls.

"I'm Ned," the boy declared with a smile. "What's yer name?"

"Nathaniel."

Nice to meet you." Ned placed a finger diagonally across his chin. "How'd ya get that?"

Nathaniel's face grew hot as he glanced down at the floor, "I fell into a river."

Ned's eyes widened, "Off a boat?"

Nathaniel shook his head, "Jus' walk'n through it with my sister."

"Ya like pirates?"

"What're those?"

"Scalawags who sail the seven seas!"

"What's a scalawag?"

Ned's eyes widened, "Ya don't know?"

Nathaniel shook his head.

"They carry carpetbags to put the valuables they steal in. Pirates don't do that. They keep their treasure and swords in chests." Leaning forward, Ned pointed out Nathaniel's cotton sack. "Is that your stuff?"

Nathaniel nodded.

"Yer supposed to put it at the back of the room. That's what my daddy had me do."

"Who's yer dad?"

Ned turned around and pointed at a group of grown men standing next to the wood stove. "He's the biggest one of them."

All the men were big, **and** Nathaniel couldn't discern which one had fathered Ned. Tightening his grip on the cotton sack, Nathaniel stood up and walked to the back of the room. Spotting an assortment of possessions stacked along the back wall he walked up and placed his item among them. Looking to his left, he noticed a one-legged man sitting in a chair. Next to him, atop of another chair was a metal bucket. The man spotted the boy staring at him and smiled back. Blushing, Nathaniel turned and hurried back to the front of the class.

Plopping down in his seat, Nathaniel turned to Ned and asked, "Is this your first day too?"

Shaking his head, Ned lifted two fingers, "I've come here two times before this."

"You have any brothers or sisters?"

"Ya."

Miss Mathers walked to the front of the classroom. Immediately the chit chat hushed and everyone not seated scrambled for an empty one.

Moving to the front of the class, Miss Mathers faced the pews and announced, "Hello, scholars. I'm excited to see you all here, ready for another year. I'm sorry to be missing so many faces"—she directed her eyes to the front row—"and grateful to see newcomers." She returned to addressing the whole class. "Time is limited. I need to announce that this will be my last year teaching here."

"If we make it that long," a man commented.

"That's why we got Max posted out front," another chimed.

A murmur rippled through the older and adult students.

Miss Mather's held up her hands and the noise died down, "It is scary for all of us." She glanced at the front row. "Perhaps we should discuss such things later."

A woman stood up and shouted, "It affect the youngins lives mo' than yours!"

Miss Mather's brow furrowed. "Need I remind you, Mrs. Cobb, that my *late* brother was killed this last May?"

"Like none of us haven't lost scores of loved ones?" Mrs. Cobb retorted, "Welcome to the front line! The war may have ended up North but for us, down here, we still fighting. And it's illegal for any of us to own a gun!"

A large man stood up and shouted, "We're wasting time! Some of these youngins ain't gonna get much more opportunity other than what we got right now," he looked about the room, "Argue after we educate them little ones."

"Ya," a new voice agreed. "Let's hurry up to the learn'n!"

The student body voiced its concurrence.

"Indeed," Miss Mathers stated and waited for the noise to die down and the full attention return to her before announcing, "How many readers do we have? Raise of hands." With an index finger, the teacher silently counted the number of elevated limbs. "Good, I need several literate scholars to come to the front. You will be helping the little ones learn their alphabet."

There was a small scramble of legs and resources as the class figured out who the volunteers were going to be. Nathaniel watched a group of adults debating among themselves. Some of the ladies smiled at the little ones. One commented on how cute Ned was.

Nathaniel frowned as he thought, "I already know the alphabet."

"Then this is practice," Qi said.

"I already know it well enough."

"Then this is a waste of time."

A tall, short haired, skinny lady moved in front of his pew. She smiled sweetly down at them and tilted her head ever so slightly. Her twinkling eyes switched between Ned and Nathaniel.

"Do y'all know your alphabet?" she inquired.

"I do," Nathaniel answered.

Ned shook his head.

"Oh, good for you." She focused on Ned, "I will help you."

She took the seat next to the boy and handed over the small, rectangular book. Peeking over, Nathaniel read the faded gold font letters on the front cover: "American Elementary Speller." With the book resting in Ned's lap, the nice lady opened it up and started slowly flipping through the pages until she reached the part that had a two page spread on the English alphabet. Ned placed a single finger on the page and began tracing the capital letter "A."

Scanning the room, Nathaniel spotted Miss Mathers busy with some of the older students. One of the men who might be Ned's dad was busy arguing some point to a different man who Nathaniel considered might also be Ned's dad.

"Hello," a sweet voice said, "my name is Lottie."

Facing front, Nathaniel's breath froze in his heart. a tall, beautiful, giant lady smiled down at him.

"'s anyone come to help you with a lesson?"

Nathaniel shook his head. She gestured for him to scoot over and he promptly obeyed. Sitting down in between Ned and

Nathaniel, he felt her grown thigh take up the space right next to his own. He remained still, daring not to move. His dry breath scraped against his throat. Lottie placed an open book in front of him. He stared at it as his legs got used to its weight.

"Open it," Lottie insisted.

Opening the book, Nathaniel flipped through the pages until he came upon a page with the likeness of a pretty lady printed upon it.

"That's too far," Lottie said. "We need to start with more basic letters. Go back to the beginning."

"Who's Phyllis Wheatley?"

Lottie stared at the boy.

Nathaniel continued, "She was brought from Africa when she was a year older than me?" he looked up at her, "What's Africa?"

Lottie squinted her eyes, "You don't know what Africa is?"

Nathaniel shook his head.

"Who's your mother and father."

"My Ma and Pa."

Lottie raised a single eyebrow.

"What are their names," Qi clarified.

"Zeke," Nathaniel remembered, "Mr. Gibb calls my dad Zeke."

"Ezekiel," Lottie pondered. "Who works for Mr. Gibb? Tall guy?"

Nathaniel nodded. "Strong as a bear."

Lottie smirked, "To children, all grown men are as strong as bears. Is your father here today?"

Nathaniel shook his head. "He's taking care of the stock. But he'll be coming to night school when we get back. Jane says sometimes they switch and Pa comes in the morning."

"I see. Jane's your sister?"

Nathaniel scanned the room until he spotted Jane in the back near the metal bucket. Pointing a finger, he declared, "There she is."

"I see. Perhaps someday I can have a word with your father."

Nathaniel's eyes widened. "Did I do someth'n wrong?"

"Heaven's no," Lottie retracted, "but that's also part of the problem. You are ignorant of Africa due to no one teaching you." She leaned forward and gently pinched a portion of Nathaniel's baby soft cheek skin; goosebumps erupted all over him. "Africa is the lineage of all of us beautiful black people," She released him. "It is a big continent on the other side of the Atlantic Ocean, south of Europe."

"Is it bigger than America?"

Lottie touched her chin, "I'm not certain."

"It is," Qi interjected.

"Why did you never tell me about Africa?" Nathaniel thought.

"You never asked," Qi replied.

"So," Lottie glanced down at the text, "you can read this?"

Nathaniel nodded.

Lottie squinted her eyes again, "What does that sentence say?"

Shuffling in his seat, Nathaniel focused on the words. "She was bought by Mrs. John Wheatley, a Boston lady, who chose her from a crowd of robust Negroes, although she looked feeble and slender, because of her modest appearance and pleasant face."

Lottie's eyes were wide. "Wow! That's fantastic!" She studied him like a carnival game. "You've never been to school before?"

Staring at her beaming smile, he answered, "I learned from my Pa's ABC's book and"—he leaned in and whispered—"I stoled his Bible and read that too."

She whispered back, "Well, I'm sure God will forgive thee for such a transgression." Raising her voice back to a normal volume, she said, "What an absolute gift you have!" She placed her hand on the book and asked, "have you ever read this book?"

Nathaniel shook his head.

"Read through it then," Lottie said. "There is much to learn."

Nathaniel flipped the page.

"If you have any questions."

Nathaniel looked up at her.

She hesitated. "It's alright to ask them."

Nathaniel nodded.

"If you have a question ask me," Qi interrupted.

"Uh…"Nathaniel looked down at the floor then raised his face and asked aloud, "What's your favorite food?"

Lottie snickered, "What?"

"I want to ask you something that I didn't already know."

Lottie smirked then giggled, "Well, I love sweet potato pie. My grandmother made the best. Especially on a cold night. With a nice hot cup of cider."

Nathaniel flipped all the way through the book. "What do you study?"

"Oh, I'm working on some mathematics."

Nathaniel looked up from the book. "Arithmetic."

"Don't tell me yer also a bona fide genius with numbers as well."

"I don't know if I am or not. I didn't know I could read until I tried and did."

Lottie sighed. "I wish it were that easy for me."

"Can you help her with her numbers?" Nathaniel thought.

"No," Qi answered.

"No! Ned!" the short-haired lady commanded. "Pronounce it again!"

Lottie and Nathaniel looked at each. Lottie shrugged and pointed down at the text.

She cocked her head, struck by a thought. "Did they ever teach you about the United States?"

Nathaniel shrugged. "I know I live in Alabama. An' Montgomery is north of us."

"Montgomery is west of us."

"But Pa said he had to go *up* to Mon'gom'ry. Up is north."

"He mus'ta been use'n an expression," Lottie explained. "Not saying it actual-like."

"Oh," Nathaniel said before thinking, "Is that right, Qi?"

"Montgomery is forty miles south-west of here," the spider replied.

"Do you know that you live in the South?" Lottie asked.

Nathaniel nodded.

"Did you know that the southern states used to be a part of the Confederacy?" She lifted a finger as she listed, "Virginia, Mississippi, Tennessee, Arkansas, Louisiana, Texas, North *and* South Carolina, Georgia, Florida," she continued the count by lowering her fingers. "Virginia, and Al-ah-bam-ah! There was a war less than a decade ago. They fought the northern states. It was the Union against the Confederacy and the Union won."

"Ya, my parents said that. They said it was the war that emancipated us."

"Yes. Freedom and it turned us into fodder."

"Father?"

Lottie giggled, "No, its fodder, ef-oh-dee-dee-ee-are. It means like something you can just use up and git rid of. Usually there is a lot of it." Her smile faded. "Two of my older cousins were killed. An' then I got another cousin who was killed in Colfax this last spring." She looked down at Nathaniel, "Ya heard about the Colfax murders?"

"Alright!" Miss Mathers projected as she walked to the front of the class. "Everyone's attention up front."

A group of gentlemen stood up and walked out of the building.

"We will now begin our Bible lesson." The teacher continued. "I need volunteers to come to the front of the class."

Lottie poked Nathaniel with her elbow and whispered, "Go."

Nathaniel blushed. "Why don't you?"

"I've been up there a thousand times." She turned and faced him, "You should go."

"Qi?" Nathaniel thought.

"Do what you want."

Standing up from the bench, Nathaniel took a step forward.

"Come forward, volunteers," Miss Mathers beckoned.

The sounds of butts shifting in seats echoed off the wooden walls. Nathaniel walked up next to the teacher. She looked down at him.

"Nathaniel?"

Nathaniel looked up at the teacher, "Yes?"

With an index finger, she traced a circle in the air. "Turn around."

A few giggles rippled through the class as Nathaniel spun around. Blood rushed to his head as he faced the sitting crowd. Everyone watched him, including the other volunteers approaching the front of the class.

Miss Mathers leaned over him and asked, "Are you sure you want to read out loud in *front* of the class?"

"Uh…"

From the back of the classroom, Mrs. Cobb stood up and shouted, "Let the child learn!"

"Fine." Miss Mathers stepped away from the small boy.

A line formed around Nathaniel, putting him in its middle.

The teacher stepped in front of a skinny young man and held up her hands. "We have enough."

The man halted his step and quickly reversed it. Another person sat back down on their pew. Nathaniel looked over the whole class. They were all smiling at him, as though he were already doing something extraordinary.

A grown man hovered over the boy and asked, "Ya sure you want to be up here?"

Nathaniel shrank back.

"John," a smiling Lottie called from the front row, "Let him show ya."

John snapped his eyes over to Lottie. "Aren't the older students supposed to sit in the back of the class?"

Holding up her hands, Lottie stood up and admitted, "Ya got me."

John continued to side-eye Nathaniel. "Isn't this your first day?"

The boy stared.

"Obviously he will do splendid," John muttered as he strode over to an open spot in line.

With a large Bible in hand, Miss Mathers scurried to the front class. Opening up the book, she flipped wildly through the pages until she found her intended target. Handing off the scriptures to the first reader, the teacher leaned in and whispered something in her ear.

Turning to face the class, Miss Mather's projected, "We will now commence a reading of Job chapter forty. Everyone listen with a keen intent for we are going to discuss these verses following the reading." She nodded to the lady holding the Bible.

She spoke in a slow staccato, "More-ever, the Lord answered Job and said, 'Shall he that con-ten-deth with the Al-migh-ty in-struct him? He that Re-prov-eth God, let him an-swer it,"

The student handed the big book over to the next scholar before instructing them, "Read two verses then pass it on."

The next reader spoke with fluidity, "Then Job answered the Lord, and said, 'Behold, I am vile; what shall I answer thee? I will lay mine hand upon my mouth.'"

She handed the text over to the skinny mustached adolescent.

Handling the big book with ease, the man projected, "Once have I spoken; but I will not answer; yea, twice; but I will proceed no further." He dropped his voice and slowly built volume over the course of the sentence. "Then the Lord answered out of the whirlwind and said." He knelt down and offered the book to Nathaniel. "You want me to hold it open for you?"

Nathaniel nodded appreciatively.

He focused on the book. "Where am I supposed to start?"

Giggles rippled through the crowd. The mustached young man pointed to verse seven.

Focusing on the words, he tried his best to project, "Gird up thy loins now like a man."

"Can't hear," someone called from the back of the room.

Nathaniel practically screamed, "Gird up thy loins now like a man! I will demand of thee and declare unto thee! Wilt thou also dis," he tripped over the word but recovered, "Annul my judgment? Wilt though condemn me, that thou mayest be righteous?"

People erupted into cheers and clapping. Tall, old scholars he did not know patted him on the back. Somewhere in the background, Lottie was confirming to another student that it was indeed the boy's first day.

"That's incredible," the mustached man said as tears welled in his eyes. "My grandfather learned himself how to read. But he was almost forty when he did it and he had to keep it a secret."

Nathaniel's beaming smile flickered. Someone started ringing a loud bell.

"Alright!" Miss Mathers projected. "Alright! Settle down."

Student returned to their seats. Nathaniel's heart was still thumping like a drum, his stretching smile had yet to fall from his face. The classroom was full of bright faces, all beaming at him.

When it was quiet enough, John leaned over and announced to the girl standing next to him, "Continue the reading."

The mustached man offered the Bible to the girl. Taking the Bible, the girl searched the pages for where to begin.

"Where did you leave off?" she asked Nathaniel.

"That's alright," Miss Mather's stepped in. "We covered what we needed to cover." She walked over to the girl holding the Bible and took it back. "We can now discuss what we just read." She turned and addressed the classroom, "Does anyone have any observations on this passage?"

The room was filled with a solid silence.

With a sigh, Miss Mathers reopened the Bible and quickly found Job 40, "Shall he that *contendeth* with the Almighty *instruct* him?" Looking up from the text, she scanned the room. "Anyone have any thoughts on this?"

"This is such a waste of time," Qi commented.

The teacher continued, "It means who are we to instruct God? Who are *you* to instruct God? God's will is holy and perfect and who is anyone of *us* to condemn *Him*?" Lowering her eyes back down to the text, Miss Mathers continued, "In this chapter, Job had all these riches. He was a faithful servant of God and he didn't have to worry about food or shelter. And then one day God allowed the Devil to destroy everything Job had. We all know the story, the Devil took his wealth, family and finally his health. The chapter before this Job had questioned God as to why He would allow such a thing." She scans the page for another section. "In the next chapter God says, 'Canst thou draw out Leviathan with a hook?'" she looked up at her class. "Can any of y'all fish out a Leviathan?" She shook her head and some of the class mirrored her. "We may not know where God's plan is leading us, but we can trust in Him that it is His plan." Closing the book she placed her hand on its cover, "according to His Holy word in the scriptures."

Nathaniel felt the urge to clap but hesitated when no one else did.

"Don't listen to her," Qi said.

Does anyone of us have the *authority* to question God?" the teacher said.

"Her mind is not in good health," Qi said.

Uneasiness settled inside Nathaniel's belly. Walking up behind

Miss Mathers, Nathaniel grabbed her skirt and gave it a gentle tug. She jumped back, taking hold of the part of her dress that the boy had been just holding.

"Can I sit down?" he asked.

"Fine," she answered before addressing the entire reading line. "You may all take your seats now."

John coughed to himself as he returned to his seat.

"I my only hope that we can all learn something from Job," Miss Mathers continued scanning the room. "I need the little ones to get slates and start working on writing the alphabet and numbers. I will need two volunteers, *different* from before, to do that for me. The upper class, we will work on geometry."

The little girl in the dirty dress hopped off the pew and made her way over to the far wall. Another small boy followed after her. Nathaniel looked at Ned who looked right back at him. With similar rhythm, the boys slid off the pews and walked to the far wall. They caught up to the girl and boy who were busy picking out the best slates from the limited bunch. When they moved on to picking chalk, Nathaniel moved up to pick next but Ned was quicker. When Ned moved on to chalk, Nathaniel discovered that the final chalkboard was missing a section of wood. Grabbing the slate by its broken side, he turned to the left and picked up a piece of chalk out of an old wicker basket. Returning to his seat, he saw that Ned was now standing in front of the pew, utilizing it like a table. Setting his chalk next to Ned, Nathaniel peaked over at his friend's work.

The mustached man walked to the front of the class, followed closely behind by a tall, older girl. All of the youngins turned around to face the new adults looking for their attention.

"I'm Robert," the mustached young man introduced himself.

"I'm Mary," the girl said.

"Did anyone get cloths to erase the chalk?" Robert inquired.

Every child shook their head.

"I'll grab a few rags." Robert gently touched Mary on the shoulder. "Get them started."

Mary blinked and smiled. "I'll be fine."

As Robert made his way to the far wall, Mary turned and

addressed the youngins. "Does everyone know how to write each letter of the alphabet in order?"

One child nodded while the others either shook their heads or remained motionless.

Mary leaned closer to the one boy and asked, "May I borrow your slate?"

With both hands, the child held up the requested offering.

"Thank you."

She took the slate and carefully inscribed each of the twenty six letters of the Roman alphabet before holding it up for all the children to see. After finishing she pointed to the first letter, "They are a bit small. I want y'all to focus on one letter at a time, it will give you more room. Use my board as a reference," she said as she handed the slate back to its original owner. "I'm gonna get you a fresh one. Guard this one for me, okay? Make sure all of your friends who want to see it get a chance to look."

The boy nodded and then looked down at the flawless rendition of the alphabet laying in his lap.

"Did you get a slate?" the lady asked a different child.

Facing the pew, Nathaniel stared down at the blank slate in front of him and thought, "A." Bringing the tip of his chalk down on the board, Nathaniel drew a straight line at an angle. Then he drew a related line going in the opposite direction. Then he connected the two angles with a horizontal line.

"That looks like an 'H,'" Qi commented.

Nathaniel frowned.

"Do it again. Your muscles will learn," Qi confirmed.

"Jus' try it again." Robert stood in front of the boy, offering a rag. "That's how you learn. I didn't get it right on my first try."

Accepting the offering, Nathaniel erased the markings on his chalkboard and tried again.

"Interesting," Robert commented. "So you self-taught yerself how to read but you've never learned penmanship?"

"Reckon so."

Robert smiled, "I'm glad you're learning something today. They should have you teaching the class."

Nathaniel smiled back.

"Your 'A' looks a lot better," Qi said.

Nathaniel tried his skill with a 'B.'

"You should try doing the smaller version of the letter," Robert commented.

Nathaniel looked up at the young man.

"Know what? Never mind. Try lower case tomorrow. Just stay focused on the capitals today."

Nathaniel went back to practicing. When he reached 'Z,' he started over from the beginning. When he was busy scribbling a 'Q,' Miss Mathers moved to the front of the class and clapped her hands together.

"Alright, scholars," she announced, "it's time for a half hour recess. You may eat your lunch now or later. During afternoon recess, if anyone has any questions for me I will be at the desk preparing for our later lessons."

The room erupted into a thousand noisy conversations. Leaning over, Ned loudly asked, "Y'ver play town ball?"

Nathaniel shook his head.

"C'mon," Ned said as he grabbed his friend's hand, "I'll show ya!"

With his arm stretched forward, Nathaniel followed Ned into the flow of people exiting the schoolhouse. Standing just outside the building and just out of the way of the departing crowd was a group of five men. The only one among them sitting was holding a shotgun while the other four stood in a semi-circle around him. As the boys passed by one of the standing men reached his hand back behind him and grabbed Ned.

Pulling the small child near, the adult leaned down and asked Ned's left ear, "Learning a lot?"

Ned nodded.

"Good boy." The man let go. "Run along."

Ned continued at his previous pace, slightly wrenching Nathaniel's arm in its socket. Dashing to the right, they ran alongside the schoolhouse until it ended and the meadow opened up. The horizon ended after the vast field reached a far off tree-line. To the left some yards out was a well with several people standing around it. Up ahead children of all sizes were busy claiming their personal portion of a cluster of large oak trees. To the right standing next to the back of the schoolhouse was a clique of tall boys. They gathered around a large tree stump with many roots growing out of the ground. Ned didn't stop running until both he and his friend were directly in front of the tallest adolescent of the pack.

The second tallest one noticed the boys and addressed Ned. "Wanna play?"

Ned nodded.

"Yer friend too?"

Ned nodded.

"Y'all know how?"

"I do, he don't."

"Books don't know how to play? Ya gonna teach him?"

Ned nodded.

"Alright, why don't you two cover the field and ya explain him the rules while yer out there."

"Can I swing?" Ned asked.

"Later, after ya explained him the rules."

"Okay, fine," Ned tapped Nathaniel on the shoulder and gestured for him to follow.

They ran far out, almost to the trees. Where Ned stopped, Nathaniel did likewise. Looking up, he spotted Jane standing on some branches really high up in a tree. She was fiercely busy, shouting obscene gibberish at the boy throwing pebbles at her.

"Face this way," Ned explained.

Facing the schoolhouse, he spotted the group of tall boys still arguing over who was on which team and which of those teams was going to swing first. Four tall girls moved nearer to the squad of arguing players and three of them engaged the boys in in the debate while the fourth assisted a one-legged man with traversing the terrain. With a crutch under his right armpit and his left arm wrapped around the girl's shoulder, the pair hobbled over to the tree stump where the man sat down upon it. When he was fully settled, he placed his crutch behind him and then cupped his hands together. The young lady then joined up with the still debating players. The leader boy pointed to where Nathaniel and Ned were standing. The entire group took a brief glance over at them before returning to their conversation. The cluster divided in two, with one section drifting towards the field and the other moving up against the wooden panels that made up the back wall of the schoolhouse. The group near the school formed into a line and the young lady at the front picked up a long stick and walked up to the stump.

Ned pointed a finger at the swinger. "If she hits the ball and the ball comes near us, we catch it or if we can't catch it, grab it and throw it to that guy"—he pointed at the tall boy standing next to the almost equally tall stick staked into the ground beside him—"and he gets her out. Three to four outs and the teams switch and *we* try to hit the ball."

"Three or four outs?"

Ned shrugged. "If one team is losing really badly, we might give them another out." He pointed at the swinger. "If she makes it past the first safety stick"—Ned's voice built and peaked with excitement —"she's gonna keep charging onto the second and third and then make it back to the stump without getting out, she scores a point!"

"Oh? And that's bad?"

Ned threw up his hands. "Of course its bad, don't you understan'? We don't want *them* getting *any* points."

A loud wooden crack split the air over the field. The thrower dove for the ball as it rolled just beyond his reach. The boy standing near the second stick reached out and scooped up the rolling ball. In a single motion, he threw the ball up into the air. The ball peaked and then fell, traveling in an arch all the way into the hands of the lad guarding the first stick. The girl stood next to him holding the pole.

"AUGH!" Ned grabbed his face as he muttered. "She got to the stick; *she's safe!*" his eyes snapped to his teammate. "We gotta make sure she don't get no further." He pointed towards the one legged man. "If she gets back there, to *him*, she scores a point!"

The tall boy tossed the ball to the second tallest boy, the one who called Nathaniel, Books. The originator of the nickname waited for the next swinger to step up to the stump. As soon as they had picked up the bat, he wound himself up like a spring. Uncoiling he threw the ball at maximum speed. The swinger swung and struck a bunch of air.

"Whiff!" everyone called out.

The one-legged man threw the ball high up into the air. The thrower easily caught the slowly falling ball. He positioned himself to throw. Ned bent his legs and Nathaniel did the same. The thrower threw. The swinger didn't swing.

"C'mon," the thrower yelled. "That was perfect."

"Not for me."

"That's cause ya can't swing!"

"Just wait an' see!"

"I've been doin' jus' that!"

"Nathaniel!" Ma cried out, "Come eat your lunch! Jane!"

A loud crack issued from the wooden bat. Nathaniel looked back just in time to see Ned dive forward. Jane jumped down from the second lowest branch and hurried towards Ma.

"I'll be back," Nathaniel called to Ned's back before dashing to his mother.

He caught up to Ma. She had removed all of the contents of the lunch parcel and was currently unwrapping a piece of leather from around some squares of cornbread and some morsels of cooked rabbit. With a wary eye on the game, Ma smiled at her approaching children. Jane and Nathaniel both went for pieces of meat before grabbing a portion of cornbread. The rabbit was dry, but covered in congealed grease that coated the tongue, teeth and throat. The cornbread managed to be even drier, as it crumbled into bits and soaked up ones saliva like a sponge.

"How are you liking school?" Ma asked Nathaniel.

"I'm thirsty," he said.

"Finish your food and then we'll all get water. How do you like it?"

"I like reading."

"We saw that," Ma agreed. "What else do you like?"

"I wrote the alphabet."

"Very good," Ma turned to Jane. "What did you do?"

"Added and subtracted fractions."

"Very nice," Ma nodded, "Mathematics are good. That's how your brother knew Mr. Gibb was bilking yer father."

"I know!" Jane screamed as she stood up and ran off towards the trees.

Ma finished chewing before commenting, "She's gonna learn someday. You will never have such support as what your family can give you. I hope y'all won't splinter like my family did. Your father's too." She let out a sigh. "Ready to get water?"

Nathaniel nodded. Ma led the way back to the schoolhouse. They passed by the group of five men still chin wagging. The mother and son entered the schoolhouse and went straight for the big metal bucket propped up on the chair next to the one-legged man's empty chair. At the front of the class, Miss Mathers was in the midst of conversation with a skinny woman cradling a baby in her arms.

As Ma and son took turns drinking from the ladle, they could not help but overhear Miss Mathers explaining, "Come up north. You don't have to live like this."

The mother dropped her eyes as she stared blankly at the floor, "The white men band together and won't buy until we get so desperate we practically give it away."

Nathaniel drank from the ladle.

The skinny mother continued, "An' don' talk about the north like its the hallelujah promise land. There is still plenty of separation." Careful not to drop her child, she pointed a finger. "It ain't easy when you don't have a mother and father you can rely on. Especially when ya got little ones."

Ma took hold of the ladle and put it back onto the bucket, "C'mon, let's spend whats left of recess outside. "Holding her arms out, she guided her child back towards the door.

"Well," Miss Mathers replied, "what about Jamaica? Or Liberia? Be with your own kind?"

Outside the schoolhouse the group of men were still talking among themselves. Ma stopped in front of them and declared, "I declare if that pale lady was a man, I'd advise one of y'all to give him what's good for."

The men faced the statement with confused faces.

"Ya got a problem with Miss Mathers?" one of them asked.

"She's fine, jus' fine. Lord knows I owe her my free soul

'sider'n she taught me how to read an' all but some things you can just never understand no matter how much time ya spend beside it."

"Not sure I follow you," a man replied.

"I suppose I sound like some raving lunatic," Ma admitted. "Perhaps you can ask Ophelia about it," Ma pointed a thumb behind her. "She's in there right now, having words with the teacher."

The man stepped forward, "With all due respect, Ma'am, Miss Mathers is the least of our worries. Word come 'round about another lynching happened no more than fifty miles east of here."

"In the mountains?" Ma inquired.

"Not north, east. Cousin of mine who lives no more than five miles from here says he smelled smoke walking home just the other night."

A hush fell over the adults. For a second, Nathaniel thought they might have suddenly started praying.

"It's gotten worse," Ma said.

Everyone nodded.

The man with the shotgun shifted in his seat, "Don't worry about Miss Mathers. She helping more than she hurting." He pleasantly pleaded. "The real enemy out there is hurt'n an' kill'n both us anyone willing to help alike."

"Amen." said another man.

Ma sighed. "Yer righ'. But some of the things she say don't sit well with me."

"I do not know y'all's history" the man confessed, "but I do know from m'own knowings that whites can know a lot but it'll never be the same as liv'n in it."

Ma nodded and then shook her head, "It's deliberate!" She tugged on her child's shoulder. "C'mon Nathaniel, let's finish up lunch."

Nathaniel eagerly hurried away from the grown-ups. He rounded the corner of the schoolhouse and spotted the town ball game as active as ever. Ned stood behind a tall boy standing in a primed swinging position. The lady who had helped the one-legged man was now standing where the previous thrower had. She wound up and hurled the ball at the stump. With his enormous hands, the one legged man caught the throw.

"Whiff!" the team in the field cried out.

Coming up behind Ned, Nathaniel tapped his friend on the shoulder. Spinning around, Ned's face immediately brightened.

"Where ya been?"

"Lunch."

"I eat mine in the afternoon." Ned turned his head and kept watching the game.

"Can I swing?"

Ned shrugged, "Sure." He glanced over at the swinging tall boy. "If he gets on and I get on, we won't have anyone else to swing." He looked at Nathaniel. "We lost a few players. And they win'n by three points."

"What's the score?"

"Three–zero."

"Whiff!" everyone yelled out.

"C'mon, Harris," Ned clapped his hands, "get it this time!"

Harris bit his lower lip and concentrated while the one-legged man threw the ball back to the thrower. When the next throw came, he didn't swing.

"That was a beautiful throw," the girl complained.

The tall boy readied himself again.

"There's a lot of waiting in this game," Nathaniel commented.

Harris swung and a crack resounded. Simultaneously, the two runners lived up to their title. With both arms reaching out, the helpful girl dove for the ball but she only managed to deflect it.

Ned's eyes bulged as he screamed, "Yaaaaaaaaaaaaa!"

The thrower scrambled, chasing after the ball. Finally she seized her rolling target and whipped herself around, ready to throw. The two youths remained touching the first and third stick. With her eyes shifting between the stationary runners, the thrower inched back to her throwing area. Ned picked up the fallen swinger stick and readied himself. The thrower locked eyes on him and threw. Ned lifted up the broad side of the stick and the ball struck the wooden surface. It was redirected up into the air and Ned took off. It took a moment for the thrower to realize she should run for the hit ball with low expectations. By the time she reached it, Ned was already holding onto the first stick. She glared at the person on third base, who dared not try to reach the stump. She walked back to the throwing area, eyed all the runners, and then turned around to face the next swinger.

"It's your turn," Qi said.

Nathaniel stepped forward. Leaning down, he picked up the fallen stick. Focusing on the thrower, Nathaniel held the stick the same way the other children did. The ball came flying. He wasn't ready.

"Ya havta swing if its good," the girl called before looking over her shoulders. "Did anyone explain the rules to him?"

Ned raised his free hand, "I did!"

The one legged man tossed the ball back to the thrower. With a piece of hay sticking out the side of his mouth, he shifted his straw hat with a free hand, revealing a smiling face.

"Ya got this," the one legged man said, "Knock yer sister out them trees."

Nathaniel giggled as he focused on the thrower.

"Ready?" she asked.

Nathaniel nodded.

She threw a good pitch.

"Whiff!" everyone cried.

"Almos'" the old man said as he threw the ball back to the thrower.

"We could experiment," Qi said.

"What?" Nathaniel thought as he readied himself to swing.

"Relax, stay in this position. I'll help you hit the ball."

Nathaniel thought incredulously, "You will?"

"Yes."

The ball flew through the air, Nathaniel found his arms moving into a swinging motion. He barely caught a glimpse of the ball striking the stick. It sailed high up into the air. It peaked and then fell and bounced off the church's roof.

"Run!" Qi commanded.

Nathaniel took off for first base.

"Stop!" several players, shouted, including some of his teammates.

Nathaniel came to a skirting halt. His eyes shifted from the thrower to the first base guard.

"What?" he stammered.

"Play's dead," the thrower explained. "That's a bad hit. If it goes behind you its out of bounds." She turned and yelled at Ned, "You did a terrible job teaching him the rules!"

Ned's smile flickered. "I taught him about guarding the field."

"But ya didn't teach him anything else?"

"He ate lunch!"

The old man sitting on the step shouted, "Someone's gonna havta go get the ball."

The thrower pointed at Nathaniel, "You go get it."

"But I didn't know."

"You hit it."

Nathaniel crossed his arms, and muttered "Fine," before turning around and marching off.

As he neared the edge of the building, Ned's father emerged into view, carrying the ball in his hands.

"Any team need an extra player?" he inquired.

Jumping up and down, Ned's smiled and flailed his arms and squealed, " We do! We do! We need an extra player!"

Ned's dad analyzed the closest players, "Am I swinging or guarding?"

"Swinging!" Ned continued and pointed to his friend. "You're next after Nathaniel!"

"Alright, who's throw'n?"

"I am," the helpful girl held up her hands.

Ned's father tossed her the ball.

"This doesn't seem very fair," she mumbled.

"What's a matter?" Ned's dad asked as he walked over and stood beside the one legged man's stump. "Scared we gonna run away with it?"

"Ya," she answered.

The thrower watched Nathaniel walk back to the stick and pick it up.

"I'll make sure to let Nathaniel know to go easy on ya," Ned's dad winked.

Picking up the stick, Nathaniel readied himself. The thrower eyed him up and down. She glanced behind to make sure her teammates and opponents were in their proper places. Winding up she snapped her eyes forward as she hurled the ball straight at the stump. The ball flew through the air at an odd angle. Stretching his arms out, Nathaniel extended the stick as far out as it would go.

"Whiff!" people exclaimed.

Stumbling forward, Nathaniel blushed.

"You don't have to swing at the bad pitches," the one-legged man said.

Nathaniel's eyes snapped up to the stump sitter. "What?"

"You only have to swing at the good throws," Ned's dad interjected. "You *don't* have to swing at the bad throws."

Nathaniel looked back and forth from each adult, "How do I tell the difference between a good throw and a bad."

"If it doesn't hit *you*," the man pointed a finger, "*and* if you have to move your feet to hit it, its a bad throw."

"House rule here is if I can't catch it, its a bad throw," the one legged man chuckled.

"Can I have my ball back?" the thrower complained.

"We're explaining the rules," the man sitting on the stump yelled back, "Can ya grab the ball and throw it to back to my grand daughter, Violet?"

Walking closer to the schoolhouse, Nathaniel reached down and picked up the stationary ball. Turning around, he chucked it up into the air. Gravity dropped it right on top of Violet, who easily caught it. Nathaniel watched the thrower exhale before coiling herself up like a spring.

Ned's father stepped back as Nathaniel took position next to the stump. His eyes focused on the thrower. Uncoiling, she pitched. His hands were flung into orbit around his body. The stick's curving trajectory collided with the heavy ball. The sound sent shockwaves through the air while the vibration knocked the stick out of Nathaniel's grip. He took off running. Without slowing the boy reached out and grabbed hold of the first stick. Slamming on the brakes, he felt the ground pop as the first stick came free from its hole.

"I broke it!" Nathaniel panicked.

Looking around, he noticed that no one was paying the slightest bit of attention to his vandalism. The thrower held up her hands as she dashed for the stump. Ned laughed like a maniac as he twisted around her and headed for the stump. Catching the ball, Violet turned and desperately tried to tag the small boy who was quick. Ned leaped up into the air and stomped on the ground just in front of the stump. Their entire team cheered, including the one legged man on the stump.

Ned's father yelled across the field, "Nice hit, Nathaniel!"

"Yeah, Books," The boy who had first referred to him as such called, "great hit!"

"Nice going!" Harris chimed.

Nathaniel lifted up the stick.

Ned broke out into laughter that became very contagious.

Ned's father turned back and asked the old man, "Ya got the hammer?"

"Yes I do." The old man reached behind him.

The bell tolled. An audible groan rose up from all of the children. With a fraction of their previous vigor, the kids descended from the oak trees or wandered in from all over the field. Ned's father jogged over to first base and offered Nathaniel a hand. When Nathaniel took it, the adult pulled him to his feet.

"I'll take care of the stick," Ned's father insisted, "you run on back to class."

"Oh." Nathaniel let go of the stick.

Wandering after the scattered students, Nathaniel noticed the stream of the moving student body bottlenecking around the edges of the schoolhouse. Suddenly he noticed Ma walking beside him.

"Do I still need to sit in the front?" he asked.

"Yes, dear. It's so you can see. You'd be too short in the back." As they walked, she pulled him close and kissed the top of his head.

Out of the corner of his eye, Nathaniel spotted Violet assisting the one legged man to stand up. With the assistance of a wooden crutch and her shoulder, the pair made slow but steady progress back toward the front of the schoolhouse.

Separating from Ma, Nathaniel returned to his pew. Not too long after, Ned popped a squat on the seat next to him. Craning his neck, Nathaniel spotted the old man hobbling over to the empty chair near the water bucket. The old man plopped himself down in his seat before placing his crutch on the floor. Thanking his grand-daughter, Violet returned to her seat. The old man looked up and immediately spotted the boy staring at him. Blushing, Nathaniel quickly faced forward.

"I hope everyone enjoyed the break," Miss Mathers announced. "Let's get right back to it. I need more volunteers. Who has not helped the little ones yet?"

Harris and Violet moved to the front of the class.

Nathaniel looked up to the one legged man's progeny and asked, "May I use the outhouse?"

She nodded. "Come right back."

As Nathaniel passed by a pew at the back of the room, Lottie stood up and addressed him, "Where ya going?"

Looking over at her, Nathaniel pointed to the exit, "Nature calls."

Lottie covered her mouth. "Do you know where it is?"

Nathaniel shook his head.

Sidestepping out of pew, Lottie took his hand. "I'll show ya."

Leading him out of the schoolhouse, they passed by the chin-wagging men and crossed the dirt road. Stepping through a gap in the stone wall, Nathaniel spotted the tall, thin, rickety building. Then a gust of wind had them both smelling it. Pinching his nose, Nathaniel looked up and saw Lottie wrinkled her own.

"Do you have something to wipe yourself with?"

Nathaniel shook his head.

"Well," her eyes focused on the nearby stone wall, "get yourself a smooth stick or some leaves, be sure not to get anything with bristles."

Nathaniel shuddered as he looked around until he found an appropriate stick. Moving to the outhouse, he opened, entered and carefully secured the door closed. With his nose still plugged

Nathaniel sat down a planed wooden board with a hole in its center. Trying his best not to breathe, he finished up as quickly as possible. Dropping the used stick down the hole, he departed from the rustic lavatory. He headed back to the waiting Lottie and she led the way back into the schoolhouse.

Nathaniel returned to the front pew and practiced his numbers and basic addition until the teacher announced a switch to spelling words. Nathaniel spelled every word correctly, even if he could barely read his own writing. He had not gotten through very many three-letter words before the teacher called for another switch.

"The next subject will involve the entire class." Miss Mathers explained. "I need two volunteers."

Two male scholars assisted Miss Mathers with retrieving a map. When they reached the front of the classroom, the teacher instructed the men to hold the map up while she completed her lesson.

"This is Alabama," Miss Mathers announced as she tapped the portion of the map with a long polished stick. "North of us is Tennessee, to the west of us is Mississippi, east of us is Georgia, and south of us is mighty wet." She shifted her pointer. "This is Indian territory." She moved her indicator again. "Down here is Mexico." She waved her hands in front of the map. "All the rest of this is the United States, thirty seven states."

"Don't forget Canada up there," someone called from the back of the room.

"Canada is not a state."

"It's a country."

"It is not part of the United States."

"It's still important! I got fam'ly up there."

Right, thank you, yes, Canada is up there. Alright." She held her stick like a baton as she faced the class. "I am going to call on scholars to come up, one at a time, and answer a question pertaining to geography."

Multiple hands shot up from the student body.

"I will call on you," the teacher reiterated.

Nathaniel thought, "Your map is better."

"Indeed," Qi said.

"You can look at the whole planet."

"Indeed."

"Where is Vermont?" the teacher asked as she handing the pointing stick over to a scholar.

Taking hold of the pointer the student tapped the correct section of the map.

"Can I ever do that?" Nathaniel thought.

"I don't see why not."

"Anyone know where Lincoln is located?" Miss Mathers questioned. She lowered her eyes and scanned the front row. "Y'all have any idea where Lincoln would be located on the map?"

A child from the second row exclaimed, "There ain't no dead president on the map."

The room erupted into hilarity.

From the back of the room an adult explained over the noise of the dying laughter, "Lincoln is the capital of a state."

The children said nothing. Ned raised his hand.

"Yes?"

"Illinois?"

"Nope, wrong. Anyone else?"

"Do I know the answer?" Nathaniel wondered.

"It's Nebraska," Qi replied.

"Nebraska!" someone called from a few rows back.

"Yes, thank you. The capital of Nebraska is Lincoln. Alright," Miss Mathers projected, "it's time for another break. Please eat or drink if you have yet to do so. It's difficult to learn on an empty stomach." The teacher's tone dropped as she addressed a specific scholar. "Sarah, is the water bucket empty? Does it need to be filled up?"

Standing up, the classroom shuffled about. The room cleared much more slowly than the first time. More people lingered inside. The helpful granddaughter helped her grandfather hobble to the door. Ned was gone and so were Ma and Jane. Standing up, Nathaniel stole glances at the teacher and Sarah as they lingered near the water bucket.

Nathaniel headed for the exit. The group of men was now dispersed but the one with the shotgun was still sitting guard, a smelly pipe dangling from his lips. Scurrying to his right, Nathaniel ran alongside the side of the schoolhouse until he reached the field. Ma sat among the spectators.

When she spotted her son her face brightened. "There y'are!" she declared.

"I waited for everyone to clear out."

"Smart," Ma said. "Ya gonna play?"

Nathaniel glanced over at the game. Short, little Ned stood out as he stood next to a cluster of tall young men and tall full-grown men. Nathaniel bit his lip.

"Maybe you'll have a better time with Jane over in the Oaks," Ma pointed in the direction of the trees.

Nathaniel turned and walked closer.

"Watch out for the ball," Ma shouted, "it can hurt real bad!"

Nathaniel wandered closer to the trees. Looking up, he spotted Jane climbing up to some of the highest of the branches. The boy who had been throwing pebbles at her before was standing even higher than her.

"Just wait till I get you, you red coat scum!" Jane declared. "You will rue the day you ever heard the name Esmeralda Voodoo, witch queen of the pirates!"

The boy laughed as he feebly flailed a long, thin branch at her.

Jane struck his leg with her own stick. "Ha! I chopped yer leg off. Now yer a peg leg! Ya gotta hop around!"

Nathaniel watched the boy hop from one thick branch to another.

"This looks like an awful idea," Qi said.

Nathaniel stopped his approached.

"He could fall on you," the spider observed.

Stepping back from the trees, Nathaniel watched as the boy slipped and almost fell from the tree.

"Save me!" he shouted. "Esmeralda I see a sea monster beneath me. I'll give you all my gold an' treasure!"

"Nay!" Jane shouted back. "You be-est a traitor, Josiah Cutthroat! Down to the wicked watery depths with thee!"

Holding on, the boy yelled and would have started sprinting if his frantically running legs were not in midair. A crack filled the air and Nathaniel immediately faced front. A ball sailed through the air, and the man guarding the second stick jumped up. Snagging the ball from the air, everyone except the runner's team cheered.

The boy in the tree screamed as he let go, "I'll get you, Esmeralda witch!"

Jane pointed her sword. "It's Esmeralda *Voo-Doo!*"

As soon as the boy landed, he sprinted around to the front of the tree and climbed up. Already he was nearly back to where Jane was holding out.

"Yer dead," Jane insisted.

"I came back from the dead," he answered smugly.

Jane shook her head, "Can't do that, the dead can't come back from the wicked depths, its like an extra bad prison in hell for extra bad people. Not jus' for the regular sinners."

"Fine, I'm not Josiah Cutthroat anymore, but the royal commander of the Navy and I have imperial orders for your arrest!"

Jane stood up and flailed her sword. "Only a worst dog traitor than a cutthroat traitor is one that's loyal to the crown. On guard, you smelly ol' rat!"

"An insult! On guard!"

The crack of the stick striking the ball echoed across the field. Nathaniel whipped his head back around just in time to see the ball go rolling in between the legs of two full-grown men. Nathaniel jumped to his feet but his legs failed initiation when he watched a young lad scoop up the ball and chuck it at the first stick. The ball went sailing past the intended target and the runner took full advantage of the opportunity. Ned's dad came dashing across the field, he touched second base and didn't miss a step as he charged on to third. The one legged man shifted forward and stuck out his hand. Ned's dad spotted the old man holding the ball and stopped his run at third base.

"C'mon, Charlie!" the one legged grandfather called, "C'mere, I got somethin' for ya."

Charlie squawked out a single laugh before shouting back, "I keep forgetting an old timer like you can catch a cold in the middle of summer."

The old timer threw the ball back to the thrower. Ned stepped up to bat.

"Watch his tricky half hits," the old timer called out.

Glancing back, Ned put a finger to his lips and shushed the tattletale. The thrower threw.

"Whiff!" everyone decreed.

The one legged granddad tossed the ball back.

The thrower threw.

"Whiff!"

The old timer threw the ball back.

The thrower wound up. Ned held the stick up. The ball struck the broad side of the stick and bounced straight up into the air. The thrower dashed forward and jumped, catching the ball in midair.

"Gone!" multiple people yelled.

"Out!" Others exclaimed.

Ned shoulders slumped as he walked back to the end of the line. Another adult picked up the stick and readied himself to swing. The thrower threw and a crack echoed throughout the field. Charlie charged for the stump while the other running adult dashed for first. The lad who finally picked up the ball, hurled it at the stump. After a single bounced, the old timer caught the ball but it was too late to stop Ned's father stepping on the ground just in front of the stump.

"Yer out!" the granddad beamed.

"Out?!" Charlie twirled around. "I was safer than a rigged bet."

With a huge grin on his face the granddad held up his thumb. "Get outta here," he turned and looked at Ned. "Next!"

Ned stepped closer to the stump.

"What's the score?" the thrower inquired.

"It's a tie," the stump sitter answered.

"No its not!"

"What's the score then?"

"Four to three," the thrower looked back at the outfield, "right?"

"Sounds fine. Hurry up and throw before Mathers tolls the bell."

The other team was in the midst of recounting the score when the bell tolled.

There was a little more pep in everyone's step as they moved back to the schoolhouse. Nathaniel sensed that the day was winding down.

After Bible study, Miss Mathers prayed, "Lord, keep us all safe. These are trying times. We all know to trust in you, Lord, but You know how difficult it is to remain faithful in the midst of such a time. Keep your children safe. Keep them safe from the other children who do not recognize their own kin in Jesus. Do not let the Devil complete his evil works. Amen," Opening her eyes and adjusting her voice, the teacher continued, "That concludes our first school day. I hope all of you will be here tomorrow or better yet are staying for the evening class. God be with you. You are dismissed!"

Conversation and butt shuffling erupted all over the classroom.

Ned turned to his friend and asked, "You staying for night school?"

Nathaniel shook his head, "I don't think so."

Ma's voice distinguished itself despite the noise, "There you are!"

Both boys looked up. Ma and Jane stood awaiting the boy's full attention. Jane already had her cotton sack tied around her shoulder and waist.

"Did you make a friend?" Ma inquired.

"This is Ned," Nathaniel gestured.

"Ned," Ma smiled, "I believe I know your father."

"Yes, Ma'am."

"Well, we must be going, it was nice meeting you, Ned. Tell yer folks I said hello. Come along children."

Ma led the way out of the schoolhouse.

"Good evening, Miss Mathers," Ma announced coldly.

"Bye, bye," Nathaniel called out, "thanks for all the learn'n!"

Giggles rippled through the shuffling crowd.

"Yer child is such a gift," a woman called from nearby.

Nathaniel hid his face in his Ma's leg while she answered, "Thank you. He *is* my treasured son. God has blessed him greatly."

Nathaniel looked up at his mother. She kissed him on the forehead.

When they reached the first intersection, many families went in different directions and the crowd split. The group continued to dissipate until it was only the three of them passing in front of Gibb's Manor.

"What's for dinner?" Jane wondered aloud.

"Whatever Pa has managed to cook. I pray he went hunting."

The three had not made it to the porch steps before Pa opened the front door.

"Y'all mak'n so much noise, I heard y'all a mile out," he teased. "Y'all have a good first day?"

Emerging from the trio, Ma met Pa at the top step and planted a long kiss on his lips. Pa slipped a hand around her side.

Jane pinched her nose, squeezed her eyes shut, and squealed, "Gross!"

As the duo completed their embrace, Jane avoided the steps as she climbed onto the porch.

"Is there dinner?" she asked.

Pa nodded before addressing his son, "Ya learn a lot today?"

Looking up at his father, Nathaniel nodded.

"You should've gone 'stead of me today," Ma said as Jane disappeared into the shack. "Everyone got a real kick out of him reading full verses on his first day."

Pa patted Nathaniel on the shoulder. "'atta boy!" he stood up looked back at his wife, "It was good you an' Jane saw it." Pa broke out into a broad grin. "Nothin's ever gonna top when we tol' Gibb off about the money he owed."

"'tis true," Ma agreed, "but see'n' John get all upset at a chil' read'n finer than he," Ma wooted and laughed. "Ya should've seen his face! Would that I could sketch a likeness of him!"

They laughed heartily and Nathaniel snickered quietly.

"I can imagine," Pa chuckled.

"I'm hungry," Nathaniel said.

Ma finished up laughing. "Ya got anything?"

Pa winked. "I may have cooked something up for y'all's first day."

"Rabbit?"

"Squirrel corn chowder."

"Chowder? Where'd ya get dairy?"

"Not tell'n."

"Ya got a secret cow I don't know about?"

"C'mon," Pa waved to the air, "let's go inside and eat some." He turned around and headed back into the shack. "Nathaniel, ya read anything interesting today?"

As he followed in the wake of his parents, Nathaniel answered, "I read about a lady, Phyllis Wheatley."

"What's she do to be worth write'n 'bout?"

"She lived in Boston and had a pleasant face."

"At least she has a pleasant face," Pa chuckled.

Nathaniel laughed too.

12

With a belly full of sausages, eggs, croissant, jam, butter, honey, and two just barely burnt pieces of toast, Beechcroft stepped out onto Fifth Avenue. Buttoning up his coat, he eyed a street cleaner applying his trade to a recently deposited pile of shit. Raising up a hand, the Englishman did not wait long before a cab driver approached.

"I need to go to Houston Avenue," Beechcroft stated.

"Which part?"

Beechcroft reached into his jacket pocket and withdrew a piece of paper. The cabbie smiled.

"I meant Greene Street," Beechcroft answered.

Pulling out a cigar, the gentleman replied, "Greene Street or Houston, I can take thee to either or."

Beechcroft entered the cab.

"Greene Street it is," the cabbie announced as the wheels rolled them away from the curb.

The vehicle did little to ward off the cold save for minimizing the time spent in it. A violent scent invaded Beechcroft's nostrils as the air grew thick.

Leaning out the window, Beechcroft shouted up. "Do I smell smoke?"

"Yep."

The cabbie slowed to take a corner that led to large intersection. A colorful crowd blocked the large open junction of several streets. Beyond the crowd, a building was engulfed in fire. Flames and smoke flung themselves from the open windows. A man hung by his hands out of a third story window. He shouted down at the people below. Bells tolled, vibrating through Beechcroft's head. A unified cry rose up from the crowd as the man let go.

"It may take a little bit longer than expected," the driver said as he turned the cab and headed down one of the only unblocked streets. Bells tolled off in the distance, growing louder the further from the crowd they traveled.

A long red wagon came dashing into view, followed closely behind by several dalmatians. The cabbie kicked on the break as his horse came to a trotting stop. With barely an inch between the vessels, the emergency vehicle maneuvered around the taxi as it charged towards the flames. Leaning his head out the window, Beechcroft looked back and watched the firemen. Removing the brake, the cab continued on.

Not too long after the driver announced, "We're here."

Beechcroft waited for the cabbie to come to a complete stop before announcing, "A little further up."

"This is as far as I go."

"I'll tip you," Beechcroft shouted.

"I need to go check me home's not burnt down!" the cabbie replied.

Beechcroft exited the vehicle. "How much do I owe?"

Executing a U turn the driver stopped all traffic as he immediately merged back into it. With a single sovereign in his hand, Beechcroft watched the vehicle disappear. Disrupted drivers cussed and shouted at the departing maniac as they quickly regained their lost speed. Pocketing the coin, Beechcroft assimilated into the pedestrian traffic.

Up ahead, he spotted a group of smartly dressed dudes congregating outside of an apartment chatting with a lone woman. Standing a distance off from the group, Beechcroft glanced at the quaint building, squished in between two wider and taller complexes. From the other side of a glass window, a blonde haired child watched the talkative group currently assembled in front of her building. Following the child's stare, Beechcroft focused on the young men gathered around the smiling young lady.

With a coy smile, the lady leaned in and whispered yet loudly enough for everyone to able to hear, "Why don't we get ourselves out of the cold. We have a nice warm fire inside."

"I don't mind saying so," one dude commented, "but we are in need of more than one femme belle."

"There are plenty more angels inside. Including several who could learn ya a thing or two about the French language."

After watching the group meander through the front door, Beechcroft quietly followed in after them. Warmth swept over the Englishman and he unfastened his coat. He followed voices into a bright, drawing room with plenty of cushioned seats and a roaring fire. Everyone was already engaged in a conversation, save for two ladies.

A freckled-faced redhead with a skin tone paler than a snowflake stood up and quickly closed the distance between her and newcomer. "Oy, love. What might yer business be?"

Making direct eye contact, Beechcroft spoke clearly, "I have a proposition."

A blonde woman with piercing blue eyes came up and hugged the redhead from behind, resting her chin of her chum's right shoulder. She said, "I'll bet ya a dollar I can guess what it is."

Beechcroft smirked. "Actually, I doubt you would."

Without releasing her hug, the blonde girl shrugged. "Try me."

"I am looking for a companion to travel the regions of this fine country that lay southwest of here."

The other two gentlemen were led by their hands through a door at the back of the room.

"Won't you have a seat?" the redhead asked.

"Thank you."

The chair creaked as Beechcroft settled his weight upon it. The redhead sat on one of the large armrests, placing her feet over Beechcroft's left leg.

"Seems to me," the blonde said as she pulled up a wooden chair and sat down in front of the pair, "that yer as far south as ya need to be."

A smirk darted across Beechcroft's face. "I am looking for someone who would not mind leaving New York behind indefinitely. I am traveling in a south-westerly direction. I am not sure for how long, but I am willing to pay a dollar each day until my journey is completed. Should my journey take less than ten days I am willing to pay a minimum of ten dollars. I will be riding first class whenever possible and taking care of any expense my luxurious lifestyle incurs."

The redhead studied Beechcroft from head to toe. "My, my, that does sound like quite the offer," she looked at the blonde. "Doesn't it?"

"Sounds to me yer looking for a wife," the blonde commented.

The redhead looked at the Englishman. "I couldn't just up and leave. But I can show ya one hell of a time right here."

"That is the answer that I will probably hear most," Beechcroft shrugged, "but I only need one person to say yes. Do either of you know of any girl who might be interested?"

"Where ya staying?" the blonde asked.

"Winsdor."

"Shit," the redhead whistled, "heard they got running water in every room."

"That's true," Beechcroft nodded.

"There's a few bimbos 'round here who'd I'd pay *you* a dollar a day to take out of town," the blonde commented.

A laugh escaped the redhead's lungs. "Y'oughta take Millie Jean."

The blonde girl's eyes and smile widened. "We got jus' the gal for you."

Beechcroft studied the women's faces. "I do not wish for a troublemaker."

The blonde crossed her arms. "Yer wishing for someone who's fed up with *this* town but does not have the means to change their situation, *an'* ya want them to *not* be a troublemaker?"

Beechcroft looked down at the rug.

"They'll be putting you in the ground before ya find anyone match'n yer criteria."

"Millie's fine as long as she drunk." the redhead added. "She's only an unruly churchbell when she been sober for too long."

"Liquor ill. She laudanum too," the blonde nodded, "an' that toothache remedy."

"She got no mo' teeth to remedy."

Beechcroft grimaced, "She's got no teeth?"

The blonde shrugged, "Most men don't mind."

A young stranger entered the room, stealing everyone's attention. "Pardon my interruption but is Saltwater Taffy here today."

"She's occupied at the moment," the blonde answered as she stood up from her seat, "but I could take yer message to her."

"I was uh…hoping," the young man mumbled as the blonde took him by the hand.

The blonde led the lad through the door at the back of the room.

Pulling out a coin, Beechcroft offered it on an open palm. "Where does Millie Jean reside?"

Accepting the payment, she turned and pointed out the window. "She lives a few numbers down that way. Easy enough walk." She lowered her hand. "Thirty-two Greene Street. Not that knowing the number will do you much good. I doubt its got any recognizable feature that hasn't rotten off. You should recognize it by the broken windows with young bastards hanging out of them. Though I suppose she's boarded 'em up for the winter."

"Does she have many?"

"Windows?"

"Bastards."

The redhead shrugged. "All of them old enough to walk are either working, begging, or stealing."

"Ah." Beechcroft offered another coin. "This one is for your friend. I would like to stand."

The redhead stood up to allow the Englishman to follow suit. Testing the grip of his cane, Beechcroft buttoned up his coat before tipping his hat to the redhead. He headed for the exit.

Upon opening the door, the cold embraced him like an old

friend. Looking up at the sky, beyond the various streams of smoke, a cloudless blue ocean floated. A thought crawled over his mind, sending a brief flutter of panic up his spine.

Stealing a quick glance behind, Beechcroft lifted up his cane and shouted, "Taxi!"

An empty cabbie to pull over.

"Where ya headed?" the driver asked as Beechcroft planted his ass in the seat.

"Thirty-Two Greene Street."

"Sure thing."

The horse powered wheels moved them into the active traffic. Beechcroft watched the building numbers slowly decline.

Up ahead a quivering voice boomed and trembled over the loiterers and pedestrians. "Repent of yer wicked ways!"

Leaning his head out the window, Beechcroft spotted a preacher standing on a soap box in the middle of traffic. Each driver did their best to avoid getting the zealot tangled up in their spokes and hooves.

Spittle flew from the preacher's bearded mouth as he shouted, "The Lord doth not abide in the mix'n of races and genders! You are no better than *animals, animals I say!* The *creatures God created* for *man* to have *dominion* over! Not to *be*! Beg forgiveness, *kneel* and *beg* forgiveness *at the cross*! You are sodomites! You have turned this fresh new land into Gomorrah!"

"Woah," the driver called as the carriage reached the rear of the bottleneck of traffic.

"He sure can captivate an audience," he mumbled.

A sparse, spread out crowd gathered. Mostly made up hard working mothers and small playing children all stopping to listen. In front of a large alleyway a group of unshaven gentleman inspected the preacher's lesson on fire and brimstone. They wore matching colored scarfs tied about their top hats or wrapped around their legs. One of them patted his double-barreled shotgun while another burst into laughter.

"You exchange money for sin!" the preacher continued. "And you exchange it so you can lay with *animals*!"

"Oye!" an Irish girl called out. "Sounds like ya coul' use a bit of a brush up."

Only the innocent did not laugh aloud.

The preacher shouted even louder, "*God damn* yer loyalty to the devil!"

Three tall gentlemen with matching colors emerged from the alleyway and walked beside the line of halted carriages. Approaching from behind, the leading man kicked the back of the preacher's knee and the speaker crumpled into the arms of the other two men. The two dragged the sermon away while the third man kicked the soap box out of the street. In unison the drivers released their parking brakes.

"Unhand me, sinners! I am a servant of *GOD!*"

One of the children grabbed the discarded soap box and set it down precisely on the edge of the sidewalk.

Standing up upon it, the lad shouted, "Now you all have to listen to me!"

The traffic quickly cleared. Beechcroft kept his eyes fixed on the alleyways filled with different groups of ruffians wearing similar colors. Most of them were in conversation with women dressed in large winter coats and hats. They usually lingered just outside several buildings.

The carriage came to a stop. "We're here."

Beechcroft studied the closest building, which proclaimed the number thirty-one above its front door.

"Its on the other side of the street, sir," the driver said.

Turning his neck Beechcroft caught sight of a dilapidated building just behind a broken-down wrought-iron fence. A rectangular strip of snow covered the open portion of space in front of the house. The front door was set several yards back from the curb.

Beechcroft looked down at the wet, cold, shit covered cobble-stone. "I'll give ya a good tip if ya park me on the other side."

Momentum thrust Beechcroft back into his seat as the cabbie guided the horse and carriage across active traffic to reach and park on the other side of the street. When he regained his breath, Beechcroft promptly opened up the door and set his feet on solid ground. Paying the cabbie a sovereign Beechcroft faced his destination. It took him several seconds to spot the front door.

From above, a sweet, shrill, feminine voice yelled, "Mister, ya got the wrong house."

Looking up, Beechcroft caught sight of a young blonde woman leaning her upper torso out of the second story window.

The blonde lady's mouth did not move but the same voice continued speaking. "Yer kind of parlor houses are on the other side of town,"

Beechcroft's eyes continued searching upward until they reached the fourth floor, where another female face was peering out from a different window.

"Are you Millie Jean?" Beechcroft asked.

The girl on the fourth floor shouted, "No, sir, but she live just above me. What's a good looking gentleman such as yourself doin' asking after the likes of her?"

"Do you know where her current whereabouts would be?"

A shrill laugh burst from the girl, quickly followed by, "Haven't heard a peep from her in over a day. Must've sold 'nough stock to outfit herself for a whole week. She's pro'ly two days into a five-day coma." The girl leaned on the railing. "Be a shame to miss out on good times while yer wait'n on her."

A group of young sailors stopped in front of the home.

One of them approached, scratching his crotch and yelling, "You there, got any *pink* nightgowns?"

The blonde lady yelled back, "Who ya think ye'z? Ya haven't even asked a girl's name before yer tell'n'er what t'wear?"

"Paul," Paul stammered as he reached the front door. "Wha's yers?"

"Charlotte, but all my friends call me firecracker."

One of the other sailors cheered, "'atta boy!"

Firecracker leaned even further out the window, "if ya can find yer way up here, I might let ya pick out a fresh outfit for me."

"Meet us at the dance hall when yer done," another sailor added.

The rest of the gang carried on while Paul moved passed Beechcroft and disappeared into the building. Lagging behind the sailor, Beechcroft entered the building. The sailor climbed the stairs but ascended no further than the second floor. Beechcroft continued on. His vim was challenged as he reached the third story. It continued to struggle until Beechcroft had to stop at the bottom step of the fourth-floor stairwell. Leaning against the railing he took a moment to catch his breath.

"I wouldn't trust that railing if I was you," a lady's voice warned.

Letting go of his support, Beechcroft turned his head and looked up at the lady standing at the top of the stairwell.

"I'm Sarah. Millie's neighbor. Who told ya'bout her?" Reaching into his jacket, Beechcroft took out a flask. Unscrewing the cap, he took a swig.

Sarah raised both hands up like a catcher. "Cap it, I'll catch it,"

Fastening up the top, Beechcroft tossed the flask. Taking a small step forward, the girl snatched the alcohol from the sky. With practiced motion, she uncapped and drank.

After swallowing, she appraised, "That ain't cheap shit."

She wiped her mouth on her sleeve. Her eyes wavered for a second before focusing on the stranger. Cracking a smile, she descended the stairs.

As she placed a foot on the last step, she offered back the flask, saying, "Millie takes anyone she can. Fewer and fewer every day. When she makes money she spends it on a pharmacy." She casually placed a hand on Beechcroft's shoulder. "There are much more pleasant people to spend yer time with. She all used up. Why not spend the night with someone fresher?"

"I'm her father."

The flask slipped through Sarah's fingers. She scrambled to halt any spillage.

When she finally grabbed hold of it, she lifted it into the air.

"I— I'm sorry," she stammered as Beechcroft retrieved the whiskey stained container. "I didn't know."

"Sorry it smells like whiskey," Beechcroft mumbled as he wiped the flask with his silk handkerchief.

When the flask was properly dry, Beechcroft drank more heavily than Sarah had. Tears welled up in his eyes. "I can't even remember the exact year I began this journey." He looked down at the floor-boards. "So long ago." He shook his head. "My wife and I sent her to boarding school. She got bored. She ran off. We suspected a handsome devil of tempting her. We suspected he had smuggler friends who brought them to America. I've hired so many detectives, waded through countless horrors, all to find her." He looked up at the next flight of steps. "Now I've finally found my baby girl."

Sarah retrieved a thin metal case hidden in her breasts and pulled out a cigarette. Placing it in her thin lips, she manifested a match and lit it on the railing. She inhaled deeply and then exhaled for just as long, filling the hallway with smoke. The scents of tobacco and whiskey mixed with the lingering rot.

Sarah's lower lip twitched as she confessed. "I'm sorry 'bout what I said before. Had I realized," She took a deep drag. "She told me she was from the south."

Beechcroft shrugged before loudly mumbling, "She's always been a spoiled, lying bitch."

Sarah squawked.

"But she's blood and *her mother* misses her," Beechcroft **lied** as he struggled to stand. He reached for the railing but then recalled its unreliability. Sarah's eyes followed him as he processed each step to the fourth level.

She yelled up, "Watch out for her n*."

On the next floor, Beechcroft slowly walked alongside the railing. At the bottom of the fifth stairwell, the Englishman stopped to catch his breath.

From above but beyond sight, a deep voiced male spoke. "What's yer business?"

"I wish to speak to Millie Jean,"

"Let me see yer face."

"I doubt that's a good idea."

"Do I know you?"

"I don't think so. You don't sound familiar."

"Then I ain't got no quarrel with you."

"Well," Beechcroft pondered. "That's good."

"Let me see yer face."

The bottom step creaked with Beechcroft's weight. The next

step creaked even louder. After the next few steps, he caught sight of a tall, bulky negro sitting in a wooden chair. One hand patted the butt of a shotgun while the other gripped its metal barrel. The Englishman's right hand moved for the inside of his jacket but he hesitated.

" What's your name, sir?" Beechcroft inquired.

" Tin. Folks call me differen', an' to my family I go by Peaches." He pointed a bony finger at Beechcroft, "You ain't folks, an' you ain't family, so what do I go by? "

"Tin."

Nodding his head, Tin leaned back in his chair. "Exactly." Pointing with the shotgun, Tin indicated the far side of the fifth floor. "There some chairs in that corner. Grab one." He gestured to the spot next to him with his gun, "Sit."

When Beechcroft finally triumphed over the final step, he wanted to kiss the floor but a brief study of the floorboards quickly cured that impulse. As he caught his breath, he stared at the shadowy corner where water damaged chairs had been thrown. Beechcroft challenged the final short distance head on. He quickly returned to Tin's side and plopped a rickety seat down. The chair screamed as it accustomed itself to the new weight.

"Bet ya a dollar that chair breaks," Tin commented.

"I'll pay a dollar for a better chair."

Standing up, Tin marched into the corner and returned with the healthiest looking seat in record time. Beechcroft quickly upgraded and handed over a sovereign.

"The fuck is this?"

"English currency."

"Oh," Tin commented as he pocketed the coin in the front pouch of his overalls. "Pounds worth more than a dollar. You a high roller?"

"Indeed."

"You need'n protection tonight?"

"That all depends on how feral Millie is."

Letting out a laugh, his face grew serious. "Ya really interested in seeing her?"

"I am, why?"

"You ain't her usual type. Most poor sons a bitches pawing at Millie are trying to trade something they stole for a roll in the hay."

"Oh."

Tin nodded his head. "Few days back some dude bastard traded a bottle of laudanum for as long as he could go for. Haven't heard from Millie since. Even after he went. Ya might be here for a while."

"Ah," Beechcroft turned his head, sort of making eye contact with Tin. "It's been days? Should someone go and check on her?"

"Ain't no one but family 'lowed to see her right now."

"Are you family?"

"That's a stupid question."

"You're her family, correct?"

"Of course!"

"Then you can go in and I could follow you."

"Why should I let you go in there?"

"I'll give you another coin."

From a few levels lower Sarah's voice interrupted Beechcroft's response, "Fuck off, ya pissed bastard!"

Tightening his grip on the gun, Tin stood up.

"Damn it, Tin! " Sarah shouted, "y'up there?"

The sound of footfalls rapidly ascending the stairs bounced off the shaky walls. Leaning forward in his seat, Tin tilted his head and listened to the intruders approaching footsteps.

"Jack," Tin shouted, "I told ya not to come 'round here!" The footsteps stopped.

"Tin!" a quavering male voice called back, "what are ya doin' here? I heard ya was fired fer bein' a dirty **black bastard**!"

Tin ensured both barrels were loaded. The click the gun made as its barrels snapped closed echoed throughout the building. The footfalls resumed but this time they were descended twice as fast and moving in the exact opposite direction.

"I'm gonna paint the walls with yer blood!" Tin screamed as he made it to the next floor in a single bound.

The entire building shook as Tin landed. His desperate steps punished the carpentry and his heavy jumps shook the very architecture.

Standing up, Beechcroft walked over to Millie Jean's door. Any noise he made opening it up was lost in the chaotic cacophony coming from below. The smell struck him. Covering his face with his collar, Beechcroft peered into the room. There was barely any light. Every window was covered, entirely or mostly, by a blanket and or some sheet of tattered textile. Despite the brisk air, it was thick with musk. There was no doubt in Beechcroft's mind that the shadowy corners were infested with mold. Tilting his head, Beechcroft tried to listen for breathing.

From down below a shotgun went off. Someone screamed.

The floor squished as he took the first step into the room. His next step kicked something solid, sending it clattering across the floor. After the object came to a stop he heard snoring coming from the smelliest side of the room. Taking out a box of matches, Beechcroft added a tiny, flickering light to the darkness. A shadowy lump lay upon a bed. By the time he reached the side of the frame, the match had burned down. Striking another match, Beechcroft lit a nearby candle. A form lay underneath a pile of thick blankets.

Reaching into a different pocket, Beechcroft pulled out a vial and uncapped it. Pulling back the closest part of the stained, thick blankets, he discovered a pair of legs wearing ripped up stockings. Recovering the legs, Beechcroft moved to the other end.

Folding back the damp blanket, he revealed a narrow, wrinkled, pretty face. Beechcroft placed the vial underneath the face's nose and counted to eight. The instant the girl's eyes snapped open Beechcroft blew out the match. She groaned.

As he retreated to the bedroom door, he corked the vial and returned it to its rightful spot. When he exited the room he ensured that the door was placed precisely back where it had been before. Moving back to the chair, he did the same thing to himself.

Tin's approaching footsteps were much quieter now. When he finally reached the fifth floor, Beechcroft tossed him a coin. The coin bounced off the his chest and clattered on the top step. Trusting the shotgun to a single hand, Tin bent down and retrieved the money.

"What this for?"

"You deal with Jack often?"

"Jack, Tom, Dick, Harry," Tin pocketed the coin. "There's always some pissed bastard try'n out the same bright idea."

"Indeed," Beechcroft said as he took out his flask and offered it to the acquaintance.

Walking over to the Englishman, Tin took the flask, sat down in his chair and drank deeply.

Looking down at the weapon, Beechcroft inquired, "You shoot Jack?"

"Winged him." Tin fed the hungry gun then closed up the weapon with a satisfying metallic click.

He placed the gun across his lap, aiming it away from the guest.

"How do you pass the time?" Beechcroft inquired.

"Time pass jus' fine on its own."

Letting out a sigh, Beechcroft slumped into his chair and for a split second was convinced his seat was going to break. He tried letting time pass.

"I warned ya."

Beechcroft glanced over at Tin.

Tin shrugged. "Wait'n on Millie is a full time job."

Beechcroft went back to staring at the ceiling.

For a split second, Beechcroft could not believe he had almost fallen asleep, but when a loud female voice snapped him awake he realized he must have been at least dozing.

"Tin!" a female voice cried, "Why ain't these candles lit?"

Both men twisted their heads back to look.

"C'mere, an' comfort me, Tin!" the voice continued. "It's dark."

Tin stood up, "Ya heard noth'n."

He entered the room and secured the door behind him. Beechcroft strained his hearing. Low indecipherable voices spoke. After a few minutes the door burst open and Tin emerged.

"She's ready."

Beechcroft stood up as Tin took his seat. Entering the room, Beechcroft noticed a few candles had been lit. The room had looked a lot nicer before, but at least he saw all the obstacles in his way. He made quick work of the distance between himself and Millie's bed.

Pressing his cane into the mushy floor, Beechcroft announced, "I have a proposition."

Millie Jean laughed, "I bet I can guess where it is."

"I am offering an opportunity for you to be my traveling

companion. I am traveling across the country. Exactly how far I am not completely certain of at this present moment. I will have to study and learn at each destination I reach. I do not even know how long this journey will last but I am willing to pay a dollar a day. Should my trip end before ten days have been accrued I will pay a minimum of ten dollars. Should my journey last longer than ten days, I will pay a dollar for each additional day. I am asking for assistance with luggage and geography. Along with the salary I will be covering the expenses incurred by traveling first-class."

Millie picked up a half full bottle, "Know what a Pullman Car is?"

"I've read about them and I have ridden on comparable brands in London."

"It's divine, I rode one when I went to Chicago." For a moment, she lost herself in the memory, before snapping out of it. "When I came *from* Chigaco, to *here*. Anyway, where are we headed?"

"The capital of the United States. From there I must decide whether to head towards Philadelphia or head down towards Florida. It is a decision that I cannot make without first traveling to the next destination hence why I cannot make assurances regarding how long the trip will take. Do you speak any Spanish?"

Millie shook her head.

"Hopefully it won't come to that."

Millie spoke softly, "Where are you staying?"

"The Windsor."

Millie whistled with a pitch that pierced Beechcroft's brain slightly. "Prove it."

Beechcroft reached for his wallet.

She quickly sat up. "Take me to your room!"

Beechcroft froze save for his mouth. "You'll do it?"

"Yes. If ya can prove yer staying at the Winsdor. I read they got water in every room, hot *and* cold!"

"Thankfully it is kept in pipes. Do you need to get dressed? Do you need some time to gather together some rags?"

"I..." Millie Jean picked up a nearby glass bottle. "Show me your wallet."

Beechcroft pulled out his finely crafted leather pouch. Opening it up, he showcased all of the colorful bills and well folded documents residing inside. He sealed up the leather pouch and hid it away back inside his jacket.

"Many things can be purchased," Beechcroft analyzed the room.

Millie lowered the bottle, "You got any new clothes with you right now?"

"No," Beechcroft

Placing the bottle down, Millie swung her ripped up stockings out of bed. Slipping her feet inside a pair of slippers, she added weight to her legs and wobbled her way up into a standing position. Wandering over to her dresser, she knocked a few things off the bureau as she placed the bottle on top of it. Opening the top shelf, she turned and wandered over to the closet. Taking a bag she returned to the open dresser.

"I can get you a new bag."

Without pausing her packing, Millie replied, "Do you have it here, with you, right now?"

"Errr...no," Beechcroft muttered as he watched her pack.

She made sure the Englishman saw her pick up her derringer and strap it to her upper thigh.

Reaching down, Beechcroft pulled up his right pant, and unholstered a small gun of his own.

Beechcroft held up his weapon so Millie could view the barrel. "Yours stamped with Philadelphia?"

"Chicago," Millie replied as she focused on fastening her luggage. "I know a cab."

"I'm ready when you are," Beechcroft insisted as he hid his Deringer underneath his pant leg. "Lead the way."

She headed through the door and Beechcroft secured the barrier behind them.

"Miss Millie!" Tin declared as he stood up from his seat. "Ya owe me!"

Dropping her bag, Millie pointed a finger at the Englishman and shouted, "I've paid you more than I owe ya."

"You know you lying," Tin shouted back. "Either ya pay me

what ya owe me or this gentleman can jus' go on 'bout his way without ya."

Beechcroft reached into his jacket. "How much she owe?"

"Two dollars and twelve cents," Millie answered.

"Put'n yer debts on a stranger!" Tin accused.

"Why not?" Millie snarled, "Yer gonna end up with his money either way!"

Holding up his left hand, Beechcroft offered three sovereigns. Tin reached out a hand and received them.

"Come along, Millie," Beechcroft ordered as he took her by the hand.

Leading the way, Beechcroft descended the stairs. He kept the lead for the first flight but eventually Millie broke free from his grip and took the lead. Her lead grew with each flight they descended.

"That was a lot easier than going up," Beechcroft stated as he balanced his heavy steps, "though there is a greater peril of falling."

Looking up, he spotted Sarah leaning on a railing, staring down upon them. Looking down, his eyes followed a fresh trail of blood down the remaining steps and out the front door.

When Millie reached the street, she shouted, "Badger? Yoohoo! Badger!"

A single horse gig pulled up next to the girl. Beechcroft's eyes were still following the trail of blood as Millie hopped into the cab.

A jolly gentleman tipped his hat. "Where ya headed?"

"Fifth Avenue, Windsor Hotel," Beechcroft replied as he entered in beside his riding companion.

Badger whistled, "Sure 'bout that?"

"Yes!"

Folding his top teeth over his bottom lip, Badger whistled and the cab pulled away from the curb. The combination of the shape of the seat and the motion of the cab drew the couple closer together. Beechcroft could barely move his arms without elbowing his new companion.

Beechcroft leaned over and whispered. "Let me hire the next taxi."

Shifting her position, Millie wrapped her arms around her new employer, freeing up space for his large appendages,

"Only if you want to."

"The hotel has a pharmacy."

Millie considered the Englishman's statement, then smiled, "Good."

All over Beechcroft's body muscles tensed and tightened. Through his thick clothes, Millie's featherweight body warmed his skin. They rocked about as the carriage rolled over the uneven cobblestone. Hot blood raced to the Englishman's head. Beads of sweat formed upon his forehead.

Covering her mouth with a free palm, Millie barely muffled a gasp with her hand as they pulled up in front of the hotel. Hopping out of the cab, Millie eyed the edifice from end to end. When Beechcroft finally managed to escape the carriage, he tipped Badger. Millie pulled out a tiny flask, unscrewed the top, and took a drink. A bellhop rushed forward and picked up her bag professionally.

Beechcroft leaned over and whispered to the back of her neck, "Jus' wait 'til ya see the inside."

"I'm staying here tonight? I'm staying *here* tonight?"

The bellhops held both doors open as the guest and his plus-one entered the establishment. Millie gasped. Her wide eyes scrutinized each shiny detail of the lobby. She stared down at the floor while Beechcroft walked up to the front desk.

"Yes," Beechcroft told the clerk, "we would like one dinner and one large soup sent up to two fourteen. Also a bottle of whiskey and a bottle of wine, top shelf. And would you happen to know of a place to get a decent dress for a lady?"

One of a group of dapper gentlemen said loud enough for the whole lobby to hear, "I do say, sir, a gentleman has their dirty laundry taken care of through the *rear* door."

The gaggle of men erupted into laughter.

"A box of cigars and some chips of ice block," Beechcroft continued, "Got all that? Repeat it back to me."

"One dinner, one large soup, whiskey, wine, cigars, ice chips sent up to two-fourteen," the clerk rapidly rattled off. "Will that be all?"

"Such lack of tact," the heckler shook his head. "Not an honorable bone in *his* obese body."

Tugging Millie by the sleeve, Beechcroft led her up the stairs and away from the lobby. They passed in front of the dining room and continued down the narrow hallway. Letting go of her clothing, Beechcroft unlocked the door and entered his room. The fire was already lit, making the room an outpost against the winter.

The moment Millie set foot in the room, she stripped off her clothing, "Where in the hell is this bath?"

Beechcroft pointed. Millie Jean's eyes darted to the bathroom a second before her legs took her there. The door to the bathroom slammed shut.

"How do I...?" she called out. "Oh, wait! Never mind."

Beechcroft removed his jacket and draped it over the back of a cushioned chair. A sigh escaped his lungs as he unbuttoned his vest. Moving around to the front of the chair, he plopped himself down. His heavy body sank into the luxurious furnishing. Leaning down, he removed his boots. A knock came from the door.

"Beverage service!" the voice from the other side called.

"Come in."

A skinny lad wearing a bright uniform pushed a small cart topped with glass bottles, glassware and a small, metal bucket of ice.

"Where would ya like me to place these, sir?"

Beechcroft gestured to the round table closest to the fireplace and the bellhop pushed the cart over. The young servant picked up a corkscrew before grabbing the neck of the wine bottle. The staff member gently stabbed the curly, pointy instrument into the soft cork before pushing and twisting. Beechcroft snatched up two ice cubes and plopped them into his glass before pouring in the liquor. Setting the bottle on the cart, the Englishman raised the full glass to his lips. The first sip refreshed and burned the tongue and throat.

"The food should be ready momentarily," the servant stated, "Do you want me to leave the bottle open or pour you a glass?"

Without halting his consumption and without spilling a drop, Beechcroft carefully nodded.

The bellhop watched the Englishman drain his whiskey down to the last drops for a brief, professional moment before his hand reached out and grabbed the open wine bottle. Taking the closest wine glass, the employee filled it. When finished, he placed the drink on the cart.

"I'll go check on your meals," he announced.

The door closed with a satisfying click. Putting down his empty glass, Beechcroft picked up the full glass and wine bottle and headed for the private bath.

Thick steam poured out of the bathroom as Beechcroft opened the door. He quickly entered and secured the barrier. Despite having to fight for each breath, there was something pleasant about inhaling the hot steamy air. Millie's face was almost hidden among the vapor and voluptuous, overflowing bubbles. When the towering Englishman came into view, Millie sat up.

She stared at the offered wine glass. Accepting the gift, Millie paused its rim just beneath her lips. She looked up at her new employer. "Ya really had me fooled."

Millie took a sip and the sip turned into a guzzle. She handed back the empty glass and Beechcroft proceeded to refill it.

"I could have sworn yer full of shit. Before ya brought me in here, I'd've been willing to bet my life that ya was lying."

With an extended hand, Beechcroft offered a full wine glass.

With nimble fingers, Millie accepted the offering. She held the glass rim to her nose with both hands and sniffed. She sipped.

"I've never tasted anything like this," Millie confessed before drinking the rest of it.

"Just wait until you taste the soup," Beechcroft remarked.

Looking up, Millie wondered aloud, "What are ya still doin' dressed for a blizzard? Come in."

"I promise I'll join after I've eaten."

"Is the food here?"

"Soon."

Beechcroft walked over to the toilet and dropped his pants. Millie plugged her nose with a free hand.

"Don't mind me," Beechcroft commented as he grabbed a few segments of the paper roll.

"Of course they got paper specifically for *that*," Millie declared with a giggle.

Beechcroft stared at her, "I'm very happy you're taking a bath."

Millie folded their fingers, save for the middles ones.

"Rude," Beechcroft chuckled as he tore off another segment of paper.

Millie looked away as the Englishman wiped his ass. Standing up, Beechcroft lowered the bowl lid before pulling on the lever. "Mine at home is nicer."

"Oh really? Where's that? In a castle?"

Beechcroft shook his head. "Stone is cold in the winter. I better go check and see if our food has arrived."

"They'll knock."

Beechcroft headed to the door, and closed it behind him. He moved around the bed left and past the lit fireplace to his right. Opening up the front door, he spotted a lad pushing a cart down the narrow hallway.

Beechcroft stepped back as he gestured towards the table. "Bring it in and leave it over there."

The moment the lad parked, Beechcroft flipped him a coin.

"That will be all."

The bellhop stood his ground, "I was told you inquired about a dress for a lady."

"I *said* ," Beechcroft snapped, "that will be all!"

The bellhop promptly exited. A naked Millie emerged from the bathroom and headed straight for the cart. Removing the circular silver cloche, she leaned her face over the bowl and inhaled the steam issuing from the bowl. Opening her lids, her eyes drank in the sight, before sinking her spoon into the soup. It was rich, creamy and densely filled with vital nutrients.

"You eat like a dog," Beechcroft said.

Millie paused eating. "Dog's don't use spoons,"

"If they did, they would eat like that."

"But they don't."

She continued to devour her soup. Beechcroft picked up a duck wing and bit into its crispy skin. He ripped off a good portion of its steaming, moist, succulent flesh. Millie leaned forward, puckered her lips, and sucked up every last trace of pureed split pea. The nearly liquefied legumes sat simmering in her belly. She picked up her glass of wine and waited to drink, relishing her full belly. She held her glass up to the light of the crackling fireplace and sloshed the liquid about.

Beechcroft ate every morsel of meat, even the cartilage connecting the joints. After reducing the fowl to nothing but bones, he chewed on a small, long piece of elbow. He spat a thin splinter of calcium onto his plate. Lowering what remained of the wing, he smelled his whiskey with ice. In unison, Beechcroft and Millie emptied their glasses before proceeding to refill them. With her cup in hand, Millie's eyes lingered on the Englishman. Beechcroft sipped his perfectly crisp liquor. The burn of his whiskey sparked a warm fire in his belly

"I tol' myself," Millie confessed, "there ain't no *damn* way in *hell* that this fine, elderly gentleman has got a room at the Winsdor hotel. Ain't no way that if this gentleman could afford to stay at such a hotel if he'd wish to be anywhere near the likes of Millie Jean." Throwing up her hands, Millie frantically scanned the room. "Well, I'm here!" Millie sipped some more wine and then her face brightened. "Oh! Cigars!" she stood up and opened a drawer in the cart. "Ya ever ridden a Pullman Car?"

"As I said before," Beechcroft answered, "we have equivalent brands of car in England."

"One time, seems like so many years ago, I took a Pullman Car out to Chicago." Millie smiled at the memory. "It was how I came out here. It was the best train ride I ever had! Ya can ask the n*s for anything at any time; day or night. At two in the morning I wanted scrabbled eggs an' hot sauce. It's fantastic! I got 'em by two-fifteen! Eggs *dripping* in hot sauce. Saved my damned life."

Beechcroft took another sip. "I'll be sure to thank the chef next time I see him."

"Mmmm," Millie added. "I would love to ride one again."

"We shall ride the best of whatever is going to Washington tomorrow."

"Washington," Millie repeated as she glanced at her wine. "DC?"

Beechcroft nodded.

"What's there?"

"Advancement in my understanding of where I need to go next."

"Oh," Millie leaned back. "What sort of conversations do you like?"

Beechcroft swished the ice cubes around in his glass. "I beg your pardon."

"What do you like to talk about? I don't want to say the wrong thing. If this is gonna be a long trip, I don't want to start off on the wrong foot by talking about something rude."

"Uhhm...I'm not a quick tempered man," Beechcroft confessed and took another sip, "I can forgive the occasional stumbling upon an unpleasant topic."

"What part of England ya from?"

"I believe I understand you. Perhaps we will get along better if we avoid discussing where I hail from. As far as you need be concerned, I was born in the countryside some hundred miles or so from London and have lived there my entire life. That is the most interesting aspect of my life outside of banking."

"I'm fascinated by banking."

Beechcroft's head fell back as laughter erupted from deep within. He quickly regained his composure and finished his glass of whiskey.

"I could talk about banking until your ears fell off," Beechcroft snickered, "but I'm afraid you would throw yourself off the balcony before I finished describing my morning routine."

Millie giggled.

Beechcroft finished his drink and reached for the whiskey bottle, "Mustn't waste good ice," he mumbled before raising his volume. "Whenever I travel, I travel like this."

"Ya got a missus?"

Beechcroft shook his head.

"Ya look'n for one?"

"Occasionally."

"Is this such an occasion?"

"Indeed." Beechcroft sipped his lukewarm whiskey. "I can order another wine bottle."

"Ya like yer girls pissed?"

Beechcroft shrugged as he sat down in the empty cushioned chair. Standing up Millie strategically relocated her ass onto the Englishman's lap. Through his trousers, the Englishman's thighs felt hard. Reaching back, Millie placed the remaining wine on the cart. Her green eyes locked onto his pale blue ones. Her hand took hold of his smooth chin.

"You must be a good card player," she said as her other hand rubbed his crotch.

Through the clothes it was difficult to distinguish anything other than hardened flesh, until something cylindrical started emerging Beechcroft watched Millie's small, long face grow closer, until her lips connecting with his. He pulled her closer as she unbuttoned his vest.

She pulled her head back from his and asked, "How many layers ya wear'n?" Pulling at his vest, her grip slipped and she fell back. Beechcroft caught her with both hands. Standing up, he placed her on her feet. Standing up, he placed her on the ground. Reaching down she unbuttoned his trousers. He watched. He felt the pants fall away from his convexed thighs and legs. She placed a hand on his leg, his skin was smooth yet rough and his muscles were hard as solid as rock. She placed another hand on the other leg. He felt like a warm statue.

Beechcroft dropped his undergarments and sidestepped one leg at a time out of them. Grabbing Millie's waist, he lifted her like a toy. Walking over to the bed, he held her over it. He aimed the tip of his penis for the slit between her legs. She tried to hide her wince as he wiggled his dick into her dry genitals. His grip maneuvered her body, trying every angle, getting the vagina a little further onto his stiff genitals with each try. Biting her lower lip, Millie shut her eyes and tried to get wetter. Beechcroft was nearly all the way in now. He started slow, raising and lowering her like a flag. After several grinding minutes, Millie let out a sigh of relief when it finally started feeling good. He dropped her, caught and lifted in a circular motion. Her arms flailed as her tensed muscles began to cramp. Beechcroft continued. A purple vein bulged on his forehead as he accelerated the rhythm, pulsating physical ecstasy throughout her anatomy. It built and built and then exploded and cascaded throughout her body. She rode the orgasm like a stone skipping on waves. Then a tsunami hit.

Sliding off his cock, the ride and the feelings came to a sudden end as she fell onto the mattress and bounced to a stop. She panted, her hands feeling her hardened nipples. Beechcroft walked back over to the cart and refilled his glass. As he drank, his manhood deflated like a giant balloon with a tiny hole poked into it.

"Think the bath is still hot?" he asked.

"I dunno..." she sat up. "Let's find out!"

Rolling off the bed, Millie headed for the bathroom. Removing his remaining clothes and shoes, a completely naked Beechcroft followed after Millie. At the threshold, Millie turned around and eyed the Englishman's physique. It looked like a mixture of muscle, infection, and irritation but there was no discoloration on the European's smooth convex body. He mostly resembled a circus strong man save for his belly, which resembled that of a rich man.

Retreating from the doorway, Millie moved up to the porcelain tub before advising, "You should get in first."

Lumbering over to the tub, Beechcroft felt the water with his fingers.

"I do hope the tub is sturdy."

Leaning most of his weight on the back rim, Beechcroft lifted his leg and slid his entire body over the porcelain edge. The water rose as he settled into the tub.

Closing his eyes, Beechcroft confessed, "I've broken my fair share of tubs."

Millie plopped herself down on his smooth, hairless skin. His hardened muscles had the tiniest amount of give. It gave Millie the impression of sinking into Englishman's body and his flesh shifting around her.

"Where did you get such strength?" Millie wondered aloud.

Beechcroft smirked, "I found it."

"I'll bet that whole bottle of whiskey don't do much to ya."

Beechcroft glanced down at the glass and finished it off before placing the empty cup on the nearby table, "Can't recall the last time I was beyond merely tipsy."

"Me neither, but I suspect not for the same reason." Millie's face

164

changed as she searched the room. "Shit, I forgot my wine." She offered Beechcroft her cutest look. "May I drink from your whiskey o' great one?"

Beechcroft gestured to the alcohol and Millie quickly snatched it off the table.

"Yer gonna have to order more."

"The night is young."

The train's engine chopped the air with a steamy, crunchy rhythm. Sitting on a bench on a wooden platform adjacent to the tracks, Beechcroft and Millie passed the time by observing the station's inner workings. Beechcroft checked a small silver pocket watch and pocketed it before wrapping an arm around Millie. Pulling her closer, he placed the top of her head just below his nostrils and inhaled deeply. Held at an odd angle, Millie could only stare blankly at the passing pedestrians.

"You smell quite pleasant," Beechcroft declared as he released her.

Her eyes drifted over the nearby commuters bustling about their days.

"That bath did wonders for you."

Sitting up straight, Millie shrugged as she continued her analysis of the rail yard. She watched the long train idling adjacent to the platform. Shifting her eyes to the front of the locomotive she spotted a white man in dark uniform exiting the cab. When his boots struck the wooden platform, a dark skinned man in a white uniform leaned out of the cab and handed down a hand sized bell.

Taking hold of the bell, the older white man walked alongside the train, swinging his arm and yelling, "All aboard! All aboard!"

Standing up from the bench the duo grabbed their luggage and headed for the train. Several dark skinned gentlemen stood alongside the cars, watching the crowd.

One strange voice specifically addressed them with directness. "Ma'am and gentleman! Are you in need of assistance?"

Beechcroft and Millie stopped and turned in the direction of the addressee. A skinny black man made quick, graceful work of the distance between them.

With his head leaned slightly forward, he stopped in front of the pair, straightened himself up and put on an even friendlier smile and tone. "Are ya traveling to Washington today?"

"Indeed."

"May I inspect your tickets?"

Shelling out his wallet, Beechcroft removed two thick pieces of paper and handed them over. While the porter leaned down to validate the authenticity, Millie squinted her eyes as she read his hat.

As the porter inspected their tickets, a sparkle twinkled in his eye. "Y'all are traveling in a Pullman Palace," he stated. "Excellent," he handing them back, the porter beamed. "I'd advise keeping these on yer persons until you arrive at your final destination, the conductor may require their presentation at any given moment. I go by Ralph." Gesturing to the suitcases, Ralph inquired, "May I lessen your burden?

"Thank you, Ralph," Beechcroft replied.

Releasing both of her suitcases, Millie said, "Lead the way, George." As Ralph picked up the luggage, she squealed "I'm so excited to see inside!"

"Please follow me," he turned and walked along the platform, heading for the caboose, "Have y'all been waiting for a long time?" he shouted above the noise of the engine.

Beechcroft pulled out his tiny, silver pocket watch. "'bout two hours."

"Oh my," Ralph answered, "If y'all had just come over when we pulled in, we would have let ya wait inside the train. If your compartment hasn't been cleaned yet you can always wait in one of the social cars."

"Good to know," Beechcroft acknowledged. "I'll remember that for next time."

"The saloon car is always open."

They had walked to nearly the other end of the train when Ralph turned right and moved in between the ends of two cars. Bounding up the steep, metal steps of a gangway, Ralph disappeared inside the car and quickly reappeared with his hands free of any luggage. Millie rushed right by the porter and entered the car. Planting his feet, Ralph leaned forward and offered the Englishman a hand. Taking hold of the offering, Beechcroft watched as Ralph leaned back with all of his weight and strength. Taking hold of the railing, Beechcroft hoisted himself up the first and steepest step. Surprised by the skinny, nimble porter's strength, Beechcroft soon found himself standing on the top step.

Standing on the ground next to the train, Ralph gestured to the door. "After you, sir," he said as he let out a deep breath. "Whenever you so desire."

Beechcroft took a few steps into the luxurious car and collapsed into the nearest velvety cushioned crimson chair. Removing his bowler hat, he took out a handkerchief and wiped his forehead.

"Are you all right, sir?" Ralph inquired.

"Whiskey."

Ralph grinned, "Very good, sir." He glanced about the room. "I'll be back promptly."

Grabbing both of Millie's suitcases, Ralph hurried down a narrow hallway. Another white jacketed employee, with hands full of luggage, entered the car. He led the charge of a family of four. Moving at a rapid pace, the porter nodded politely to Beechcroft as he passed by.

Glancing back at the young family, he commented, "Your children are very well behaved."

The parents thanked the porter for the compliment as they followed after him down the narrow corridor.

Putting away his handkerchief, Beechcroft stood up from his chair. He only managed a single step before Ralph reappeared.

"Are you ready to see your quarters?"

"Yes."

"Follow me, please."

Beechcroft followed at his own gait and the porter's speed rapidly adapted. They moved down a narrow corridor. With the space split between the walkway and private sleeping quarters, Beechcroft managed to reduce the traffic to a one-way flow.

"Here we are," Ralph announced as he halted in front of a thick curtain. Pulling the velvety textile aside, Beechcroft looked into his room. He immediately noticed that Millie had already settled into a mattress section of the polished wooden wall. Stepping inside his quarters, Beechcroft stood in the center of the rectangular space. As Beechcroft cautiously completed a 180 degree turn, Millie squished herself further into her comfy crevice

Looking Ralph in the eye, Beechcroft asked, "This the biggest one ya got?"

"They are all the same size, sir." He snapped his fingers and scolded himself briefly before addressing the Englishman. "You mentioned your desire for a shot of whiskey."

"Bottle."

The porter snapped his fingers again. "Right, I'll go see what I can conjure up."

"Please."

Stepping out of the room, Ralph drew the curtain.

"Thankfully there's no chandelier," Millie commented.

"I'd be set aflame," he said as he moved over to the other cushioned area directly across from Millie.

Millie placed a hand over her lips. Turning his butt around, Beechcroft sat down on the mattress like it were a bench.

"I'm gonna to have to learn to sleep sitting up."

"I brought the necessities!" Ralph called as he pulled the curtain back.

With a full busing tray in hand, the porter moved in between the two guests, coming to a stop near the window. Reaching out with a free hand, he twisted a knob that was built into the wall just below the bottom frame. A piece of half moon shaped wood folded down and settled into a tiny table. Placing the tray down, Ralph popped the bottle and immediately filled the two glasses. He presented one first to the lady and then to the gentleman.

After drinking the shot, Beechcroft offered back the empty glass as he insisted, "Pour yourself one."

Ralph studied the Englishman.

"I won't tell anyone," Beechcroft promised.

"Unfortunately, I only brought two glasses," Ralph said.

"Use mine."

Ralph studied the tiny cup still filled with the residual liquid, then grabbed the neck of the bottle and quickly poured himself a shot. Downing it in a single gulp, he refilled the glass and offered it back to the guest. Beechcroft traded a sovereign for the drink.

"English, same as the accent," the porter pocketed the coin, "I thank thee kindly. And if there is anything else I can get for you, just let me know. If you cannot readily find me, just ask one of us in uniform and they will be more than willing and happy to assist you."

"Thank you, Ralph," Beechcroft said as he moved closer to the window. "We are all set for now."

"A bottle of wine," Millie pipped up.

Ralph met Millie's eyes. "Any specific variety?"

"White."

"Any specific grape." He shifted his weight.

Millie stared at the porter.

"I'll see what we have." He looked at Beechcroft. "That is if it's alright with you, sir?"

Beechcroft gestured for the porter to get a move on. Ralph opened and closed the curtain with himself on the other side.

Standing up, Millie grabbed hold of the curtain.

"Going somewhere?" Beechcroft demanded.

"The saloon car."

"You just ordered a bottle of wine. And they probably won't let ladies into that car."

"The bottle of wine is for later. For when I don't want to wait around for it. And if I am stopped, so be it. I want to explore this mobile hotel. That's what all the newspapers call it, 'a moving hotel.' I wonder if they have a ballroom car."

"They have a parlor car."

"I'd prefer a parlor house car."

Beechcroft snorted. "Maybe I'll invest in one when I get back home."

Millie departed and drew the curtain.

Grabbing hold of his suitcase, Beechcroft placed the luggage on Millie's bed. Opening it he pulled out a thick piece of paper. He placed a map of the United States down on the floor. Taking out a compass from one of the suitcase's pockets, Beechcroft laid the orienteering instrument atop of the shaded shapes of color that distinctly indicated each state. Taking out the pocket watch, the Englishman placed the two circular pieces side by side. With frowning lips and fixated eyes, Beechcroft stepped back until he was able to sit back down on his own bed.

~

Sitting in a cushioned chair, Beechcroft watched himself fly by another portion of the United States. His eyes shifted to Millie and then to the approaching waiter. The staff placed a glass of whiskey in front of the Englishman. Beechcroft held out a sovereign which was quickly yet politely snatched from his fingers. The worker retreated behind the bar. Beechcroft glanced back at Millie and then at his drink.

"I am aggravated," he confessed.

Placing her empty glass on the table, Millie leaned back in her chair, "Oh?"

"Do you know any Spanish?"

"I know a lot of foreign tongues but not that one," Millie admitted, "I doubt I would be much use to you in Mexico." She looked up at him, "Is that where you've decided to go?"

Beechcroft picked up his glass. "Perhaps. I've been staring at that damn pocket watch for too long. Each turn seems to promise something that never comes. Hell, every time we go through a tunnel it bucks my concentration." Beechcroft sipped on his whiskey. "Had to get out of that room."

"Yeah, I have the same feeling." Millie held out her hand until Beechcroft handed her the bottle. "We're not headed too far west are we?"

"Southwest," he corrected.

"South is fine but not too far west, right?"

"I will go as far west as I have to. If you'd paid attention even the slightest to what I've already relayed, you would have a clue as to where we're headed. Louisiana will be the furthest west I go. I may end up in Mexico but that has yet to be determined." Leaning back in his chair, he pointed a finger at Millie. "Ya sound like ya got somethin' against the west. Y'hate cowboys?"

Millie shook her head, "Back home I got a neighbor whose first cousin an' his wife settled out in Montana." She clutched her throat with one hand and grabbed hold of a clump of her hair with the other. "Soldiers found them, their house torched and their heads scalped by savages."

Beechcroft snorted.

"It t'ain't funny! Red savages *take* fair girls," Millie pouted. "You would hate it. Barbaric. There ain't no sort of luxury out there. Money only works in a store. Out there, ain't nothing. Out there ain't noth'n but sick, ragged, an' desperate men an the ghost towns they leave behind."

"You've seen it?"

"A lifetime ago." Her zoned out eyes lingered on the nearly empty bottle. "Maybe not a lifetime but a whole childhood ago. I saw the west when I was barely older than a child." Looking up, she met her employer's eyes. "I tried my luck in Denver, but I never made it there." turning her head, she watched the landscape rush by. "When I was younger I would catch the train for sport."

"A moving train?" Beechcroft looked down at the passing ground.

"I usually waited for them to stop. And *that's* another reason why the west is such a blowhard. Ya get out there well enough, but if ya ever want to go anywhere else or come back there ain't nearly as many trains. It could take you weeks to go what should've only taken a day or two. 'specially if the damned savages are sabotaging the track. A person's liable to get stuck out there for years. Or die."

"Odd circumstance. A lot of trains must get stuck out there. Did you get stuck?"

"I didn't make it longer than twenty months." Her body rocked with the train's motion as her eyes continued to zone out on what-ever happened to be passing by. "I had fun, but it was hard. Work hard, play hard, just like the men. Dangerous work. Lotta them never came back. Maybe I did die back there?"

Beechcroft looked about the car. "I'm in your heaven?"

Millie cracked up, "I ain't goin' to heaven, honey."

Beechcroft lifted his glass, "Neither am I, I suppose"

13

Nathaniel jumped up and threw his arms up to the sky. "Knock the leaves off them trees, Ned!"

Ned snapped his head back and glared at Nathaniel. "There aint no leaves on them trees."

Nathaniel shouted, "Just knock it far so Jane's gotta *run* far to go *get* it!"

Bending his knees, Ned stuck his tongue out the corner of his mouth as his eyes focused on the thrower.

"Ya ready?" Pa's smiling face asked.

Ned nodded.

Pa threw the ball underhand. The stick connected with the ball with a crack. Ned took off running. Reaching out, Pa failed to catch the ball. Touching the first stick, Ned didn't miss a step as he dashed for the second. With her hands up, Jane stepped in front of the runner. Ned skidded. Almost losing his balance, he rolled over and scampered onto his hands and knees as he desperately reversed direction. Jane raised her throwing arm but it was too late to catch the whippersnapper. She took a moment to glare at him before tossing the ball to Pa.

Catching the ball, Pa announced, "I think I'm done for now. Anyone else want to pitch?"

Violet stepped in front of the stump and picked up the dropped swinging stick.

Qi spoke calmly, "Nathaniel."

"Yes?"

"I need to tell you something. It will cause some alarm," Qi continued. "You may wish to be somewhere private to hear what it is."

"Oh, you don't want to say it here?"

"If you stay here, you have to promise not to show any reaction."

"What do you mean?"

"You need to remain calm."

"I—" Nathaniel hesitated. "I am calm."

"Right now you are."

Nathaniel stiffened.

"Someone is tracking you."

Shivers traveled down Nathaniel's spine and his smile waned.

Turning his back to the ball game, Nathaniel looked down at the ground and wondered, "What do you mean someone is tracking me? Who is tracking me? Why?"

"A man from England. He possesses a device that knows your location. Yesterday he arrived in Chattanooga and today he will enter Alabama."

There was another crack of a stick connecting with a ball.

Placing one foot in front of the other, Nathaniel pondered this as he wandered towards the road, "He traveled all *that* way to find *me*?"

"Yes."

"Why? What does he look like?"

"I can show you his appearance tonight."

"When I dream?"

"Yes."

With his head still down, Nathaniel headed for the side of the schoolhouse, thinking, "Where's England?"

"North-east," Qi answered as her host reached the road, "across the Atlantic Ocean."

"Where am I going?" Nathaniel wondered as he power-walked like he was going home.

He passed a duet of skipping boys returning to the schoolhouse with baskets full of berries. Nathaniel made it to the rise in the path and soon passed over it.

Glancing back at the schoolhouse, he thought, "They're gonna be worried."

"We'll see them later, back at home."

"I'm gonna get in trouble."

"No, I have a plan."

"What plan?" Nathaniel started jogging and wondered, "Why am I going so fast?"

"Time is of the essence. And we need to make a stop before we get home."

Nathaniel jogged an entire mile before he lowered to a walk. He recognized the fields and the naked winter trees up ahead that hid very little of Gibb's Manor. He wanted to rest but his legs kept walking. He walked until he could clearly see a portion of the brick wall that lay just inside a once young, meticulously maintained forest.

"Climb that tree," Qi instructed, "Gibb is taking a nap inside the house and Goober is working in the stable."

As he headed for the one Qi indicated, Nathaniel wondered, "What am I doing here?"

"Getting something we need."

The instant Nathaniel grabbed the branch, the cyan dot moved to the up to the closest limb.

"What's that?" Nathaniel asked as he continued chasing the dot upward.

With a rapid ascent, it did not take long for the colorful circle to indicate the wide, flat top of the brick wall. Gripping a large, long branch with both hands, Nathaniel crawled along it like a caterpillar. Inching his way ever closer to Gibb's property, he eventually stopped and carefully planted both feet atop the wall's crux.

"The front door is unlocked," Qi said.

Turning himself around, Nathaniel gripped and lowered himself, scraping his belly on the ledge of the wall. Lowering his weight onto his outstretched arms he dangled by his fingertips before letting go. His ankles exploded with pins and needles as he landed on his feet. Hobbling on two pincushions Nathaniel winced as he tried to out-**walk** the pain. By the time he made it to the front door the discomfort had slowly receded into a dwindling pulse. Taking hold of the doorknob, he slid the door open just wide enough for himself to slip through. Entering the foyer, he gently secured the doors behind him.

To his surprise, the blue dot was indicating something dangling from a hat rack. Nathaniel stepped cautiously toward the indicator.

"Take the satchel," Qi instructed. "You will need it."

Nathaniel grabbed the strap of a leather satchel and unhooked it from the rack. Placing it over his shoulder, he noticed that the blue dot had moved to the top of the staircase. Moving to the second floor, Nathaniel took a left and found himself in a narrow hallway. He followed a blue dot all the way to a door at the end of the hallway.

Twisting its knob, Nathaniel opened the door and stepped through into a long, dark room. On the other side of the room sunlight penetrated through a set of heavy curtains, casting a muted light upon the office. A hearty scent of ash lingered in the air. To his right an unlit, stony fireplace radiated a stone-cold chill. Smooth rocks were built into the wall; dividing the sections of wall filled with framed portraits and paintings in two.

Nathaniel maneuvered around a cushioned chair and almost stumbled into a wooden cart. The glassware refracted the dim light as each brittle piece regained its balance. Stepping around the fragile items, Nathaniel came upon a grand piano.

"It's a desk," Qi corrected. "What we need is on the other side, in a drawer."

The desk was so long that Nathaniel doubted if grown men could reach across to shake hands. Nathaniel crept his way to the dot. As he drew nearer, he realized that Qi was indicating the region where Mr. Gibb would put his legs if he were sitting in his big fancy chair. Grabbing the chair with both hands, Nathaniel tilted the seat back and dragged it until his strength gave out. Stabilizing the furniture, the boy analyzed the gap and impulsively crawled into the vacant leg space. Squinting his eyes, he focused on the petite cyan dot, shining like a tiny bright blue bead. It highlighted a section of the inner desk that looked exactly like all the other portions of smoothly polished wood.

"Press it," Qi said.

Nathaniel lifted his preferred index finger and pressed the exact spot. The wood gave way as a muffled, metallic clicking sound came from inside the desk.

"You unlocked the bottom left drawer," Qi announced.

Crawling out of the depths, Nathaniel saw the bottom drawer protruding half an inch or so out from its regular position. Pulling on the knob, Nathaniel found himself staring down at a revolver and several boxes of ammunition.

"It is loaded," Qi said.

Reaching down, Nathaniel's tiny fingers wrapped around its polished grip. It was much heavier than any of the gun-shaped sticks he had shot Jane with countless times before. It was no imaginary weapon. Without even lifting it Nathaniel could feel the gun's solid mass. You didn't need to shout, "bang!" when you pulled this trigger. He caressed its metallic barrel. It would be so easy just to slip a finger through it and squeeze.

"Stop fixating on it," Qi announced as a cyan dot appeared on the satchel Nathaniel was wearing. "Put it in the satchel. Take a box of bullets as well."

Unbuckling the satchel, Nathaniel carefully placed the box of ammo in first, before resting the weapon on top of it. Buckling the belt, Nathaniel clutched it to his tummy and stood up.

"Put the drawer back."

Dropping to his knees, Nathaniel shoved the drawer back into place. Back in the depth's of the desk's inner workings, he heard the muffled metallic click.

"And the chair."

Rushing to the back of the chair, Nathaniel placed both hands on it and pushed. It slid across the wooden floor, back into its usual position. A cyan dot appeared on the door at the far end of the room and Nathaniel bolted for it. Exiting the office and taking a left, Nathaniel headed back to the foyer. After descending the stairs and departing via the front door, Nathaniel stalled when he reached the porch.

"We should exit through the back fields," Qi said.

Taking a sharp right, Nathaniel jogged alongside the manor. Looking up, he spotted the outside of the room he had just been in.

As he reached the edge of the house, Qi said, "Hold on."

Nathaniel stopped, "What's wrong?" he wondered.

"Goober is at the well. He'll be done soon."

Nathaniel went to peer around the corner of the building.

"Stay back!" Qi snapped. "He mustn't see you!"

Nathaniel froze.

"Get back."

Backtracking a few steps, Nathaniel waited, listening to every sound. He heard the trees floundering in the wind. After a solid minute, his legs got tired. Squatting down, Nathaniel continued to wait. He noticed a nearby stick, picked it up and utilized it to draw a figure in the dirt.

"Put that out!"

"What?" Nathaniel asked aloud.

"Silence."

Nathaniel felt a cold chill freeze his bones and skin.

"Do not speak," Qi instructed, "Rub that smiley face out of the dirt. What do you think Mr. Gibb and Goober are going to think if they find a face drawn in the dirt?"

"Uh," Nathaniel started to say but then merely thought.

"I don't know either, but it will be something that none of us need."

Nathaniel stared down at the crude drawing.

"Rub it out."

Nathaniel rubbed the picture with his palm, thinking, "What if they think it's a ghost?"

"They won't think of anything if they don't see anything. Goober's back inside the stable. Go now!"

Jumping to his feet, Nathaniel sprinted for the picket fence. He placed a hand on the barrier as he leaped over. Landing with momentum, he launched into a full sprint. As he continued to pick up speed, his hands clutched the heavy satchel. He came upon flat dirt fields and looking to his left, noticed he had left the brick wall a good ways back. He dashed for the thin forest that continued on when the wall had not, passed through it and ran for the road. He did not slow down until his feet were pounding down on the path.

"We need to make a detour."

"Another detour?" he whined.

"Jane's fort. We will store the gun there."

"Are we gonna fortify it?"

"No."

"Why don't we get Pa and Ma an' Jane to help us fortify the barn and then we can fend off this England ma—"

"We cannot allow this man to know we have family. You will get them all killed."

"But Pa will help us if we tell him! He has a shotgun!"

"Nathaniel, your judgment is naive. This man will murder your entire family if he has to."

"Does he kill a lot of people?"

"He is capable and I cannot risk your life. We will flee to a more advantageous position in the Talladega mountains."

"Where's that?"

"About sixty miles north from here."

"Sixty miles!" Nathaniel proclaimed, "That's far! I can't do that."

"It will take you multiple days."

"Multiple days of *walking*?"

"Yes."

"But Pa's gonna punish the hell outta me if I'm gone for that long."

"Don't worry about Pa."

"Easy for you to say."

"Nathaniel," Qi's voice shook the boy, "there is no guarantee that we are going to live through this encounter. The man hunting you is intelligent and brimming with resources. Should he get a hold of you—nay! Should he realize that you are a *who* and not a *what*, he may decide that a cadaver is much easier to study than a living child."

Nathaniel stopped and pondered the ground in front of him.

"Please continue walking," Qi pleaded.

"We're gonna run?"

"His device makes evading him impossible. His resources make it impossible to go somewhere he cannot follow. Even if you were to crawl into a tiny hole and somehow still have access to unlimited food and water, even then, he will always be able to dig you out."

"How would he know?"

"He has a device that points to you. We would have to destroy the device to give ourselves any chance of eluding him. But that would involve getting incredibly close to him. Should he discover you have legs, he will hire bounty hunters to chase you. We will not be able to avoid multiple adults for very long."

With each step, Nathaniel felt the weight of the gun bouncing off his waist. "I'm gonna shoot him?"

"Maybe," Qi replied as up ahead on the side of the road a cyan dot appeared, "Hopefully not. Go through that gap in the rock wall."

Marching through the hole in the stone wall, Nathaniel found himself following a barely discernible path. Walking all the way out into the field of rolling hills, he spotted the barn. As the boy drew closer to the structure, all of the building's crumbling attributes intensified. There was a hole in its roof that made the gap appear almost organic in its frozen attempt to consume the rest of the ceiling.

"That's Jane's fort?"

"She claims."

"There's monsters *and* ghosts liv'n there."

"I've only ever observed a family of owls. Though they can be rather aggressive."

Nathaniel made quick work of the remaining distance between himself and the barn. He entered the building via a hole in its side. No single scent was strong but they huddled together and clung to the back of Nathaniel's throat. It smelled like Gibb's stable only more unruly and way more forgotten. The gap in the roof allowed enough illumination for Nathaniel to easily navigate. He moved for the indicated stable and found it almost empty of the bales of rotting hay that covered most of the dirt floor.

"Its the driest portion of the barn," Qi said as Nathaniel laid the satchel on the most elevated portion of hay. "Pray lightning doesn't strike overnight."

"It's gonna rain?"

"Very unlikely," Qi said, "but not impossible."

The barn was cast into near darkness as a bird flew into the concentrated beams of light. Its movement cast a shadow upon the earth floor. The winged creature flew up into the dark rafters and disappeared.

"Odd time for an owl to be about," Qi commented. "Let's depart. Keep your head down. It may be angry with us."

Nathaniel headed for the hole in the side, "Are we going home now?"

"Yes. You are correct that we should avoid punishment. When the time comes you will need to feign illness."

Nathaniel clutched his stomach. "How long do I need to pretend?"

"It will be up to Ma when to take you to bed. But with vicious enough symptoms I'll bet she puts you to bed mighty quick. When you get to bed I will need you to sleep. That part should be easy."

Nathaniel replied aloud, "Uh…okay. If I'm sick, they won't punish me?"

"Ma will relate the news to Pa and Jane. They will scold you for the abandonment but you are young and sick, they will understand."

Nathaniel strolled across field, heading for the gap in the stone wall. Now it felt odd not having a heavy satchel knocking into his side with each step.

"I'm gonna shoot him," Nathaniel determined.

"That's a back-up plan. It will be difficult for you to be accurate with such a big weapon. It was not designed for a child, let alone a small child."

"Then why'd I'd take it?"

"Because you *may* need to use it. *Hopefully* you do not."

Making it onto the road, Nathaniel took a right as he thought, "What's your plan again?"

"Tonight, when you sleep, I will tell you."

He walked the final tenth of a mile and then took a right,

entering the narrow path that led back home. Hot flashes flushed his head while pain swirled inside his stomach. Clutching his lower torso, Nathaniel hobbled the rest of the way. With each step the nausea steadily increased into a dense, humid fog that clung to the insides of his belly.

Hobbling onto the porch, Nathaniel stumbled on the final step. Instinct threw his hands at the nearest beam, before his face hit the floor. Catching himself, the boy stared at the boards as he started to drool. He lurched a large portion of his lunch onto the wooden planks.

Collapsing onto a dry portion of the porch, he did feel ever so slightly better. When he slightly uncurled his body, he saw a wide-eyed Ma looking down at him. She took a cautious step forward and reached out with both hands.

Sitting him up, she rubbed his back as she softly inquired, "Wha's the matter? Why ya home so early? Where's the rest o' yous?"

With both hands clutching his stomach, Nathaniel slowly rolled himself over and nodded. With motherly reflexes, Ma spun her child's head, and aimed it away from the house. The rest of his previous meal sprayed, poured, and then dribbled from his gaping maw. A gentle gust of wind dried and cracked his lips.

"Look at my porch." Ma shook her head. "Got anymore?"

With hands holding what his neck could not support, Nathaniel stared aimlessly at the ground. A thin strand of drool dangled from his bottom lip. Finally he risked shutting his mouth and swallowing.

"I'm gonna boil some ginger. Sit here and look at the ground if ya start feel'n anythin' else start comin' up."

Nathaniel hugged himself.

"Are ya cold?"

Nathaniel nodded.

Leaning over, Ma felt his forehead, "Yer burn'n up." Straightening herself up she continued, "The moment ya don't have nothing else coming up we goin' get ya under some warm blankets,"

Nathaniel shriveled up even tighter, shivering. Scooping up her son, Ma carried her baby to his bedroom, laid him gently down and quickly covered her son in blankets. Shuffling over to Jane's side of the room, she retrieved her daughter's pillow. She fluffed up the pillow as she rushed back over to her son's side and placed it beneath his head. Nathaniel rolled over and buried his face in the pillow. The nausea did ease. He felt his own body heat begin to warm the soft bedding. The pain in his head drained while the knots in his stomach were gently sliced in two. His internal temperature burned through the coolness of the bedding. He stared at the darkness in his pillow and felt his face growing hot against the soft fluff. Lifting up his head, he inhaled a deep breath, then repositioned himself into a more comfortable position before closing his eyes. He heard Ma shuffle over to the threshold of the children's room.

The darkness behind his eyelids faded into a sheer white room. He floated in weightlessness until he realized he was standing. Walking forward, he suddenly realized that a giant spider was standing behind him. Turning around, he didn't see any sign of the arachnid. He only saw the details of the featureless white room. But, off in the distance, where the bleak horizon displayed itself, a tiny black dot stained the sheer sky. As Nathaniel moved closer, the dot grew in size. As it continued to grow in size he eventually realized it was an opening. Reaching the threshold, he peered inside and saw sheer darkness. From the back of the pitch blackness, a small bright light shined. He stared until he realized the aperture was shaped like a tunnel. Stepping forward he aimed himself towards the only light source. When he drew near enough, he realized it was the entrance to another cave. Entering the opening, Nathaniel found himself back in the usual, infinite white space. Looking straight forward, Nathaniel spotted a speck of black, way off in the horizon.

"Qi?" Nathaniel shouted, "What are you doing?"

He headed for the small black speck. With each step, it grew. It took forever for it to get any bigger. He ran. He ran faster than he ever thought his legs could go. Stopping a few yards in front of the cave's entrance, he held his breath as he listened to the silent air. Nathaniel tried to get a glimpse into the cave. Stepping closer, he confirmed that it looked just like the previous one.

"Qi," he shouted, "are you in there?"

Looking back, Nathaniel saw that the previous black speck was gone, dissolved into the single color of the environment's canvass. He faced the cave.

"Qi?"

Taking another step, Nathaniel plunged through the floor. Reckless gravity took hold of him as he plummeted through ceaseless space. Suddenly, his fall stopped as he struck strong webbing. Struggling against the sticky restraints, panic flooding his veins, he thrashed with all his strength. Leveraging the air around him, he flopped about like a fish, entangling himself even further. Suddenly, strong, thin appendages took hold of the boy. His weight drastically shifted as Qi held the boy in front of her eight eyes. Nathaniel screamed. The webbing melted off as Qi released him. Solid floor steadied the child's footing and he stopped screaming. Walking sideways like a crab, a manifestation appeared in the space the spider relinquished.

"This is Beechcroft," she announced.

Pale blue eyes shined brightly in the pale, clean shaven face of a monstrously large and tall individual. His tan jacket obscured the details of his body by covering both his torso and legs. Nearly every inch of the fabric bulged as it contained the swollen flesh underneath it. Dark brown corduroys covered his lower appendages while a pair of ivory gloves adorned his hands. Where his jacket was unbuttoned, it revealed a crimson colored vest embroidered with flowers with purple petals surrounding a bright gold pistil. A simple brown bowler covered his head while his knee high, black leather boots looked almost as tall as Nathaniel.

Stopping in front of the boy, the spider stated in a rather pleasant and hopeful tone, "I have a plan."

"What?"

"We need to travel north. We need to reach the Talladega mountains. There we can lay a trap and wait for him."

The boy's eyes snapped open. Despite the dark, the boy could see every detail of his room. Looking over, he watched the blankets covering Jane rise and fall with her breath. Placing his feet on the floor Nathaniel shifted himself off the bed and onto the floor. Kneeling down in front of his chest, he quietly unlatched the wooden container and lifted up the lid. He pulled out his sturdiest pair of overalls and placed them on the bed. Grabbing hold of his thickest long johns, Nathaniel donned the body suit, only slightly too big for him. Then, taking out his Sunday socks, Nathaniel quickly covered his feet. Picking up his Sunday shoes, Nathaniel carefully and quietly closed the lid.

Tip-toeing into the dining room, Nathaniel moved to the door and with perfect muscle memory, and slipped through it without a sound. Placing his shoes down on the top step, Nathaniel headed back inside. Turning right, he walked over to the hooks in the wall. He stared at his cotton sack for a moment.

"Jane brought it home," Qi said.

Nathaniel placed his straw hat on his head before lifting up the cotton sack. Taking it, he secured it around his body like a sash before moving to a dining chair marked with a cyan dot. Several blue dots appeared, indicating items on the shelf. Grabbing Pa's chair, Nathaniel dragged the piece of furniture as gently as possible over to the shelf.

Jumping up onto the seat like a cat, he stood up to his full height. Reaching up, he took a box of matches, an empty kidney shaped leather pouch, and a tin of jerky. Slipping each item inside the sack Nathaniel hopped down from the chair.

"Don't worry about putting the chair back," Qi commented.

He crept back to the door, pulled it ajar and slipped through. Standing at the top step, Nathaniel put down his cotton sack. Returning to the shack, he headed for his parent's room. Moving directly to the chest set at the foot of their bed, he lifted up its lid. Instinct slid his right hand down the wooden side, where the back of his hand slipped past the soft, dense stacks of folded up laundry. His fingers brushed against glass, but continued onward until they clasped around the polished hilt of a knife. Stiffening his grip, he pulled up. He retrieved the knife along with its sheath. His eyes lingered on the disrupted stacks of clothing.

"Pa's gonna be mad," he thought.

"Don't worry about reorganizing the clothing," Qi insisted. "Grab a thick wool blanket and let's move on. We still need to get tools from the shed. Carefully place the lid back."

Nathaniel carefully obeyed. With a sharp blade in one hand and a folded up blanket in the other, Nathaniel tip toed out of his parent's bedroom. Entering the dinning room, he headed for the door. Sliding through, he set his stuff down on the porch. Then took a seat on the last step and put on his Sunday shoes. They were still a little big. Ma said he would grow into them.

"Ma will kill me if anything happens to these shoes."

"No, she won't."

Looking up, he spotted a heap of shadow on the other side of the log fence. The heap stirred.

"Wake the mule last," Qi said.

A group of cyan dots lit up the inside of the three sided shed. Crawling through the fence, Nathaniel entered the stable and grabbed a coil of rope. Wrapping it over his shoulder and waist, he picked up a nearby shovel and made his way back to the fence. He climbed through and carefully loaded the items into the bed of the cart. Returning to the three sided shed, Nathaniel retrieved several feet of wire and a pickax. After a few more trips, the blue dots all but disappeared.

"You need to fill the metal buckets with water," Qi said.

Retrieving the buckets from the shed, Nathaniel marched up the hill that rose up on the right side of the shack. Stopping in front of the well, he yanked on the rope until the pulley pulled a wooden bucket from the depths. Filling up a metal bucket, Nathaniel tossed the empty wooden container back into the well. After pulling up another round, both vessels were nearly filled with water. A third turn topped them off. Latching the wiring on the metal lids shut, Nathaniel was reduced to carrying one full bucket at a time.

Returning for the second bucket, Nathaniel heard the back door of the shack burst open. Freezing in place, the boy intently listened to the heavy, slow footfalls as someone descended both of the rear steps. The back door slammed shut as the footfalls grew muffled. Nathaniel heard the familiar slam of the outhouse being utilized.

"Go," Qi insisted.

Hurrying to the well, Nathaniel retrieved the final bucket. He secured its lid, then grabbed it and hurried back to the cart. Placing it in the bed, he wiped his brow before refocusing his attention on the snoring lump of fur. The outhouse door slammed so hard, Nathaniel's heart jumped. He waited.

"Yer fine," Qi insisted. "Hitch the mule to the cart."

Turning his head, Nathaniel whispered, "Sarah?"

The mule stirred. Unlatching the fence, Nathaniel left the gate open as he moved to the stable. Sarah lifted her head up when she heard something pulling her bridle and harness off the shelf. The equipment jangled as Nathaniel moved it closer to the mule. Placing it on the drowsy animal Nathaniel quickly secured the bit into the animal's mouth. He gently yanked on the animal's reins and then winced as she brayed. He listened intently to the ensuing silence.

"No one cares," Qi said. "Let's move on."

Taking her reins, he led her out of the pen and guided her in between the two handles.

Nathaniel whispered, "Good girl."

He secured her to the cart just like Pa had done a thousand times before.

"Should I close the fence?"

"Why not?"

Closing the fence, Nathaniel looked back at the shack.

"What are you waiting for?"

"Do we have everything?"

"Yes."

"Do I get to say goodbye?"

"That would spoil the plan."

Moving to the front of the cart, Nathaniel grabbed Sarah's reins and pulled her towards the path. Her muscles tensed as she grew accustomed to her new load. The wheels turned and the pair moved forward.

"Good girl, Sarah," Nathaniel quietly validated. "We're going on an adventure. Someplace far away. We need to stick together! We gonna be the only family we got for a while now."

When Nathaniel reached the T-intersection, he followed a cyan dot to the left. As he walked, he turned his head and stared back at the shack. The bright moon shined down on the quaint little structure. Behind it, he could barely make out the distant silhouette of the oak tree. The property shrank from sight as the distance between them grew.

"Do we need to pick up the gun?" Nathaniel wondered.

"Yes."

"Should I take the mule?"

"Hitch her to a tree. Be quick and she'll be fine."

Nathaniel led the mule through the gap in the stone wall. Leading her down the shadowy yet familiar path, he stopped her in front of a group of trees and hitched her up. Alone, he trekked the rest of the way to the hilly field. He spotted the barn's broken roof and headed for its gaping hole.

"The owl is out hunting," Qi said.

Nathaniel headed for the stable and retrieved the satchel, then exited the barn and made his way back to the road. He felt a sense of relief when he spotted Sarah and quickly unhitched her from the trees. Leading her and the cart back to the road, Nathaniel felt the familiar rhythm of the weight knocking against his thigh with each step. Pressing on the satchel, he could feel the cold, solid shape of the firearm beneath the leather surface.

He passed Gibb Manor but then he took a different route and didn't go near the school. The bright moon kept the terrain in shadow save for the vague shadowy blobs of the fields, forest and road. It all felt so surreal, traveling through these familiar paths during the witching hours.

"Something happened to you," Qi said.

Nathaniel's body didn't miss a step as he tensed right up. With a sigh, he thought, "What are you talking about, Qi?"

"You know what makes Jane so special?"

Nathaniel shook his head, "You never told me."

"Jane will never get sick or poisoned."

"Really? Wow!" Looking up at the stars, Nathaniel wondered. "I can't never remember Jane get'n sick ever," he thought, "She was sick that day I worked for Gibb."

"She faked."

"What?" Nathaniel shouted.

"She acted ill. Just like you did with Ma.

Your body managed to adapt and assimilate her genetic sample.

Now you too never need fear sickness, poison, or venom. Its why your scar healed up so well."

Nathaniel touched his scar and remembered how hot and painful it had been, "Wow. That's crazy. What does that mean? Is this the reason why this hunter is able to track us?"

"No doubt he can sense how special you are."

"But what can he do about it?"

"I don't know."

"Could I talk to him for you? Tell him that it won't work?"

"I doubt he will agree to a polite conversation. I'm willing to bet that he will crack your skull open and sift through the pieces. And I can't take that risk."

Nathaniel imagined the pale blue-eyed man gripping him by the throat the way Pa had only with twice as much force and slamming his head into a big brick wall. He increased his speed and did not slow down until dawn broke.

14

The luxurious cabin barely jostled, but it was far from still. Beechcroft sat upon his bed as one might sit upon a tiny park bench. Wedging himself between the headrest and the footrest he was positioned rather snuggly. When he was exhausted enough he could fall asleep in this position. His watch would rotate in a cycle starting with his eyes focusing on the map before switching attention to the compass and then finally finishing with an obsessive stare at the pocket watch. When he tired of this, he rubbed his eyes for a while and then began all over again. Removing his hands from his face, he leaned forward and looked down at the map. The instruments jittered—barely perceivably, but Beechcroft noticed. He clenched his fist and pounded the table, sending all its contents skyward. A split second later the items landed in slightly differing positions. He reached into his pocket and pulled out a half smoked cigar. Placing the rolled up tobacco leaf in the corner of his mouth he struck a match and rekindled the smoke. Exhaling a dark gray plume, he watched it waft out through the cracked window.

The door to the room burst open and Beechcroft stood up just in time to catch Millie as she almost fell into the map. Reeling in her momentum, Beechcroft held her until she regained her unsteady footing.

One of his hands continued steadying her as she smiled and said, "Is this the right room?"

"Yes."

"Is my bed still aroun'?"

"Behind you."

Beechcroft walked her over to her side of the compartment and she flopped down onto the soft covers. Hugging her pillow, she rolled over.

"Ill?" Beechcroft asked as he sat back down on his bed.

She shook her head. Rolling back over she looked up at the Englishman. "H'yer compasses?"

"Can't tell," Beechcroft pointed to the corner. "There's half a bottle of red wine left over from last night."

"I'm doing jus' fine." Millie laid her head back. "Jus' fine. Ya' kno' you can order pharm-ma-ceuti-cals from any George?" From inside her bosom, Millie showed off a small rectangular box. "I'm saving them for later. I wanna go to a dance hall. Too bad there no dance car. Oh! But wouldn't that be splendid."

Jumping up, Beechcroft shouted, "It moved!"

"The dance car?"

"The damned *thing* moved! It's pointing south!" he stood up, "It is most definitely pointing south."

Millie sat up, "Yer balled up."

"It damned moved!" he glared at her. "That ain't southwest! That's true south. We ran out of west! We're getting closer." He threw his bulky, meaty arms around Millie and squeezed her, speaking softly. "It will be pointing east soon. We ran out of west! It's pointing true south! It will be pointing true southeast in just a moment…unless it is huge." His eyes widened. "What if it was the size of a continent?" What if it's something underground that spans the entire continent of South America?"

Letting go of Millie, he wedged himself back into his bed. Sitting on the edge of his seat, one knee bounced up and down, keeping rhythm with the locomotive's chugging, while his wide eyes remained frozen on the pocket watch.

"We are close," Beechcroft stated, "maybe within a few hundred miles."

"How do you know that?"

Leaning over, Beechcroft touched the position of New York on the map. "Because the angle," he slid his hand all the way down to Alabama, "here we can see this pointing south…southeast? We must be getting close." Grabbing the ruler, he turned it longways until it was also touching Mississippi and Georgia, then he placed a finger on Atlanta. "It can't be this far, because the pocket watch would have pointed south when we were here."

"What is the pocket watch pointing to?"

Beechcroft shot his comrade a wary glance. "My destination."

"Which is?"

"Aren't you feeling sleepy?"

"Yes."

"We are nearing the end. Should take us no longer than a month to track it down to its exact spot."

"It?"

Beechcroft nodded. "It."

15

Nathaniel missed feeling the gun knocking into his leg with each stride. After Qi instructed him to secure the satchel in which the gun was stored diagonally across his back like a quiver, the thudding stopped. But now he would have to reach way back behind himself and awkwardly retrieve the bag before he could get the gun out. More than likely, in a real situation, he would have to take the whole thing off before being able to get at it.

"Hence why we are avoiding "real" situations," Qi interrupted. "You'll be killed."

"Not if I shoot first!"

"Then other people will hunt for a murderer and execute you."

"They'll have to find me."

"We do plan on camping in the same spot for the next few days."

"They'll never find us there."

"There are many talented trackers in the area."

"But you said that I need to hide because *they* will take my stuff."

"They *could*. I said if someone sees a vulnerable child traveling alone they *may* take advantage. The opportunity is there. Therefore, remove the opportunity and avoid the risk."

"If we don't plan on ever using them," Nathaniel glanced back at the cart, "Do I have to carry them?"

"Put the satchel in the cart," Qi said. "Place it down carefully."

Nathaniel paused and unburdened himself. When he restarted, he ignored each chaffing step. Blisters and rashes rubbed where his skin was in constant friction. Closing his eyes, he continued walking on the straight path, waiting for his irritation to fade from consciousness.

With each step, he forgot about it altogether.

"How long until I rest?"

"There's an abandoned well half a mile from here, off the path a little ways," Qi said. "We should eat dinner there."

It took some time but so had every other prior step. He turned left and marched down a tiny, forgotten footpath. The path stuck out from the grounded foliage, forming into a jagged linear shape. He followed the strip of naked earth until he started passing decrepit, one-room log cabins. Some of the rooves were crumbing and falling in on themselves. Every quaint building looked elderly and abandoned.

"You should be able to see it now."

Chasing the blue dot, he found it residing on a round, stone structure that at one time had had a roof. Thankfully its pulley system appeared to still be intact. Reaching the side, Nathaniel placed one hand on the rim of the rocky structure and the other on a moist, smelly rope.

"Carefully when retrieving the bucket," Qi warned. "It may break as you pull it up. Don't fill the buckets with this water and don't let Sarah drink from it either."

"Why?"

"If you manage to retrieve some, I will bother to explain."

Grabbing hold of the slimy rope with both hands, the boy carefully pulled. Hand over hand, he felt the pulley system shift beyond its proper engineering. The bucket scrapped and dragged against the stone side as it was pulled. Stepping back, Nathaniel raised the container high enough for him to look at it. With at least one hand remaining on the rope, Nathaniel moved to the well and grabbed hold of the old bucket's rusty, wire handle. Setting it on the side of the well, a fetid odor fell into Nathaniel's nose, sending him into a retreat.

"No good," Nathaniel spat.

"Indeed, which is why it will be useful only to you."

Looking up, Nathaniel stared at the mule and then at the two metal buckets. His tongue was indeed dry.

"Save that water for the mule."

Frowning, he crossed his arms as he turned back to face the rotten old bucket.

Stepping closer, he pinched his nose while one hand scooped a tiny sprinkle of water onto his tongue. It tasted like rotten lemons mixed with Pa's morning breath after a night of intoxication.

"Would you like to numb your taste buds?"

"Yesh."

Releasing his nose, Nathaniel cupped his hands together and took another drink. The liquid was tasteless, and it went down smooth, thirst-quenching and wonderfully boring. His tongue still felt tiny specks of grit and grains of papery substances floating through the liquid. An odd vapor filled his sinuses. He washed it away with another handful of rancid water. He drank until his belly was full. With a pointed index finger, Nathaniel pushed the quarter-full bucket back into the well. When he heard it splash, he headed back to the cart.

"Alright, turn my tongue back on." His mouth tasted of rotten sawdust, mixed with chicken shit and lingering farts. "Ugh, ach!" Nathaniel crumbled to his knees. "Turn it off!" He continued spitting until his mouth fully regained tastelessness.

"Let's wait," Qi instructed. "Take some time to water the mule."

"Really? You don't want me to hurry?"

"There are some people on the road right now. But don't worry, we should reach our camping spot before the sun sets."

Nathaniel looked up at the ante-meridian sun and frowned. Taking the half-full bucket from the back, he brought it to the animal and carefully supervised her as she drank her fill. She had nearly emptied the bucket when Nathaniel removed it and finished off its final contents. It helped to peel one small layer of bad breath off his tongue. Placing the empty bucket on the cart, he removed a piece of cornbread and chowed down. Qi pointed out some hearty berries and Nathaniel dined until his mouth was filled with the ground up, scratchy tannins of dry and bitter fruit.

"Let's get started again."

Returning to the cart, Nathaniel resumed his trek, soon reaching the path and immediately bearing a left. Marching onward, he returned to his regular routine of covering ground. He saw a new version of the same old terrain repeated over and over, meadows, trees, fields, forests, some small bodies of water snaking through and running along it all.

16

"Fine specimen," Beechcroft said as he caressed the long neck of a beautiful black horse.

The skinny, mustached horse monger smiled and clapped. Rubbing his hands together like a hungry child lathering soap before dinner, a large grin appeared on his face, "I'll rent ya a horse 'n carriage for a dollar twenty, plus all the feed an' supplies ya need. Better not risk 'em get'n hunger an' feed'n off a stranger's prized flowers"—his eyes widened—"an' end up owing a pretty penny, happened to a cousin o' mine. Ended up bein' sued twenty dollars for his critters chew'n on some daffodils. Can you imagine? Daffodils."

"I wish to purchase your best two horses and carriage," Beechcroft replied, "plus a month's worth of feed,"

Removing his hat, the stable worker scratched his balding head. "Didn't ya say yer was just in town visit'n?"

"Indeed."

"Well, mister," the vendor shook his head, "'less ya plan'n on buying a place, I recommend ya rent. Else when ya get tired of them an figure on mov'n on yer gonna havta navigate this ridicu-lous livestock market that we seem to be in the midst of right now."

With the help of his cane, Beechcroft marched to a point

directly in front of the salesman and met him eye to eye. "What is your full name?"

"'Mr. Dodger, sir. Mr. Philip J. Dodger."

"Well, Mr. Dodger, what I wish to do with my money and in which markets I wish to navigate is solely my concern. I wish to purchase your two best horses and the biggest, most efficient cart you can supply."

"Don't forget harnesses," Millie pipped up. "Bridle, feed, shoes."

Mr. Dodger frowned at the lady. "*All* of our horses are fitted with shoes."

Beechcroft smiled. "What about stockings?"

Mr. Dodger's mustached twitched. "Horses don't wear stockings."

"Of course," Beechcroft trailed off. "As I was saying, I am willing to pay a fair price in full."

Mr. Dodger's frown transformed into seriousness. "Ya know what yer ask'n for is gonna cost upwards of 200, maybe 300 dollars?"

"Like I said, Mr. Dodger," Beechcroft retorted as he reached into his jacket, "I know what I wish to spend and not spend my hard earned cash on."

Within seconds, Mr. Philip J. Dodger was staring at three crisp hundred dollar bills. Taking hold of the currency, his index fingertip, middle fingertip and thumb could not stop rubbing together; feeling the friction of the crisp, sturdy paper.

"Careful that you don't rub out the ink," Beechcroft teased.

"Well,the truth is that I only sell the horses and feed but we have a partnership with Raven brothers. We're pretty much the same business. They're next door. We share newspaper advertisements sometimes," Mr. Dodger leaned in and offered back one of the 100 dollar bills, "If you intend on buying a cart with this one, you should be handing it over to them."

"Keep it," Beechcroft said. "I'll give them another."

Mr. Dodger's eyes widened. "What? Really, sir?"

"I'm not accustomed to having so many arguments about whether or not I genuinely intended to part with the money I'm extending to a gentleman." Beechcroft held up a finger. "All I ask in return is that you introduce me to the Raven brothers and then assist me with getting it all organized."

"Of course!" Mr. Dodger beamed as he retreated into his office.

Crouching down in front of a large metal safe, Mr. Dodger's narrow fingers spun the dial. The door popped open and Mr. Dodger stuffed his new money snuggly inside.

Closing it up he faced the Englishman. "Now if you and the lady would kindly follow me, I'll lead y'all directly to Raven brothers."

Moving to the door, Mr. Dodger opened it and gestured, "After you."

～

"That's the first mountain I've ever seen," Nathaniel realized. "Wow, they're big."

His eyes remained fixed on the details of the mountain range until his neck got tired. He noticed the shadows growing more defined. A blue dot indicated a portion of the forest. Exiting the path, Nathaniel guided the mule and cart through the space between the stones and trees. The cyan circles appeared almost as quickly as they disappeared as Qi gave a very detailed explanation of where to place each step. The sky had turned a dark blue by the time Nathaniel reached a colorful indicator that stayed in place. Looking up, he spotted a large, shallow cave.

"I need you to build a fire pit before the sun goes down," Qi commanded.

"Right now? I don't even get to rest?"

"Rest when you have fresh, warm flames."

With what little strength he had remaining, Nathaniel halted the mule by a fallen, hollowed-out log and hitched her to one of its smaller, still living cousins. Grabbing the shovel, Nathaniel walked around the dead tree. Squatting down at the edge of a large blue dot, the colorful circle grew and morphed into a shape that outlined the ground. Nathaniel dug his spade into the dirt.

After only a few shovel loads, Qi said, "That should be good. Retrieve some stones to put around the outside."

Outlining the freshly exposed earth with rocks, Nathaniel turned his focus to gathering various kindling, sticks, and small logs. After gathering a small pile, he constructed a tiny, flammable structure. With a single match, the boy kindled some flames and then helped them establish themselves. Taking a seat on the fallen log, Nathaniel watched the fire grow.

"This is not the cave you will be working on," Qi announced.

"No?"

"This is your home for the next few days. If it rains, the cave will provide shelter for both you and the animal. The cave you *will* be working on is not too far from here."

"When do I start?"

"After you eat and rest."

"Should I drink?"

"There is a nice river nearby that you should lead the mule to after you eat."

"Should I sleep?"

"After that, yes."

"Should I poop?" he giggled.

"Yes."

~

"Wake up."

Sitting up Nathaniel opened his eyes and looked up the stars twinkling above the tree-line. With a sigh he remembered where he was. Standing up he marched over to the cart. He picked up the pickax and shovel, then moved to Sarah's side and slid the ax into a convenient leather loop. He donned the weapons before retrieving a pouch of water and what remained of the jerky tin. Taking Sarah by the reins, he led the animal away from camp.

The land ascended, each step representing a steady and constant increase in difficuly. Leaves and needles crunched underfoot. Up ahead, Nathaniel spotted a cave but there was no cyan dot indicating it.

"Is that the one?"

"No. Grounds far too rocky," Qi answered, "much too close to camp."

Nathaniel stared at it until his legs took him away from it. He walked around fallen logs and huge boulders, anything Sarah might find too difficult.

"Okay," Qi announced, "its on top of that hill."

Nathaniel focused on the steep slopes that led up to the blue dot. "Can the mule make it?"

"Not yet, you will need to create some ramps. Tie the mule to that tree." A blue dot illustrated the one she meant.

Hitching the animal to the tree, Nathaniel grabbed the pick and charged up the steep incline. At the top, the ground flattened out for a good bit before descending down another equally steep drop. To his right, in the center of a large rocky face, was a decent sized opening, big enough for two men the size of Pa, tuck their heads down, and enter. Qi outlined a rectangular region just in front of the cave with the cyan color. Energy surged through Nathaniel as he planted his feet and raised the pickax high above his head. Allowing gravity to take hold, Nathaniel added what little extra strength he could to the pick as it sank into the ground.

"Again."

Wedging and pulling the tool from the ground, Nathaniel again raised it high above his head and let it fall. It sank even deeper into the earth. Loosening it, he swung it high up in the air and held it steady before letting the sharp end plunge into the earth. Strike after strike, he tore up the ground.

"Get the shovel."

Dropping the pickax, Nathaniel sidestepped his way down the slope. He utilized the final portion of the steep descent to propel himself forward, Speeding towards Sarah, he skidded to a halt directly in front of the sitting mule. Then, removing the shovel from the saddle, Nathaniel turned back and dashed up the steep slope. Reaching the top, he lost no time digging the spade into the ground.

"Toss the dirt onto the slopes. We need to make these slopes less steep."

Nathaniel stopped to yell, "Why?"

"Keep digging." Qi waited for the boy to return to work before further explaining. "For many reasons. Beechcroft has trouble with steep inclines, we need it to make it as easy as possible for him to get up here."

Nathaniel kept digging. "Easy for him?"

"Yes. It is crucial. We don't want him to pause and consider how difficult of an incline it is."

Nathaniel switched back to the pick and went right back to loosening up the earth. He picked and then shoveled, then picked and then shoveled. Then he picked and then shoveled. When the sun reached high noon, Nathaniel was barely waste deep. Wiping his brow, he glanced up at the nearest, brightest star.

"How long have we got?" Nathaniel wondered.

"Three to four days."

Nathaniel stared at the dirt. "You think that's enough?"

"It's what we have."

The boy tightened his grip and swung even harder.

17

The hotel employee offered a professional smile to the guests as he led a pair of beautiful black horses from the stable. Attached to the immaculate equine was a large, polished wagon covered by a large black leather bonnet. Dark iron wheels rolled the vehicle towards the bustling intersection but stopped rotating inches from the public path. The employee stood waited for Beechcroft to settle into the driver's seat before he reached up and offered over the reins. Millie moved around to the other side of the vehicle and quickly took the open seat next to the Englishman. The horses lurched forward. Her seat knocked into the back of her knees and she plopped down into her seat.

The stable hand smiled and waved as he called out, "Come back soon now, ya hear!"

Pulling back on the reins, Beechcroft steered the horses towards a large gap in between two buildings.

Millie tensed up as she clutched anything on her wooden seat she could get a purchase on and shouted, "Watch out!" Leaning out the side of the wagon, she called back, "Sorry, sir! Ma'am."

The back right wheel scraped against something.

Thickening her accent, Millie looked back and called out, "Sorry 'bout that."

They came to the end of a short road and Millie noticed street signs declaring, "Jefferson," and "Court." Moving onto Jefferson, Beechcroft's speed slightly relaxed, unlike Millie. When they finally ran out of Jefferson, they moved onto a road called Hall, for a short distance, before taking a quick right onto Wetumpra Road.

"When we lose sight of town," Beechcroft said, "switch."

Millie held on and nodded.

"I don't like driving," Beechcroft confessed.

Millie held her eyes on the road.

"I'm not a good driver."

She nodded.

18

Looking up, Nathaniel wiped his brow as he watched the moonlight peeking through the tree tops. Digging the shovel into the dirt, he grabbed the tool with both hands and flung the load out of the pit.

"You need to tie two anchors," Qi speculated, "so you can still exit after you've dug down even deeper."

"Anchors?"

"Take a long stretch of rope and tie it around a tree or boulder, then toss the loose end into the pit. Do it twice and you will not have to fear getting trapped."

Dropping the shovel, Nathaniel turned around and climbed over the increasingly steep step that led up to a slanted ramp made of compact dirt. Retrieving a coil of rope, Nathaniel walked to a nearby tree sporting a blue dot on its bark. Tying a secure knot around the plant, Nathaniel uncoiled the rope as he retreated back to the pit.

"Stop," a cyan line appeared on the cord, "slice it here."

Unsheathing Pa's knife, Nathaniel cut the rope. Carrying the severed half out of the pit and around to the cave, he tied an end into a loop and placed it around a jutting portion of rock.

"Go get the gun," Qi said.

Hurrying back to the saddle, Nathaniel retrieved Mr. Gibb's gun.

A cyan dot appeared to the left of him, as Qi announced, "Fire the gun in that direction."

Cocking the hammer, Nathaniel held the gun steady with both hands as he aimed at the colorful circle. Squeezing the trigger, the report echoed throughout the forest as the weapon kicked back and twisted itself out of the boy's grip. Branches snapped as something big fled into the night. Nathaniel's wide eyes stared at the silent gun before lifting his eyes up to the forest cloaked in darkness. Crouching down he picked up the gun and un-cocked the hammer.

"You scared it off," Qi said, "you're fine."

"What did I scare off?"

"An animal."

"What kind of animal?"

"Doesn't matter. Get back to work."

Placing the gun on the ground, Nathaniel gripped the hammer as he carefully uncocked the weapon. Holstering the weapon back into the saddle, he went back to digging.

19

"I pray there is an orchestra in the next town," Millie stated

From underneath the carriage bonnet, Beechcroft replied, "What?"

Glancing back, Millie said, "*Music.* I pray that there's some of it in the next town. Been listen'n t'nothing but a symphony of churn'n wheels. Churn'n me crazy!"

Licking his finger, Beechcroft flipped to the next page of his book, "Music would be nice."

The rotating wheels ground into the earth creating a white noise that lulled Beechcroft back into the world of his book.

"I hope there's a doctor in the next town," Millie continued. "I am with child."

Shutting his book, Beechcroft exclaimed, "What?"

"I know I am with child," she stated.

"It's *not* mine."

"Well," Millie replied, "who's else's ya reck'n it would be then?"

"No wife of mine, pure to me, has ever conceived."

"Wife?" Millie took her eyes off the road, "No wife of yers? You have a wife? In *England*?"

"Last I heard she had two children, two boys, with her new husband. They spend their summers in Italy and their winters in

France," He turned his head back and glared at the driver's neck. "If you are indeed with child, it is *not* mine!"

The following pause in conversation was filled with hooves and wheels tearing up the ground.

"Ya said before ya din't have a wife."

Beechcroft reopened up his book. "I *had* one."

Glancing over at his open-faced pocket watch, the Englishman grunted before returning his attention to the page.

20

Gripping his bundle of sticks tightly together, Nathaniel wondered, "Is this enough?"

"Can you carry anymore?" the spider replied.

Nathaniel adjusted his grip. "Yes."

"You can go back to camp and work on the one's you have, but you will need to return later and gather more."

Tying a rope around the bundle of sticks, Nathaniel walked all the way back to camp before dumping the pile of **kindling** by the fire pit. Tossing a few on the smoldering coals, Nathaniel backed away from the heat and sat down with his back against the fallen log. Unsheathing Pa's knife, Nathaniel picked up a stick in his other hand and began to whittle. Stroke after stroke he peeled the wood from the limb; shards piled up on the ground between his legs. Focusing on an end, he removed all of the thin bark. Rotating his project he transformed its shape into a point.

"That's sharp enough."

Putting down his first spike, the boy picked up the second stick and started manipulating it. His arm grew tired and his skin ached yet he continued processing the stakes.

After he had sharpened the entire bundle, Qi said, "One at a time, cook them over the fire."

Moving from his seat, Nathaniel crouched down and grabbed a spike in each hand. With each corresponding lick of the flames the wood's color darkened.

After a while, Qi said, "Rotate."

Twisting his wrists, Nathaniel roasted the rest. When the stakes were fully cooked, Nathaniel started a new pile before going back for more. When he finished, Qi had him tie them in a bundle.

Staring at the pointy end of the stack, Nathaniel considered, "Should I put venom on them?"

"You would have to catch a snake and harvest its venom. That's a lot of work and risk. Next time you shit you could rub the spikes in it."

Nathaniel wrinkled his nose. "Really? Shit? Yuck!"

"Exactly. It is yucky and will increase their lethality."

"You want me to smear my poo on each of them?"

"Yes. But you can wait for a more natural time." Her tone dropped, "Ready the mule, we need to go back to the pit."

Throwing up his hands, Nathaniel whined, "Already? No break?"

"No time."

Picking up the bundle of stakes, Nathaniel straightened himself up and carried them over to the creature. Careful not to poke her, Nathaniel commanded the mule to sit before tying the bundle onto her back.

"C'mon now," Nathaniel commanded.

Standing up, Sarah followed as he lead her on a familiar path.

Halfway back to the pit, Nathaniel stopped and hitched Sarah to a tree. Utilizing a fallen branch, Nathaniel dug a small hole in the earth before placing a leg on either side and squatted down. After wiping himself up, he pulled up his pants and returned to the mule. After getting her to sit, he removed the bundle. Returning to his improvised latrine, he dropped the bundle of sticks and one by one rolled each tip in the feces. With each stake, Nathaniel watched the shit mix with the dirt and transform into a sludge. By the final spike, he was covering them in moist, sticky earth. With extreme caution, he tied and placed the bundle on the kneeling mule. Taking the creature's reins, he stood her up and restarted the trek.

When he finally reached the pit, Nathaniel trekked up the gradual slope that led to the unfinished pit. Tapping the back of Sarah's knees, he removed the bundle. Then he carried the sticks to the front of the pit and placed them down. Moving around the pit towards the cave, Nathaniel hopped over a corner and entered into the opening. He retrieved the hidden shovel and pickax, and tossed them both into the pit. Sitting down, Nathaniel dangled his feet over the edge before carefully sliding himself forward. He plopped down into the recently unearthed dirt and picked up the pickax. Focusing on the blue dot, Nathaniel raised the tool high in the air above his hair. Letting gravity take hold of the tool, Nathaniel aimed its decent directly onto the blue dot. The pointy end sank into the ground.

"Get the spikes," Qi said.

Letting go, Nathaniel walked up the ramp and picked up the bundle. He returned to the deepest section, took a spike and pressed its tip into the ground. Picking up the full-sized shovel, Nathaniel tried utilizing it as a hammer.

"Perhaps a stone more suited to your size would be better," Qi suggested. Abandoning the pit for a brief moment, Nathaniel soon returned with a better sized hammer. Holding the spike like a nail, he struck it with the flat rock.

After a dozen strikes Qi said, "Stop. Pull it out and put a different spike in, bottom first, spiky end up." She waited for the boy to obey. "Push it in, push some dirt into the hole as well. Fill in any gaps. Bury it well. Add some more dirt. Make sure its sturdy." The spider waited. "That feels sturdy enough. Move onto the next. Same thing."

When he finished the first row of spikes, he picked up the shovel and removed a portion of the slope. When he gained enough space, he added a second row. Alternating between hammering and shoveling, he added a third, fourth, fifth, sixth, and seventh row. On the final row, Qi had himself place all but the final stake. With barely a safe space to stand in, Nathaniel took hold of one of his ropes and climbed his way out of the pit.

"Remove the anchor ropes," Qi said.

Nathaniel obeyed, removing and coiling up each rope.

21

Each rotation of the carriage's wheels churned the muddy winter ground. Sitting in the moving carriage, to the right of Millie, Beechcroft's eyes remained fixated on the time piece in his hand while Millie's only version, aside from driving the horses, were the long gray clouds, wintered trees, and the horses defecating as they walked. She envisioned their party leaving behind a trail of shit. After a few good rains there would be no trace of them having ever traveled this way.

Something stirred in the corner of her eye. Glancing over, Millie jilted her head back as she nearly caught a finger in the eye.

"Yonder!" Beechcroft declared.

Slowing their speed, her eyes followed the direction the Englishman indicated. After a brief stare, she said, "Them mountains?"

Looking up from the watch, Beechcroft's eyes followed his own finger to the mountain range that towered over the tree-line. He lowered his finger, and returned his eyes to his instrument.

"Perhaps," he said, "or beyond them." He looked up from the watch. "I should consult my map. Stop here. I need to take a bearing."

Millie pulled the horses to a full stop. Grumbling, Beechcroft eased his way off the seat; landing on the ground with a vibrating thud. Moving around to the back of the parked carriage, he stopped and waited. Millie dropped down the wagon's rear and Beechcroft accepted her offered hand. Placing a foot on the first tall step, he mustered his nimblest leg lift and landed his foot on the second step. The entire bed bent down to the ground, as she pulled Beechcroft into the bonnet. Stumbling backwards she caught herself on a suitcase. Beechcroft stood in front of a wooden barrel. Taking a document from the case, Millie unfolded the paper and placed it atop of the barrel. She retrieved a lantern and a match. Lighting a lantern, she handed to the Englishman who attached it to the bonnet's rigging. Leaning forward he squinted his eyes as he studied the large, colorful map.

He glossed over various letters he had penciled in all over the map. In each location he had written the specific degree, date, and time. As he lifted his left hand, Millie deposited a ruler into his open palm. Placing the measuring tool on the map, he lifted his other hand and it received a pencil. Tracing the edge of the ruler, Beechcroft drew a line from New York to Washington DC. Continuing to connect the various dots, Beechcroft stenciled a segmented straight line that traveled all the way down into the southern states. Setting the pencil and ruler down in Montana, he pulled out his pocket watch. His fingertip pointed at their current position on the map.

With widening eyes, he declared, "It could very well be in them mountains!"

Millie turned pale, "Great."

His face beamed with delight. "It's gotta be here." His smile flickered. "Though it could very well be beyond the mountains."

Millie side eyed the map. "But," she uttered, "it's definitely not in Mexico?"

Beechcroft burst out laughing before pinching her cheek. "It's definitely not in Mexico!" His bright eyes lingered on the map.

"Should I go unhitch the wagon?"

Beechcroft traded his smile for ponderous concentration. Snatching up the pocket watch, Beechcroft turned his back and descended the steps. He planted his feet on the ground, turned to his right and considered the mountain range. Glancing between the peaks and pocket watch, he reconfirmed the direction.

Stepping down from the wagon, Millie Jean joined in beside the Englishman.

"Is that where you need to go?"

Beechcroft nodded. "Indeed."

"Shall I unhitch the horses?"

Beechcroft scratched his gristly face. "No," he finally stated, "I want a hot meal and a good rest before I go gallivanting through a wild wintry forest."

Millie stared at the muddy ground. "Winters are nothing down here."

Beechcroft shrugged. "Let us go find a good, kind, *hospitable*, christian neighbor."

Millie nodded and pointed with her thumb, "I think I saw one a few miles back."

"Let's hope they have a spare room."

22

Gathering up long thin branches, Nathaniel wrapped dried ivy around each stick before placing it in a grid like formation over the top of the pit. Soon it started resembled a brittle roof or floor. Then he switched to even shorter and thinner sticks and continued placing them. Bit by bit, section by section, the gaps were filled in with long, thin sticks. Using the shovel as best he could, he scooped up piles of fallen leaves and set them beside the pit. With his hands he tossed the rotting foliage onto the grid of sticks.

"With your hands," Qi instructed, "toss handfuls of sandy dirt on top of the leaves."

Kneeling on the ground, Nathaniel dug into the ground and scooped up dirt he had previously loosened up. He tossed the rocky debris onto the layer of organic litter and sticks. Working his way around the perimeter of the pit, Nathaniel ensured each inch was uniform.

"Remove and coil up the two ropes," Qi instructed.

Nathaniel obeyed, untying, coiling up and placing the anchors onto the mule. "In the morning light we may want to touch up a few spots," Qi announced.

"In the morning? You said he's nearby."

"They came the closest they've ever come today," Qi admitted, "but Beechcroft wants to rest before hiking through a strange wilderness."

"So they're not coming tonight?"

"No."

Letting out a sigh Nathaniel blurted, "You could've told me! I thought they gonna come up on me at any moment."

"You got a lot of work done. Let's go back to camp and get some rest."

23

"Just don't make 'em think yer some carpetbag bunko," Millie insisted as she drove the horses down a vaguely marked dirt path.

Up ahead, the travelers spotted a middle-aged woman sitting in a rocking chair on a porch, cradling a bundle in her arms. The lady watched the approaching black wagon like a hawk. When they drew within yelling distance, Millie slowed the vehicle to a near stop.

"Good afternoon to ya, Ma'am," Beechcroft tried his best.

"Howdy, stranger," the woman called back.

"Is the man of the house in?"

The woman hesitated in her rocking rhythm. "Ya from the bank?"

"No, Ma'am," Beechcroft quickly answered. "I was wondering who this property this belongs to."

"Yer *not* from the bank?"

"No, Ma'am."

"Well, yer reside'n on the property of Mr. Edward Ferguson, an' Mr. Edward Ferguson is currently indisposed, on the other side of this here wall, having himself a nap."

Out of the corner of her mouth, Millie whispered, "Call her Mrs. Edward Ferguson."

Beechcroft's accent thickened like a sauce on high heat, "Well, Mrs. Edward Ferguson, my companion and I are in need of accommodating quarters this evening, and considering our alternatives have decided to seek out whether such accommodations are being offered here. Now I am fully willing and committed to paying full and well for whatever expenses I may incur. My companion and I are hungry and thirsty from our travels and I would be more than willing to pay the price you deem reasonable."

Mrs. Edward Ferguson leaned her long neck back and shouted, "Pa! Come on out here."

The silence that followed was deafening.

"Paul George?"

From within the farmhouse, an older boy's voice yelled back, "Yes, Ma?"

"Wake yer father! Tell him there's business out here. Not the bank!"

"That yer baby?" Millie inquired.

The woman's eyes snapped to Millie, "It is," she stated bluntly, before smiling sweetly at the child and continuing in a more tender tone. "Jus' had this little 'un no more than two months ago."

Beechcroft glanced over at Millie.

"Why don't y'all pull up a little closer, take the load off yer critters."

Millie flicked the reins, "Appreciate it!"

The horses walked forward until Millie commanded to stop them with a "Woah!" Dismounting, she quickly led the horses to a post. Beechcroft carefully and slowly stepped down from the carriage.

"Seems to me ya could stand to miss a few meals," Mrs. Edward Ferguson commented before turning her attention to Millie. "Come sit up here in this seat." She indicated the wooden chair next to her before glancing over at the Englishman. "Not sure if any of our chairs got the strength for ya."

The front door opened with such noise that Millie paused her journey to the offered seat. Dressed in trousers, faded overalls and a loose white shirt, Edward Ferguson's tall, muscular body strolled out onto the porch. His fiery green eyes glared at Beechcroft. The porch trembled as Edward's bare feet propelled him down the steps. He offered out a hand to Beechcroft who promptly accepted. The Englishman felt the agricultural worker's strength.

"I'm Edward Ferguson, this is my property," he released the handshake. "Got the deed to it. What y'all here for?"

"I was hoping to rent a room from ya for the next few evenings. I'm willing to pay top dollar." Beechcroft reached inside his jacket and retrieved a wallet. Pulling out a bill, the Englishman handed the currency over to the man. "Perhaps a down payment will clarify that I am not being metaphorical."

Taking the ten-dollar bill, Edward Ferguson stared intently at the greenback. Squinting his eyes, he lifted it up to the waning sunlight.

Stuffing the bill inside his front pocket, the farmer announced, "Tell Paul George he sleep'n in the stable tonight. These fine folks will be using his bedroom for the evening." His eyes addressed his missus. "Tell Margaret to make two more servings for dinner." Edward turned and headed for the open front door.

"Where ya headed?" Mrs. Edward Ferguson demanded.

"To put some damned shoes on."

"Paul George!" Mrs. Edward Ferguson called out, "com'n'on out here!" She spoke more conversationally. "I call out to the children, 'cause if Eddie does it, they know somethin' be up."

Millie giggled.

The mother addressed Millie, "Where you from?"

"I'm from Georgia."

"Ya'll come from Georgia? Atlanta?"

Millie shook her head, "South of there."

Mrs. Edward Ferguson nodded, "Ed's got a cousin who moved out there some time ago. We've never had the time to go an' visit anywhere but righ' here."

A tall boy, no older than fourteen politely scrambled onto the porch. When he came to a stop, he stood up straight, awaiting direction.

"These here folks are gonna be staying in yer room tonight."

A flicker of objection passed over the lad's freckled face.

"Don't bother arguin' 'bout it. Show 'em their room and make sure

218

they comf'able. Ya might also wan' take a extra blanket an' pillow out to the stable fer yerself."

Paul George looked up at the guest and then down at the floor. "If y'all would follow me."

"We need to hitch up these horses," Beechcroft replied.

"Paul George, lead them to the stable."

Paul George had only made it halfway down the porch when Edward Ferguson dashed from the house, insisting, "I'll take yer horses to the stable!"

Paul George froze as his father dashed around him and planted his heavy boots in front of the horses.

"If you insist," Beechcroft replied as he stood up. "I need to gather my things," twisting his torso, Beechcroft grabbed his suitcase and pulled it through the bonnet. "Ya need anything Millie? *Anythin'* of *value?*"

Grabbing her carpetbag, Millie jumped down from the back of the carriage. She quickly passed Beechcroft and made her way up the porch steps. When Beechcroft was steady on the ground, Edward Ferguson led the horses and wagon towards an open building on the edge of the property.

"Paul George, take 'em to where they be staying," Mrs. Edward Ferguson said.

The lad led the way through the front door and into a hallway. As soon as Paul George set foot inside his home he increased his pace. By the time he reached the end of the hallway, it dawned on him to be courteous. When the guests caught up, Paul George led them into a room filled with steam, smoke, and buzzing with active cooking. In the midst of the blurry scene, a young lady bustled about, moving between a stove top and a table covered in corn, peppers, lettuces, cabbages, and beans. Pausing her hurried pace, she stared at the lad as he escorted the strangers through the kitchen and into a washroom. Through the scents of soap and water at the back of the room were two doors, one of which was much draftier than the other.

Opening the warmer of the two doors, Paul George looked back at his audience and declared, "This is it." He led them into the quarters and waited until they completely filled up the room before continuing. "It's not much, but its the closest room to the…the uh place…where you do the thing…t's only a few steps outside the back door."

"Thank you so much," Beechcroft declared. "I would like a nap before dinner."

"If y'all need anything else," Paul George nodded, "I'll be helping with dinner."

The room was so crowded that Millie had to leave first before the lad was able to exit.

Re-entering the room, Millie closed the door behind her and loudly objected, "Don't sit in his only chair, you'll break it."

Standing up, Beechcroft retorted, "then I'll buy him a new one."

"You already have," Millie replied as she laid down on the bed, "Ya know yer overpaying by a lot—and I mean a *lot*?"

Beechcroft pointed a finger at the bed. "Don't sit there, I need it."

"Really?" Millie moaned as she rolled off the bed.

Plopping his suitcase down, Beechcroft said, "Overpaying buys a different level of service." He faced her. "Giving someone an entire bill cuts out any ideas they may have of cutting yer throat to get their change back. And I *hate* the sound coins make when they jangle around in a pocket."

"Then just give them to me. It must be nice throwing all that cash around. How young were you when ya came to know such wealth?"

"It has made certain things very convenient," Beechcroft answered as he splayed a map out on the bed.

Placing the compass and watch beside one another, Beechcroft took a ruler and aligned it with the angle of the single handed time piece. He stared at the region that lay near the ruler's second inch mark.

"It's in them mountains," Beechcroft stated, "It must be in those mountains." He bit his lip and scratched his gristle face. "Or maybe even before the mountains," he trailed off.

"Great, can I lay on the bed now?"

Turning his head, Beechcroft stared at Millie. "I suppose."

As soon as he gathered up the map and devices, Millie plopped herself down on the bed.

"I don't suppose it would be considered rude to ask to dine in here."

"They probably don't want you to get food all over the floor."

"Hmmmph, even after I've paid good money?"

"You can alwayds rub that in their face. They may end up deciding to murder us in our sleep."

"Think they would?"

"With all them li'l ones run'n 'round?" Millie shook her head, "I'll bet they got a dozen even smaller ones hidden in every nook n' cranny."

"Maybe they'll put 'em to work dig'n our graves during dinner."

"Maybe you should mention that you have friends waiting on you further up ahead."

"That's wise." Carefully turning his body, Beechcroft analyzed the room. "I miss the Windsor."

"Me too."

24

Spotting the predator, the rabbit jumped to its feet and ran. A wire, looped around the animals chest cinched, abruptly stopping its progress. Rushing forward, Nathaniel grabbed hold of the wire and yanked. The rabbit bared its teeth as it tumbled off balance. Removing the wire from the spike, Nathaniel swung it; lifting his prey off the ground. Spinning the catch in a circle above his head, he waited until the prey was good and dizzy before he carefully placed it on the ground. He gripped its ears, pulled back the dazed critter's throat and sliced his blade across it. Blood drenched the front of the fur coat as screeches exploded from the rabbit's lungs. Kneeling on the back while pulling the ears back further, Nathaniel encouraged the blood to escape more quickly. The frantic rebellion reached a crescendo before promptly dwindling. When the squirming had stopped completely, he loosened his grip and untied the cinch. Holding his dinner by its ears, Nathaniel wiped the blade before sheathing it. Carefully not to drip on himself, Nathaniel made his way back to camp. Placing the cadaver on the fallen log, he unsheathed Pa's knife. Blue dots illuminated all four of the animal's limbs.

"Amputate."

Nathaniel sliced Pa's blade through the skin and reached the bone. Leaning his weight on the knife's edge, Nathaniel listened to the crunching snap as his knife finally made it through the calcium. Moving onto the next leg, Nathaniel worked his way through the next set of fur and bone. The upper paws were much easier.

When he had fully removed all of the rabbit's limbs, Qi indicated the Gut, "Cut there and then loosen the skin before severing it in two."

With a quick cut, Nathaniel dug one hand into the warm, bloody flesh. Loosening and slicing his way around the rabbit, he gave the creature a sort of inverse belt. Putting down the blade, he removed the rabbit's bottom half as one would take off a pair of pants. It was almost scary how little resistance the body's largest organ gave as it was fully removed from the creature's exposing its muscles. Grabbing the thinnest and sturdiest spike, Nathaniel speared it up through the animal. Then he went over to the cart and retrieved a bundle of wild thyme and a few huckleberries. Returning to the rabbit, he wrapped the herbs around the meat and mashed the tiny fruits into the flesh. After reigniting the fire, he held the stake over the flames like a fishing rod. He listened to the heat warming the moisture.

When it started to sizzle, Qi instructed, "Rotate it."

Nathaniel did so.

"Why am I cooking it?" he wondered aloud. "Can't I eat it raw?"

"Yes, but it will taste better. You can take a bite now."

Pulling back the stick, Nathaniel leaned in and sunk his teeth into the warm but still raw meat. Tearing off a chunk, he occupied his teeth with chewing while his hands returned to roasting the rabbit. The air filled with the refined smells of cooking. As the amount of escaping steam faded, a dark layer of flavor crisped up the protein. Every breath was a tease of thyme, berry, and succulence.

"Alright," Qi said.

Opening his mouth, Nathaniel pulled his meal closer to his face.

"Careful," Qi raised her voice, "give it a chance to cool."

Nathaniel could have cried as his hands held steady the deliciousness that was dripping so very close to him.

"You've done excellent, consistent work," Qi said. "You deserve a reward. Because of you we have a real chance at survival."

Nathaniel's stomach growled. Listening to his belly, Nathaniel stared woefully at his food.

"It should be fine now."

He sank his teeth into the steamy, cooked meat. Reducing a limb to a skeleton in less than a minute, he threw the bones into the flames. He pulled every ounce of flesh from the carcass. Scrapping and digging his teeth against the rodent's skull, Nathaniel pinched his jaws together and ripped tiny morsels from its cheeks. He bit into a joint full of cartilage, ripped it from the carcass, and chewed on the gummy material. After finishing each limb, Nathaniel scoured its torso and ribs for more. When a full minute had gone by without discovering any more flesh, the boy tossed the final bulk of the creature onto the fire. Sitting on the ground, Nathaniel leaned his back up against the hollow log. He watched the greedy, hungry flames darken the carcass. Bones cracked as the body turned black and then crumbled into coals.

"Where's the guy?" Nathaniel asked aloud.

"He's resting."

"In a hotel?"

"No, a local farmer is sheltering him."

"That's nice of them."

"They got paid."

"I wonder what Pa, Ma an' Jane are doin'."

"You can ask them the next time you see them."

"But you know. You can see them right now."

Qi was silent.

"You could tell me."

"They are worried about you."

Nathaniel felt a flash of heat swell through his blood.

"It is to be expected."

"They send out a search party?"

"Of course."

"They tell everyone at school?"

"Who else would the search party be made up of?"

Nathaniel frowned. "Its not right, putting them through all this."

"I think you should get some rest."

"I'm not sleepy."

"Need I remind you that all *this* is so that you may one day return to them, and *not* in a box."

"A box?"

"A coffin."

Another set of shivers cascaded down the boy's spine.

"You and Sarah will sleep in the shelter," Qi continued. "It's going to rain tonight."

Nathaniel grumbled.

"You don't have much time before it starts."

He watched at the fire pit's waning coals. Standing up, he moved closer to the fire and picked up some logs. After placing a few on the fire, Nathaniel took the rest and stored them inside the hollowed out center of the fallen log. Moving over to Sarah, he unhitched her and led her to the cave. He secured her to one of the cart's wheels before laying down underneath the slated cart that acted as further shelter. Sarah laid down. Nathaniel scooted up the animal's furry back. He felt her warmth melting into him. She smelled like the shack. Wrapping himself up in a blanket, Nathaniel snuggled up close the mule and slept through the rain.

25

The rain fell off the porch roof in heavy sheets. Raindrops ran together, forming into walls as they traveled down to the ground. Beechcroft watched the water fall, listening to the continuous, thunderous splash it made as it struck the ground. A long puddle formed in front of the porch, created by years of eroding downpours. Beechcroft took a sip of the bitter, hot liquid. The beverage trickled down his throat, warmed his chest and woke him up. His frown deepened.

"I'm not going out there today," he stated.

Millie lifted a small tin cup to her lips.

"Mountains don't travel far," he added.

Millie shrugged, took a sip, then lowered her cup and said, "Is that what you've been looking for? A mountain."

He shrugged. "Sure."

"Someone stole your family heirloom, a mountain, from London and transplanted it to Alabama? And you've finally caught up to where they put it?"

"Don't be ridiculous." Beechcroft punctuated his sentence by snapping the time piece closed. "There are no mountains in London."

Millie giggled and shrugged, "I must entertain myself somehow. It's a bore bein' in the dark."

"I'm sure." Beechcroft stepped back from the edge of the porch. "But even with better light, not all will necessarily be illuminated."

Mr. Edward Ferguson opened the front door and strolled out onto his moist porch with heavy booted footfalls. With a steaming tin of coffee, the farmer ended his strides and leaned against a wooden beam. Taking a quick swig of his caffeinated mud, his eyes darted between the Englishman and the southern New Yorker. They both waited for their host to speak.

After another gulp, Mr. Edward Ferguson pointed his free hand at the British alien, "Y'all goin' out today?"

"Afraid not," Beechcroft replied. "We plan on trekking through the local wilderness and do not need to be hindered any further by bad weather."

"Stay'n's gonna cost."

Straightening himself up, Beechcroft faced his host square on. "My good man, are you implying that I have already incurred more than ten dollars' worth of services and goods and that more money is required to cover any further addition to my bill?"

Mr. Edward Ferguson nodded.

"I spent more than ten dollars in *less* than a day?"

Mr. Edward Ferguson nodded.

Beechcroft crossed his arms. "What's the greatest amount of money that you have ever earned in a day?"

Millie butted in. "How much do we owe you?"

Mr. Edward Ferguson looked at the lady. "Another ten."

"Another ten?" Beechcroft repeated flabbergasted. "You—"

Millie instantly interrupted, "Are so kind to allow us to stay." She looked at her employer. "I've seen you throw hundred dollar bills out for lesser quality product."

Beechcroft glared at his employee. "*This* is the last bit of money you are ever going to gouge from me, Ferguson!" he declared as he reached into his pocket. But then he thought better of it and reached into a front pocket of his purple vest. The sound of coins clattering on wood filled the air as Beechcroft tossed them all over the porch. As soon as Mr. Edward Ferguson realized the litter was money, he stooped down and scrabbled to gather them all up.

Squatting on his thighs, the farmer counted the coins in his calloused hand, "I only got nine."

"One rolled into a crack," Beechcroft said and he strolled into the house. "Have one of yer bastards dig it out."

26

"I t feels weird retracing the same steps," Beechcroft broke the silence. "After breaking new ground for so long."

Millie nodded as she listened to the horseshoes tearing up the moist ground. Her eyes lingered over the details of the surroundings. Beechcroft recognized a particularly big rock. He looked upon it as a friend and rode past it as he had done a few days prior

"You shouldn't've helped that gouger," Beechcroft stated.

Millie glanced over at her employer. "That so?"

"Perhaps, at some point, I'll get someone to pay him a visit."

"Mmmmhmmm."

"Mister Edward Ferguson," Beechcroft mocked, "the bastard doesn't need to be rewarded for being such a lying, greedy gouging bastard."

"That so?"

Beechcroft widened his eyes. "*You've* conducted yourself in a professional manner, unlike him. If he really needs the extra money, there is a good and proper way of going about it."

She shifted up both eyebrows. "Is there?"

"Indeed. No one need be rude about their financial position in life," he explained. "It doesn't help the overall *anything* when one is rude."

"A working girl can get herself killed or worse if she is rude to the wrong man."

Beechcroft shot her a quizzical look.

"This *thing*," she questioned, "is it going to change your life?"

Beechcroft pondered for a moment. "It just very well might."

"Really? How? Will people never be able to be rude to you again?"

Beechcroft studied his employee for a good moment before answering, "I must have the first look."

"What?"

"I need to go first. Alone."

"Yer trampln over my question *and* make'n another stipulation?"

Turning his head, Beechcroft stared straight ahead. Reaching into her saddle, Millie brought out a flask.

After taking a long, deep drink, she held the container just below her chin as she asked, "What that mean, 'ya gotta go first?' After all this journey'n ya gonna leave me behind at the final stretch?"

"You may come see it later," he shrugged. "I wish to make the maiden voyage alone."

She pulled on her reins. "Should I turn back?"

Beechcroft halted his horse and faced his employee. "To the farm?"

"You wanna be alone."

"Travel with me to where we stopped before. Stay there and look after the horses."

Millie pointed. "Yer gonna hike through all 'em mountains all by yer lonesome?"

"Yes."

Millie took another sip. "I've seen yer natural gait. You'll be gone till tomorrow night."

"Regardless, my wish remains."

"What you looking for?"

"Remember when you asked me about what topics to not bring up?"

Millie shook her head.

"Well you did, and this is one of them."

"Fine," Millie closed the flask and put it away. "Boss."

Kicking her heels in, Millie snatched the lead. The distance between the two riders grew. She moved so far ahead, Beechcroft almost lost sight of her, but he managed to keep one eye on her all the way to the point they had stopped at before. Pulling off to the side of the road closest to the range, Beechcroft carefully dismounted. With both feet planted safely on the solid ground, he consulted his pocket watch. His eyes shifted between the pointing hand and the mountain top. With a grunt, he pocketed the time piece before untying his satchel from his saddle.

"Ya should bring someone else. Hire Mr. Ferguson to go along with you."

Beechcroft's brows furrowed. "Are you daft? I'd rather bury him."

"Hire Paul George." Millie hesitated. "If something happens to you, I'm alone."

"I've had many years—Beechcroft corrected himself—no, *decades*, of experience. I will be back."

"Well, be quick about it." Crossing her arms, she looked up at the sun. "I don't want to spend the entire day picnicking on the side of the road with no way of know'n."

"Know that I *will* be back."

Millie stared at the ground. Beechcroft took several steps forward. Stopping just in front of his employee, he leaned in and planted a kiss on her forehead.

"I won't abandon you," he whispered before declaring. "I'll take my time and I *will* be back."

Pulling out his revolver, Beechcroft ensured the weapon was fully loaded before placing it back in its holster.

Looking up, Millie raised an eyebrow. "Ya plan'n on use'n that?"

Beechcroft smirked. "It is a wilderness out there. Loud noises are good for scaring off feral creatures."

"Is it a watch?"

"Is what a what?" Beechcroft asked as he holstered his pistol.

"That thing you stare at, is it a watch?"

Beechcroft slowly nodded. "It's a watch."

"What kind of time does it tell with only one hand?"

Beechcroft eyed his employee. "The type you find."

"Yer find'n time?"

Beechcroft pondered for a moment and then nodded.

"You really do think I'm daft."

"No, I don't think yer any dafter than anyone else. I just don't have an entire school year at my disposal to teach you everything that you would need to know in order to understand the complexity of what is going on."

"Well, God damn!" Millie stomped her foot. "I know I must seem like..." She trailed off for a good solid second before her eyebrows furrowed and she shouted, "Go be off on yer merry way then!"

Opening up a pouch in the saddle, Beechcroft retrieved a tiny music box that seemed even smaller inside his large palm. Mounted on the top of the box was a figurine of a dancing bear. It was posed with an arm raised and curved above its head while the leg not on the ground kicked out at the air. As the Englishman wound up the devices tiny ratchet, Millie's eyes fixated on the dancing animal as each wind slowly twisted it backwards. The instant he released the tension, the tutu-wearing caniform danced. Both humans held their breath as they listened to the ensuing silence.

Cocking his head to the side, Beechcroft listened for a moment longer before inquiring, "Hear it?"

Mirroring the Englishman, Millie tilted her head, "What?" she shook her head, "I don't hear noth'n."

Smirking, Beechcroft replied, "Yer not an animal after all." He turned his broad back to her and strode off towards the woods. "Be back in a trice," he called.

Leaves crunched beneath his heavy footfalls as he marched through multiple generations of ruddy pines. Glancing behind, he barely saw the road through the trees. Walking some way further, Beechcroft's eyes snapped down to the bear as its dance came to a dwindling halt. He slowed his pace as he carefully wound up the ratchet before releasing it. The figurine resumed its rigid jig. Pulling out the pocket watch, Beechcroft aligned his orientation with the hand before continuing.

The terrain grew steeper, and the battle for each step grew constantly more grueling. Breathing harder with each corresponding breath, he put on the brakes and watched the dancing bear twist and twist down to a full stop. Beechcroft fully wound it back up before moving on. Without slowing much, he pulled out his pocket watch and ensured that his steps continued, taking him closer to his intended target.

Looking up ahead, he noticed a boulder blocking his direct path. Beechcroft complained the entire way around it, only ceasing when he reached the other side. Checking in on the timepiece, he confidently strode deeper into the forest. Weaving in between the trees, he trekked his way up the ever more steeply ascending path, the terrain growing even more wild too.

Making his way around another large rock, Beechcroft stared up at the sloping landscape. His eyes rested on a fallen log and he redirected his steps towards it. Planting his butt on the dead trunk, he wound up the music box to its limit before setting it down.

He reached into his pocket and pulled out a tin can. Popping the top revealed a portion of preserved corned beef. Lifting a spoon from his jacket, he scooped a bit of the gelatinous, meat to his lips and ate it. It tasted like condensed, coagulated, meat swill. Both the flavor and texture were weak. Even a dash of pepper or a pinch of salt would've helped tremendously. He swallowed, trying his best to avoid it touching his tongue, before biting off another smaller chunk. Gulping it down whole, he hurried to finish. When he reached his goal, he tossed the empty container behind him. He took out his flask and took a deep swig. Looking up at the sky, he gurgled before swallowing the contents of his mouth down into his stomach like a flushing toilet. Shivers rippled along his spine. After taking a drink of water, he slid off the log and resumed his walk. He stopped to wind up the bear before re-calibrating his heading.

Up ahead he noticed he was moving directly at a small but sheer cliff. Moving to the right, he noticed that the compass was still indicating the cliff. Around the side of the cliff a steep but steady slope led up to an elevated area surrounded by rock. After a second triple check, Beechcroft huffed and puffed his way up the slope. Reaching the top, he immediately felt the need to rest. Sitting on a nearby boulder Beechcroft studied the area of dirt and then he noticed the cave smack dab in the middle of the rocky wall in front of him.

Glancing down at his pocket watch, his heart skipped a beat. He confirmed and then quickly reconfirmed that the single hand was pointing directly at the cave. He triple and quadruple checked. Standing up from the boulder, he took a step closer.

Keeping his hands and arms frozen and his eyes steady on the pocket watch, Beechcroft twisted his upper torso until the indicator no longer pointed at the cave. He studied the pocket watch's single hand swing back to its original indication. Looking up from the time piece, Beechcroft stared at the cave. With great effort, he bent over and picked up a pebble. Straightening his back, he wound up his hand and chucked the tiny stone into the opening. He listened to the missile clatter, and again checked the pocket watch's orientation.

"I hope it's not too far inside," Beechcroft thought as he stepped forward.

Suddenly, the world plummeted upward. He felt the lackluster strength of numerous twigs snapping beneath his weight. The ground swallowed him like a rock dropping into a lake. Jagged branches scratched his eyes as he plunged into complete darkness. For a split second, his freefall gained velocity, before a multitude of sharp, sturdy points caught his falling body. His flesh exploded with pain as his cracking bones blunted numerous points. He tasted blood as several teeth splintered and or were knocked free from his gums. Time and gravity relentlessly pressed on him like a masseuse, anchoring him deeper onto each stake. He bled profusely.

Panic mustered all of Beechcroft's strength into his arms, legs, and knees as he threw every ounce of strength he had into his limbs. As he strained his injured muscles, the blood in his mouth grew hot and his tongue was drenched in the wet, dripping taste of living iron.

Tears streaked down his cheeks as his lungs erupted, "YYYYYYYEEEEEEEEEAAAAARRRRGGGGGHHHH-WWWWAAAA!"

He felt several of the stakes' grips shift and loosen. Fighting for each upward centimeter, Beechcroft managed to tear his top half up and away from the points. He tried to twist as fresh pain and creeping exhaustion sapped his determination. As the giant Englishman toppled over, spikes both old and new tore new holes in his side. One of his legs twisted as it uprooted and snapped a stake. He squeezed his eyelids shut and screamed. Opening his eyes, he saw a room full of darkness save for a patch of spotlight streaking through the hole in the ceiling. He tried to wipe his mouth, but a sharp feeling in his arm stalled the movement. The pain lingered in his limb until it faded and rejoined the rest of the body's pulsing agony. Clearing his throat, he spat out warm blood and sucked up oxygen with desperate breaths. The earthy, moist air tasted of organic, rotting shit.

"Is he dead?" Nathaniel wondered.

"No."

Nathaniel specifically listened to the present silence. Placing a hand on the large boulder, he leaned forward and peaked his head around the rock. "What about now?"

"No."

He stood up, "Can he hurt me?"

"Not without a lot of help."

Nathaniel stared at the entrance to the cave. Despite the distance and angle, he managed to make out a large hole at the front of the camouflage.

"It worked," Qi announced, "he's dying. As good as dead."

Beechcroft's screams rang in his head. Standing up, Nathaniel approached the cave's threshold.

"Careful," Qi cautioned as a cyan rectangle highlighted the region directly in front of the cave, "a misstep is still lethal."

Stopping at the brink, he poked his head outside and looked up into the sky. The wind rustled the naked tree limbs swaying in the air. Glancing down, his eyes fixated on the gaping hole. It stood out like an ink splotch on a blank piece of paper. A few broken branches stuck out of the hole at odd angles. One tiny, wooden limb lost its balance and tumbled down into the darkness.

"Dy-ing," Nathaniel thought.

"He is bleeding out. He will die."

"How long will that take?"

"Twenty-four to thirty-six hours."

"I can shoot him."

"Indeed, but wait until after you have dealt with his companion. She will hear the gunshot and get spooked."

"She can hear it?"

"Yes."

Nathaniel tensed as he thought he heard something. "Was that him?"

"He's harmless now."

"Should I," Nathaniel backed away from the pit, "feel bad?"

"You are alive. He is dead. We continue. He doesn't. If you wish to feel bad, so be it."

"I thought this would be different."

"How so?"

"Dunno," he shrugged, "just different."

Shuffling closer to the left side of the cave, Nathaniel jumped over a cyan corner, landing on solid, unshaded ground.

"Who's there?" a voice from underneath the camouflage inquired.

Nathaniel froze.

"Hello?" the swollen voice whimpered. "Someone, anyone there?"

"I thought I'd feel relieved," Nathaniel thought, "unburdened."

"There's been some sort of mistake," the Englishman begged.

"Let's be quick with the companion," Qi commented as a cyan dot appeared.

Jumping to his feet, the boy dashed down the slope. Sprinting past Sarah's usual hitching spot, Nathaniel progressed over the familiar ground. Leaping over obstacles he's become familiar with and placing practiced steps, he made good time as he neared camp. Qi diverted him from his usual route, instead sending him in the direction of the road. With gravity at his back, he focused on nimbly avoiding all of the woodland obstacles.

"You can slow down," Qi advised. "We have time. No need to break an arm running like a lunatic."

His right foot tripped over a stone and panic flooded through his blood. Reflexes reached out and caught a nearby tree. Utilizing his momentum, Nathaniel simultaneously shoved himself away from the ground and regained his balance. Accelerating, he emerged from the woods and came upon a road. He skidded to a stop, put his hands on his knees and panted like a dog standing on its hind legs. Turning his eyes to the left, he found the cyan dot on the horizon amid a group of grown trees.

"The companion is on the other side of those trees," Qi explained.

When breathing stopped being so uncomfortable, Nathaniel walked in the general direction indicated. His mouth tasted of sandy desert as he marched around a bend in the road. Up ahead he spotted three silhouetted figures. Two animals and a human were camped by the side of the road. The human was obviously feeding the larger animal while the smaller busied itself with some of the local foliage.

"She has a derringer in her left boot," Qi confided. "Let's keep this as quiet as possible." A blue line indicating the area just beside the path. "Keep to the tree-line."

Departing from the road, Nathaniel weaved through the trees. Cautiously he closed in on his target

"Now don't go on eat'n nothin' toxic!" Millie Jean scolded. "I don't want to hear no bellyaching from Mister Senior Scrooge about his two hundred-dollar horse bein' no better than a common belly-ache. You *know* he's liable to charity ya off to the closest glue fac-tree without even a second thought." Turning her head, she addressed the smaller horse. "Why don't ya c'mon over, I won't let yer sister eat every last bite of apple."

Nathaniel placed each hand and foot purposefully as he crawled in between the pines. Brushing aside a clump of bushes, he spotted the companion just beyond a fallen log. He crawled forward and pressed his body up against the dead tree. Lifting himself barely off the ground, he continued his prone progress alongside the barkless trunk. When he reached the end, he peaked around the edge.

"Greedy beast," Millie laughed as she scolded the biggest horse. "I've never seen such hog'n."

Millie wore a thick riding jacket and skirt. Free of any restriction, her hair fell from her head, covering up her neck and some of her back.

"Aim your first strike at the back of the knee," Qi illustrated with a cyan dot. "When she falls you will gain access to her throat."

Unsheathing Pa's knife, Nathaniel watched the lady go into her bag and retrieve another apple. He rose up into a squat, then crept forward. The horse chewed on the delicious fruit. Energy surged through him as he took a step and plunged the knife into the back of Millie's left leg, exactly on the blue dot, just below her knee. The blade hadn't completely finished sinking in before she burst out screaming. Pulling its head back, the horse fought its reins as its caretaker fell to one knee. In a single motion, Nathaniel pulled the knife out and sank it into the side of Millie's neck. Stepping back, the boy widened the wound as he withdrew the bloodied weapon. Clasping her wound, Millie spun around and focused on the knife-wielding child. Reaching out, she stumbled forward as she grabbed for him. Nathaniel side stepped her grasp, leaned forward and slashed a line across her forehead. Blood spilled down her face, blinding her eyes. A wail escaped her lungs as her hands tried to wipe her vision clean. Smearing the blood, she lost her balance and fell.

She rolled over on her back and reached for her boot.

"Fall back," Qi commanded and Nathaniel did not wait for any details. "She's going for her derringer."

Vaulting over the log, Nathaniel stopped his retreat and braced himself against the barrier. Sheathing his knife, he drew the revolver. Rolling over onto his back, he cocked the hammer and clutched the gun while he watched the sky with wide, terrified eyes. He waited and waited, listening for any footsteps. His imagination visualized her face appearing and towering over him.

"She's gone," Qi announced.

Nathaniel sat up. Sheathing his blade, he stood up and took careful steps around the log, keeping his sights lined up with Millie's fallen body. When he reached the woman, a cyan dot appeared at the base of her skull, right where the spine started.

"Stab there," Qi said.

"You said she's gone."

"Make certain."

Shifting the gun to his left hand, Nathaniel pulled out the knife.

Taking a step forward, Nathaniel dropped to one knee as he thrust the blade into the base of Millie's neck. Her entire body twitched before slumping further into the ground.

Standing up, he wiped the blade on his trousers. He put away the knife, then carefully un-cocked and holstered the pistol. Leaning forward, his fingers wrestled the derringer out of her warm hand. Unloading the firearm, he quickly pocketed the bullets and tiny gun. He made his way around the cadaver, squatted down and picked up a half-eaten apple. Moving up to the biggest horse, the boy extended a hand, offering up the half-finished fruit. The equine's long, sniffing snout honed in on the food. The animal lifted its top lip, revealing its upper row of teeth, as it crunched down on the apple. Three bites later, the snack was no more. Bending down, Nathaniel picked a bouquet of grass and offered it up to the animal. The smaller horse whined, the bigger horse stiffened but refused to hesitate.

"Take rope," Qi said, "tie it to the cadaver."

Moving around to the side of the horse, he removed a coil of rope from the saddle and allowed a loose end to drag as he walked back to the corpse. Nathaniel tied a slipknot, pulled her boots together and looped the cord around them both. Tightening it down, Nathaniel wrapped the limbs tighter, loopingthe rope around her legs several times before securing them with a final knot. He walked back to the small horse, unhitched her and led her over to the bigger horse. Hitching her to the larger one, Nathaniel tapped the back of the big horse's knees. As the creature knelt, Nathaniel unhitched its reins from the tree before mounting up. Powerful muscles tensed as strong legs lifted up the animal's torso, making Nathaniel feel weightless. Leaning forward, he pet the horse before wrapping his arms around its tree trunk neck. He listened to the creature's deep breath.

"Ready?" Qi asked.

Squeezing the thick mane with all his strength, the boy leaned forward and whispered in the creature's ear, "Come on." He straightened up and took a tighter hold of the reins, "Hyah!"

The horse started for the woods, dragging the body behind. Before the smaller horse's reins could cinch, she stood up and followed after her sister.

"Is this how Beech-croft came?" he asked aloud.

"Doesn't matter."

"I'm curious."

Entering deeper into the woods, Nathaniel spent most of the trip with an eye on the corpse being dragged behind the horses. Every so often he had to dismount and untangle the body from whatever obstacle it managed to get caught up in. Several times he had to retie her legs.

"Lose the smaller horse," Qi said, "*Carefully* guide this big critter to just in front of the pit, move past the pit and then go down the other side. That should drag her to right in front of the pit. Then all you **must** do is disconnect her from the rope and then push her in."

Nathaniel lined the biggest horse up with the slope before dismounting. Moving over to the medium horse, he unhitched the mare and led her over to a group of trees. Anchoring the creature to the plants, Nathaniel returned to the horse and mounted up.

"Hyah," the boy called as the horse took off.

"Woah," Qi called and Nathaniel calmly imitated her sound.

The horse slowed as it rode up the slope, in front of the pit and down the other side.

Halfway down the other side, Qi cut in, "Stop the horse, disconnect the rope here."

Unsheathing Pa's blade, Nathaniel spotted a line and severed the rope. Dropping the loose cord, he allowed the horse to step forward, relieving it from the awkward standing position it had been stalled in.

"Hitch her up too," Qi painted a blue dot on a tree.

Tying the horse to the indicated tree, Nathaniel dismounted and returned to the front of the pit. Squatting down and leaning forward, Nathaniel grit his teeth as he put all his weight into pushing. The cadaver was mighty heavy.

"Careful," Qi warned, "don't slip and fall in."

The body barely budged but it was enough to shift Nathaniel's balance, pulsating a blast of panic throughout him.

"Take the rope, move to the cave, and then you can pull her in," Qi instructed. "It will be a much safer technique."

Grabbing hold of the rope, Nathaniel made his way around the pit. Hopping over the left corner of the pit, he took a few steps into the cave. Turning around, he tightened his grip on the rope and pulled. He threw all of his weight into it, fighting for each step deeper into the cave. The corpse slid. One of its legs fell into the hole but the other one got hung up on some of the remaining camouflage. Alone in his tug of war, Nathaniel imagined tying his end of the rope to a large round boulder and being able to push it off a cliff. Branches snapped underneath Millie. She tumbled through the hole and disappeared from sight.

"Mill-eeeeeeeeeeeeeee!" Beechcroft screamed at the top of his gurgling lungs, "Nooooooooooooo! Mill-eeee, can you hear me, Millie? Please talk to me Millie! Tell me *something*, Millie!" The strength in his voice waned. "We have to get out of this, Millie," he whimpered. "Millie jean, please." Then he shouted furiously, "I demand to *know who is responsible for this*!"

"Let go of the rope."

He did.

"Take the shovel and a new rope."

Hopping over the corner of the pit, Nathaniel went around the pit and down a slope to where the horse was hitched. Retrieving a new coil of rope and the shovel, he returned to the front of the pit.

"Start filling."

Placing down the rope, Nathaniel dug into the dirt. Lifting up a load, he tossed it into the hole.

"What have I ever done to you?" Beechcroft demanded. "Who are you!?"

Dig and toss. Dig and toss. Dig and toss. Dig and toss. Nathaniel rubbed his itchy, blistered hands together before getting back to digging and tossing. Dig and toss. Dig and toss. Dig and toss. Hit a rock, move onto the next spot. Dig and toss.

"I need a doctor!" Beechcroft mustered. "I will pay good money for a person to go an' fetch a doctor for me! Better yet, t-take me to a doctor!"

Nathaniel filled in more dirt.

"What have I done to you to deserve this? I demand to know!"

After a while of filling and listening to Beechcroft's rambles, Qi announced, "We can shoot him now."

Nathaniel froze.

"Only animals will hear."

Placing the shovel on the ground, Nathaniel bent his arm back as he reached for the leather satchel tied across his spine like a quiver.

"Use her derringer," Qi advised. "It will be easier for you to handle."

Reaching into his overall's front pocket, he pulled out the tiny firearm. He moved to the closest, flattest boulder and carefully loaded the weapon. The blue rectangle shrunk down to a square.

"You'll need to remove that camouflage to get a clean shot."

"Outline him with color and I'll shoot him through the camouflage."

"The bullet might get deflected."

"I have a second shot."

"And then what?"

Nathaniel shrugged, "Then I'll use the revolver."

"Take one shot, make it count," Qi said. "He's not going to be happy after your first miss. He may try to shoot back."

Nathaniel walked over to the blue square. Crouching down, he dug his hands into the sticks, leaves, and ivy and started grabbing and disassembling the false ground. It was easy work, mostly involving twisting the foliage until the sticks buckled and fell.

"Hello?"

Nathaniel sped up his digging. He put a small, squarish gap in the camouflage and then worked on making it bigger.

"Who are you?"

Looking up from his work, Nathaniel spotted Beechcroft's pale blue eyes staring back at him.

"Is someone there?"

"He can't see me," Nathaniel whispered to himself.

"Who's out there?"

Drawing the derringer, Nathaniel aimed the barrel beyond the gap in the camouflage and at the pale blue circle. Letting out his breath, he gently squeezed the trigger. The gun bucked in his hands as a bullet rocketed out of the chamber. The sound was loud, but over quickly. The following silence filled the traumatized air like water rushing from a blown-up dam.

"He's gone," Qi confirmed.

"Gone, or dead gone?"

"Dead gone."

Placing the gun on the ground, Nathaniel went back to digging away the sticks.

"Secure your weapons," Qi said.

Nathaniel unloaded Gibb's revolver and Millie's derringer before placing them both in the bigger horse's saddle. Retrieving the rope, he secured it to a local tree before tossing it into the largest front hole. Taking hold of the cord, Nathaniel turned around, leaned back and carefully walked backwards down into the pit. Landing on a dirt covered Millie, Nathaniel stooped down and pulled at the closest stake. He searched for the weakest spike, removed it from the ground, and utilized it to dig out the bases of the remaining stakes. Slowly but surely he cleared out a path to the dead man. The corpse's left eye had been replaced by a dripping, bloody socket while his right eye was vacantly zoned out on nothing in particular. Reaching the front of the corpse, Nathaniel cleared the area of all spikes. Leaning forward, the boy slid his hand into the Englishman's jacket. His grasped a thick, leather object, and pulled his arm back, revealing a wallet.

"Too bad you will be unable to spend it for several years," Qi said.

Opening up the wallet, Nathaniel stared at its dense innards. The amount of 100 dollar bills and 100 pound notes explained its weight.

"Why?" Nathaniel demanded.

"If you show any adult vendor that kind of money, they'll simply steal it from you. You need to grow a bigger body before you try spending that kind of cash."

"Can't Ma or Pa spend it for me?" Nathaniel reckoned.

"They will want to know where you got it from."

"*They*," Nathaniel snorted, "are going to want to know so much."

Next Nathaniel unholstered Beechcroft's ivory-gripped revolver but didn't bother removing the gunbelt.

"Such an odd weapon," Qi commented.

A cyan dot indicated Beechcroft's left boot.

"Those are too big for me," Nathaniel mumbled.

"Concealed inside his boot is a Deringer."

Nathaniel carefully slid the boot off of the Englishman's foot, revealing a leather strap wrapped around his bulging ankle, holstering a small gun.

He removed it from the holster and Qi said, "Unload it."

Unlatching the barrel lock, Nathaniel tilted the gun allowing both bullets to fall into his overall's front pocket. Placing the unloaded weapon on top of the rounds, Nathaniel continued rummaging through the corpse. In the next pocket, he retrieved a hefty, rectangular metal box with the words, "Windsor Hotel, N.Y.C." etched into its side.

"It's a lighter," Qi stated.

Sliding it into a back pocket, Nathaniel noticed a small wooden box laying next to his knee. Taking hold of the unknown, his eyes studied the strange, heavy container. In the dim light, he analyzed the circular opening cut into the top of the device. He turned it over and a gear fell out and bounced off his foot.

"It cannot be fixed," Qi said, "drop it."

"What is it?"

"It utters a high frequency that keeps away animals but is too high-pitched to be heard by humans."

"Oh."

"Right now it's broken rubbish and we can't fix it. Throw it away."

Nathaniel tossed the broken piece into a far corner of the pit. A blue dot indicated a coat pocket. Reaching into the cadaver's outer-most layer, Nathaniel pulled out a round tin. Holding the container up to the light, Nathaniel read, "Spam."

As Nathaniel pocketed the spam, Qi announced, "We're done pillaging."

Nathaniel studied the Englishman's bloody attire. "It's too bad none of it fits." His eyes zoned in on some of the blood stains. "Should I sample his genetics?"

"No!" Qi *shouted*. "He is poison!"

Nathaniel frowned as he shouted, "You've said I can't get poisoned!"

"Remember how I said that nothing from earth can harm you?"

Nathaniel shrugged. "Sure?"

"His genetics are not from earth."

"Oh. Where they from then?"

"Don't know. Neither of us have ever left earth."

"What's so bad about not-earth things? Aren't you not from here?"

"I'm as from here as you. We are done in here in this pit. Please exit."

Turning around, Nathaniel moved to the wall and grabbed the dangling rope. Careful not to spill his loot, he walked himself up the dirt wall. As soon as he set foot on solid ground, he headed for the shovel. Digging at the pit's bending edge, he worked his way around the perimeter. By the end of his second lap, he'd dislodged most of the camouflage. By his third lap, all of the sticks, leaves, dirt, and ivy had slid into the pit. Then he moved onto the right slope and started cutting into it and tossing the dirt on top of the crumpled camouflage.

When he took a dinner break, he sat on a boulder, eating the last half of the spam. He chucked pebbles onto the wavy, botanical layer of debris that had once resembled the natural ground. After filling his belly, he tossed the empty tin into the pit before picking up his shovel. It took much less time to fill then it had to remove. When everything was covered with a substantial amount of dirt, Nathaniel walked over the top of it. He pressed down every portion, stomping down and tightening gravity's grip on the inanimate matter underneath. Nathaniel applied another loose layer of dirt on top of his footprints. Then he dropped his shovel and tears came flooding to his eyes.

"I want to go hoooooooooooome," he wailed as he wiped his eyes. "I'm sick of being tired and dirty and cold! I want to go hoooooooooooooommmmme," he howled.

"That is eighty-three miles away."

The tears poured down, drenching his cheeks in warm, salty water. He wept, feeling a tension in his chest slowly drain. Time and tears drained a previously undetected yet enormous stress that grew inside of him. After several minutes he simmered down to a whimpering sniffle. Rolling his fists into balls he rubbed his itchy eyes.

"You did excellent work today, Nathaniel," Qi commented. "No one noticed. A certain farmer is now the proud owner of a beautiful carriage and nearly fifty dollars in groceries. I doubt he will mention anything to anyone."

"They're beautiful," Nathaniel admitted.

"The animals."

"Yes," Nathaniel nodded. "They are peaceful. Powerful beasts."

"Indeed."

Walking over to the larger horse, he unhitched her and guided her to her sister. Hitching them together, he led them down the mountain and back to camp. When he reached his shelter he allowed Sarah to properly introduce herself to the new arrivals in the trio's native tongue. Hitching up the horses with lengthy ropes, he focused himself on retrieving the dry logs hidden inside the hollowed, fallen tree. With the help of the pickax, Nathaniel created a good amount of dry kindling and soon had a fire going. The flames melted a burden from the boy's chest.

After warming himself through, he took the trio of animals down to the river. Standing in a row, all four of them drank. Glancing back at the waning flames of camp, Nathaniel cycled through drinking the river, keeping an eye on the fire and watching the thirsty animals.

Looking up at the sky, Nathaniel wondered, "Is it going to rain tonight."

"Not likely."

Returning to camp, he sat down and supped on a full can of sardines. With a tiny pan, Nathaniel boiled himself a cup of wild thyme tea. Placing the boiling beverage on the log, he zoned out on the flickering flames as he waited for his tea to cool. When his patience faltered, he grabbed the cup and placed his lips dangerously close to the steaming liquid. Vapor and scent filled his nose as he took the first sip. The heat spread from his esophagus and stomach, warming his entire anatomy. He blew a puff of air onto the tea before risking another tiny sip. It was the best cup of tea he'd ever tasted.

As the afternoon continued, the horses settled down. Seeing the animals readying themselves for a nap, reminded the boy of how tired he was. He finished his cup, then moved to the unhorsed cart and removed the blanket from its bed. Moving to where the horses had gathered, Nathaniel placed it over two of the horses.

"Don't sleep in between two large horses," Qi scolded. "After all you been through, yer gonna end up crushed between two sleeping horses."

Staring at the big, beautiful horses, it didn't seem like a bad way to go.

"Shared body heat is a good idea, but nap next to Sarah: she's less likely to roll over and squash you like a bug."

At his rope's end, Nathaniel unfolded and covered the mule with the blanket before slipping in beside her and wrapping an arm over her furry back.

27

After a long day full of harvesting, Nathaniel took a swim in the river. Jane splashed him unfairly until he found himself quitting the game and running back home in defeat. His wet pants clung to him, slowing him down, and growing heavier with each footstep. He grew exhausted and craved a nap.

Up in the sky, a moving cloud uncovered the moonlight that streaked through the towering oak tree's foliage. Its strongest, longest branch protruded outward from its trunk. Swinging in midair just underneath the woody limb were two bodies. Bending cords connected the two necks to the branch. Their faces were discolored and swollen. Pa's purple tongue resided in a limp position that covered up most of his bottom lip. Ma still had eyes. They were almost popped completely out of the skull.

"What happened?" the boy demanded.

"Gibb discovered his gun had been taken," Qi explained. "He blamed your father."

"Where's Jane?" Nathaniel demanded. "I don't see her."

Faster than a blink, the scenery transformed, placing him inside a forest. In front of him, Jane lay against the trunk of a tall tree. Her eyes were closed and her lower half had been torn off and dragged several feet away from her.

"After she bled out," Qi said, "coyotes got to her."

The scene melted away, replaced by the blank, white room. Qi emerged from the transparent mist and stood before the child.

Standing up, Nathaniel pointed a finger at where his sister had just been. "Show me what Gibb did."

"It won't help you."

"And *that* did? SHOW ME! I DEMAND YOU SHOW ME!"

"You've seen enough," she paused. "Maybe when you're older."

"I'm gonna kill them!" Nathaniel screamed. "I'm gonna kill them all."

"No. You will focus on the mission. It is all we have now."

"I'm gonna bleed 'em," Nathaniel snarled. "I'm gonna rip their eyes out and feed 'em their gizzards! I'm gonna *wreck* an' *destroy* their homes, set fire to their *wives* and—and—and rip out their children's tongues!" He crumpled and wailed, "God, I hate them!!! I hate them!"

Nathaniel screamed and pinched his skin. Grinding his teeth he jumped up and stomped down on his right foot with his left. Pressing each of his fingernails into his flesh, he etched linear streaks into his face. Pulling at his hair, he crumpled to the floor.

His eyes snapped open. He saw a starry night sky. His face wasn't bleeding. His body didn't hurt. The longer he stared, the more shining dots he noticed. Sitting up, Nathaniel looked around. He counted three equines and a cart before he remembered where he was. His hands felt the dead leaves he lay on. Pulling up a clump, Nathaniel opened his hand and let the wind knock them out of his palm.

"Was that a dream?" he asked aloud.

"It's the best way I can describe to you what happened to your family," Qi answered.

"Lie!" Nathaniel clenched his fist, "It's not true!"

"Afraid so," Qi confirmed, "I will calculate where we need to go next."

"We're," Nathaniel let it sink in, "we're not going home?"

"That would be unwise."

"I can bury them."

"Unnecessary."

"I buried two strangers!" Nathaniel shouted.

"That was necessary."

"My dead family isn't?" Nathaniel jumped up, fists up, ready to fight.

"Very unnecessary. We are not going back to see them and risking a similar fate. We need to move on. There could be another Beechcroft out there. *He* came out of nowhere, with advanced technology that even I couldn't hide from. We came *this* close to being killed. He would have shucked our brain and eaten it like an oyster. And now, I don't know if there are others like him out there. My previous assumption that you should take the time to grow into a bigger body before we initiate the mission was an error. I wasted time."

Unsure what to do with his anger and sadness, Nathaniel picked up and tore apart the dry, dead leaves.

"Get some rest," Qi commanded. "I have some ideas as to whom we should pursue next."

Nathaniel picked up a stick and broke it. The horses stirred in their sleep. The biggest one had raised its head and was now staring at the child. Nathaniel looked into its concerned, dark eyes. His muscles turned to jelly as he laid down on his back. He looked up at the stars, slowly let his eyelids close and plunged into dark, dreamless sleep.

ABOUT THE AUTHOR

Dan Allen grew up in rural New Hampshire, bouncing between Colorado and New England for a few years before settling back in Boston where he currently resides with his partner and a demanding cat. Dan attended culinary school at Johnson & Wales and continues to work as a chef in the Boston area catering and restaurant business. His everyday life experiences inspire him to look beneath history's surface and imagine what was and what could be. For more of his content please visit danallenmake.com.

ACKNOWLEDGMENTS

For those interested in the books that inspired and educated me throughout the writing of this book please read the following:

All God's Dangers: The Life of Nate Shaw (Ned Cobb) by Theodore Rosengarten.

Beloved by Toni Morrison

All God's Children: The Bosket Family and the American Tradi-tion of Violence by Fox Butterfield

Contraband: Smuggling and the birth of the American Century by Andrew Wender Cohen

Unspeakable Awfulness: America Through the Eyes of European Travelers, 1865-1900 By Kenneth Rose

Bodies and Souls: The Tragic Plight of Three Jewish Women Forced into Prostitution in the Americas by Isabel Vincent

Rising from the Rails: Pullman Porters and the Making of the Black Middle Class by Larry Tye

Thomas Nast: Cartoons & Illustrations with Text by Thomas Nast St. Hill

Sin in the Second City: Madams, Ministers, Playboys, and the Battle for America's Soul by Karen Abbot.

How to be a Victorian: A Dawn to Dusk Guide to Victorian Life by Ruth Goodman

The Trouble They Seen: The Story of Reconstruction in the Words of African Americans edited by Dorothy Sterling

www.ingramcontent.com/pod-product-compliance
Lightning Source LLC
Chambersburg PA
CBHW051338020726
47501CB00007B/2158